THE TRUCKER'S WIFE

The Complete Set

BY EMBER PENN

An Original Publication From EMBER PENN

THE TRUCKER'S WIFE

Episode One

TAKING THE WORLD BY STORM

One

"How long will you be gone this time?" she asked, flipping her long blonde hair over her shoulder and resisting the urge to cross her arms. Rayne looked up at her husband with a failed attempt at a smile. Giving up the pretense, she pressed her lips firmly together. She could still taste the remains of the cherry-flavored lip gloss she'd applied earlier. *For no good damn reason...as usual,* she thought. *Stupid of me to spend the money on it to begin with. I'm the only one who's tasted it since I bought it.* She cringed when she realized if Joe did taste it, he'd probably bitch about her spending money on stupid shit. They were on a tight budget, and her meager teacher's salary didn't help much. And since this was summer, and she'd opted for the nine-month pay schedule, she wasn't being paid at all. She was trying to find a part-time job for summer, but she'd been unsuccessful so far.

"It's another long one, Rayne. I've got to make California in three days. Drop my load there, then swing over to pick up a load in Arizona and bring it back," Joe answered in an irritated voice, while throwing a stack of clothes into his duffle bag. He didn't even turn around to answer her.

No respect, she thought. *He really just doesn't give a shit anymore. Why won't he just talk to me?!*

"I wish you'd drop your load here before you leave," she mumbled under her breath, her lame attempt at telling him she was in need of... well, *sex.* For nearly three months now, he'd avoided sleeping with her—sometimes literally—and she was seriously horny.

"Excuse me? I didn't hear you," Joe said. He turned around and raised his eyebrows, as if daring her to say it again to his face. *Yeah, he heard,* she thought. *And he knows how hard it is for me to ask...why is he being such an asshole? Just freakin' forget it then.*

Rayne cleared her throat. "I said, I wish your boss would let you stick around for more than one day before sending you back out on the road."

But it was more than the boss asking him to go... and they both knew it. Joe *wanted* to get back out on the road. He had an itchy foot and couldn't turn down a run lately, no matter how much she needed or wanted him at home. The few days a month that he was here, he all but ignored Rayne. Most of the time she didn't even know he was coming in. He just showed up—like today.

When he'd come through the door unexpectedly at four o'clock, she couldn't help but hope, once again, that he might miss her enough to spend some *quality* time with her. Rayne had rushed to pull together a good home-cooked meal, fed him, and quickly cleaned the kitchen.

Then, while he stretched out on the couch, she'd spent the last hour in the bath, shaving herself just the way he liked it—or used to like it. She left just one tiny little strip down the middle, nowhere close to her "little man in the boat," as he *used* to call it—that he *used* to drive her wild by nibbling on.

She'd also ran the razor over her legs, even though she'd just shaved yesterday. Now they were definitely smooth as silk. She'd taken her time rubbing in chocolate body cream until her legs smelled as good as they looked, and brushed her long wavy hair out, the way he liked it.

She'd thrown on a short white teddy nightie and a pair of angel-white panties and practically pranced out to entice him into the bedroom, only to find out he'd taken a call from his boss and agreed to go right back out in the morning on another long haul. Now Joe was packing when he'd barely had time to unpack.

He sighed, making it obvious he didn't want to have "the talk." She couldn't blame him, and she was tired of asking the same old questions anyway. *Do you still love me? Don't I turn you on? Don't you enjoy my company?*

Deep in thought, she chewed on her lower lip. All she really wanted right now was some good, hard loving before he left. That simple. But she was too proud to outright *ask* for sex. Why the hell should she have to? She was his *wife* for Pete's sake.

As she watched him roll his eyes at her and turn back to his packing, she knew it wasn't happening—again. *What the hell is wrong with us?* she wondered, and then mirrored his sigh.

He quickly turned around. "Are you mimicking me?"

Her brows furrowed in confusion. "What? *No*," she answered. She seriously didn't even realize she'd sighed right after he did... Oh shit, he was going to use this to start a fight. He was looking for something—anything—just to be able to leave mad. *This is becoming a routine with him lately, for some damn reason. But if I point it out, it'll just be worse,* she thought.

Rayne shook her head, further denying his stupid ass accusation.

"So *I* sigh... and then *you* just magically sigh too? What... it's contagious? Like a freaking yawn or something? I'm not stupid, Rayne. You're pissed off that I'm leaving again."

Here we go, thought Rayne as she slumped onto the bed, ready to hear his tirade.

"I go out there and stay on the road, never getting to sleep in the damn bed I pay for, under the roof I pay for, and enjoy the luxuries at home that I pay for, just so you can sit at home painting your fingernails and watching Netflix."

Rayne bit back her retort. She worked, too. She couldn't help it if she was in one of the most underpaid professions in the country. He acted as though her meager salary was non-existent. But she knew better than to bring that up right now.

• • •

"Not any freaking appreciation from you. Look at ya right now. Wearing that ridiculous nightgown. You think that still looks good on you? I bought you that *five freaking years ago*, Rayne!" Joe screamed, waving his hands in the air. "You think you still look good in that shit?"

Rayne gasped, and clinched her fists. Her mind raced. That's why he won't have sex with me. Her neck warmed and for the first time, she felt like a fool for wearing the little nightie. She crossed her arms over her chest. "You think I'm fat?" Her voice hitched on the last word.

Joe turned around and met her eyes, his attention caught by the hitch in her voice. He blew out a long breath and his shoulders slumped. He turned his back on her. "No, Rayne. You're not *fat*. But you're not super-skinny like you were when we got married. I didn't mean that at all... I'm just... I can't..."

His words trailed off as he continued his packing, although a little slower, as if he'd lost his train of thought. "I shouldn't have said that. I'm sorry," he finally continued, without looking at her.

Rayne stood up and turned around, not knowing what else to say to him and his half-ass apology. She stomped into the bathroom, slammed the door behind her, and locked it.

Joe turned and looked at the closed door and dropped heavily to sit on the edge of the bed. His face fell into his hands. He sighed, long and heavy and then ran his fingers over his face and through his hair. As he stood up again, he shook his head and continued to pack, with his shoulders slumped.

Two

Looking into the full-length mirror on the back of the door, her eyes travelled over her reflection from head to toe and filled with tears.

No, I'm not a hundred and fifteen pounds anymore. When I was that skinny, you used to try to fatten me up, she thought. Now she was healthy... not crack-head thin, but definitely not fat. *I still look good in this. Don't I?*

She turned around and bent over, looking over her shoulder at her peek-a-boo panties. Her legs were still smooth, and her ass was still pretty damn firm for twenty-eight years old. Actually, it made her horny looking at it. She wiggled it slowly, and then much faster, doing the dreaded "twerk" just see how it looked. *I still look hot, asshole.*

And obviously she wasn't the only one who thought so. She still got looks and whistles nearly everywhere she went when she was alone. It didn't matter what she wore, either. Jeans, shorts or a skirt still turned heads—except her husband's. He barely gave her a passing glance.

Rayne faced the mirror again and slowly lifted the nightie over her head, so that she stood only in her panties. Her stomach was still flat and smooth. She worked for that flat stomach three times a week at the gym. She prided herself on it, but knew it wouldn't last if Joe ever gave her enough sperm to actually have a kid. She and Joe had tried unsuccessfully for two years to conceive. It had taken a toll on their sex life, and they'd both silently given up any talk of having children for the past year. Maybe it would just happen on its own. But now, she wondered if the reason he sometimes pulled out was because he didn't want her getting pregnant after all. That would mean she'd get fatter...

No, she thought. *I am not fat. Something else is wrong with Joe. He didn't mean it.* She argued with herself, and didn't have to go too far back to justify her looks. Just yesterday, the college boy at the grocery story had carded her for a bottle of wine. He'd asked her for her license *and* phone number, and gave her a little wink. She'd giggled when she passed her license and he'd seen her age. The poor boy had stuttered all over himself and tried without success to stop looking at her tits.

That was perfectly okay with her though, she liked looking like she was still in her early twenties.

She stared at her breasts. They were huge. *My jogging partners*, Rayne thought, trying to lift her own mood with her own little inside joke. She raised one in each hand, feeling the weight of them. No, she wasn't a super-skinny model type, but she wasn't a large woman either. At five-foot-five, her breasts were almost too big for her—the *too-big tits* he'd paid for five years ago, even picking out the size and shape himself, when things between them had still been hot and heavy. *Hell, he paid to play, and this is the most action they've seen in months*, she thought. *Talk about ME wasting his money.*

She thought back to the days when all it would take to get him into bed was a look. He'd come in from a long trip, and the first thing Joe would say was, "Let me see 'em."

Night or day, she'd head into the bedroom, where he'd follow and peel his shirt off. He'd drop it onto the floor and kick off his shoes and socks as he hurried to get situated in the middle of their big bed, always starting with his pants on, sitting up against the headboard.

While they'd always enjoyed variety in their sex life, their latest routine (if you count up until a year ago at the latest) had started with Rayne taking her normal place standing directly in front of him and slowly stripping off her shirt and her bra. She loved watching his jeans getting tighter and tighter as he'd watched her. She would take her time lifting one of her breasts, and then leaning down to slowly run her tongue around her nipple. Then she'd do the other tit, squeezing them both in her hands. By then she could see the bulging tip of his him peeking out from his waistband, and usually that was when he'd groan.

That first groan was her cue to drop her pants and panties. She'd hurry on that part, because the next part drove him mad. She'd kick her clothes away and spread her legs while still standing, and with one hand still groping a breast, she'd lick two fingers of the other hand and slide them into herself, putting on a show for him—not that she didn't enjoy it herself.

Her efforts never failed to prompt him to lift his bottom and skivvy out of his jeans, while keeping his eyes on her. Once his clothes were off, he would crawl to the end of the bed, and she'd turn around and back up a step until she felt the calves of her legs against the soft blanket, all while her fingers were still inside of herself, working madly. She'd bend over to give him a birds-eye view of her girl-parts up close and personal. She could always hear him breathe in deeply, loving her scent. She could even feel his breath against her hot, wet cunt. She knew without turning around that he would be using one hand to stroke himself while watching at this point.

She wiggled and grinded with her fingers still inside until she was close—sometimes too close—and then Joe would pull her backwards onto the bed and take her. *Take her hard.* She took a pounding on those nights, and she loved every minute of it.

* * *

What the hell? Rayne thought. *Why am I torturing myself like this? It hasn't happened that way in over a year. Those were the old days!* She shook her head at her memories, and sat down on the bathroom counter, cursing herself for remembering their old routine and getting herself wet.

"Stop thinking about it," she told herself in the mirror. *This is getting me nowhere.*

The last year hadn't been that way at all. The few times he had given her any, it was a pump and dump. *But damn, back when it was good, it was so damn good,* she thought, and felt the tears wet her eyes again, and wondered what went wrong.

Did I change that much, or did he?

Rayne stood back up and looked in the mirror. "You *are* still hot," she said in a whisper, "even if he doesn't want you anymore."

A loud knock on the door startled her. She snatched the nightie and wiggled back into it, swearing to herself to never wear it again after tonight.

"Rayne! Did you remember to buy my deodorant? I told you I was out and needed some when I came home," Joe yelled through the door. "I've got to have it for this trip. I'll be gone nine days!"

Shit!

"Ummm… I haven't been to the store. If you'd have told me you were coming home today, I would've gotten it," she answered through the door.

"Dammit, Rayne! I need it. Now I've got to go out on my one damn night home and get it myself. Can't you do anything right? If you can't even do what I need you to do at home, you need to at least try harder to find a part-time job while you're out for the summer! Help me out on some of these bills."

Rayne sighed, and gave in. "I'll go out and get some right now," she yelled through the door. *What bills? Why all of a sudden does he so desperately need me to be making more money?* She knew better than to ask right though. She opened the bathroom door and walked past him. *I swear this feels like just an excuse to fall asleep before I get in the bed so he can avoid touching me. But maybe I'm just sensitive and paranoid.*

"It'll take me an hour to get there and back…" She was hoping he would just say forget it. Surely he could pick some up somewhere on his way out?

"Just go to the truck stop two exits up. They have deodorant." He stood glaring at her with his arms crossed. "I just came from there on my way home. I saw they had my brand, but I *assumed* you'd already gotten me some, like I asked you to."

She hurriedly pulled off her nightie and slipped on jeans and flip-flops. "You'll wait up for me, right?" she quietly asked, as she turned around to face him, with no shirt or bra yet, hope still winning in a fight against pride. *Maybe he'll notice me. Maybe he'll see I'm not fat. I'm still sexy… Say something, Joe…*

Rayne stood still, waiting for his answer. It seemed time stood still too. The husband standing in front of her was not the kind, loving man she had married… That man had been quietly slipping away for the last year. She watched his already red face transform into a grimace, and saw a vein ticking in his neck. So very angry—all the time lately. *And this time over a damn stick of deodorant? For real? His excuses for being pissed off are starting to get lame.*

She could clearly see he was just itching for a heated fight, when all she hoped for as she stood half-naked, self-consciously baring her breasts for him, was a hot roll in the bed before he left again. One good night to re-ignite the flame for them. *Hell, a spark would do. Anything… just give me something,* her eyes begged.

Joe looked at her in exaggerated disbelief, his eyes never leaving her face, as if she wasn't standing there topless. "Hell no, I can't wait up. I've got to leave here at six in the morning, Rayne!"

Her pride wounded again, Rayne swiftly turned around and gave him her back before he could see the hurt on her face. "Fine. Have a good trip then. I'll drop your deodorant in your bag." She snatched her bra and T-shirt off the dresser and stomped out of their bedroom.

"Fine! Thanks!" he yelled in response.

Three

She hopped into his truck because it was parked behind her car, blocking her in. She felt like a fool driving it. Joe and his buddies had camouflaged it themselves last winter for hunting season. Now it looked as if someone had glued different colored leaves all over it—not a professional job to say the least.

Within minutes she hit the interstate, the fastest way to Walmart avoiding the traffic lights. Joe would be in bed and fast asleep by the time she got back, and he'd be gone when she woke in the morning. Her eyes filled with tears as she wondered what was wrong with the two of them. It couldn't be about something as stupid as forgetting deodorant. Their problems had been sneaking up on them for almost a year.

Rayne kept trying to ignore her suspicions that he was getting it on the side, because when would he? He was on the road all the time. If he didn't have time to stay home for a few days a week, he sure didn't have time for a girlfriend on the side.

Her thoughts went back through his accusations that it could be her—she was a burden, a money pit. But she tried very hard not to spend an extra buck unless it was absolutely necessary. Except for the gym, she rarely spent any extra money, and that was his idea anyway. Now it made sense. He

• • •
11

wasn't worried about her health. He probably just wanted her to lose weight, the sneaky bastard. Well, to hell with him. This is the way I am. I'm just *not* a twenty-two year old starving model wannabe anymore! Those days are over. We freaking grew up… and with that came a grown-up body.

If Joe's problem was with her body, there was nothing she could do about that, although that thought made her sigh. She wasn't going to get any smaller. Back when they got married, she had been barely more than a girl. She was a woman now. A woman with a healthy appetite for sex, too.

Maybe Joe has a problem? she thought. *Maybe he's too embarrassed to tell me he's having issues with his equipment.*

As she drove, her eyes glanced over at the sign announcing The Quick Dip Truck Stop at the next exit. She was in the wrong lane. She was so used to routinely driving to Walmart, she'd almost forgotten Joe said she could get the deodorant at the truck stop. She looked behind her to see a car sneaking up in the slow lane. She couldn't tell how far behind it was and hoped she had time to whip over. Getting back to Joe quicker might mean he'd still be awake, and they could talk.

She cut the wheel just in time to make the exit. *Shit*, she thought, and looked into her rearview mirror to see if she'd cut anyone off.

The car passed and blew its horn at her.

Phew. What the hell is wrong with me? I'm not going into a damn truck stop for deodorant! She could've wrecked her car. She should have just went on to Walmart. She didn't like the idea of walking into the truck stop alone anyway. *Dammit!*

Four

She rolled to the top of the ramp and looked to her right. There was The Quick Dip. She laughed to herself at the irony. What she wouldn't give for a *quick dip*! She'd had a nagging, aching need deep inside that nothing had been able to take care of for months. It grew even worse now, after Joe had come home and she'd gotten her hopes up—again.

While she sat at the stop sign, letting her mind wander to sex again, she saw a girl walking in the parking lot, coming from the big rigs parked in the trucker's lot. Curious, she turned right and slowly drove in, steering into a safe parking spot near the door that allowed her to still watch the girl as she headed toward the station. She rolled down her window for a better view.

The girl was young—younger than her anyway—probably twenty-three-ish. And she was pretty. No, she was smokin' hot and thin like Rayne used to be. But not *too* thin—just slender. Long dark hair fell in loose waves past her shoulders, and curves offset her angles in all the right places. Wearing a white shirt and very short cut-off hip-hugger jean shorts with flip-flops, she looked as if she didn't have a care in the world and was exactly where she wanted to be. She looked confident. Rayne envied that look.

As she came closer, the station lighting lit her up. Her skin glowed with a beautiful dark tan. Rayne could see the nipples of her small but perky boobs through the transparent tank top the girl wore. They bounced with every step, and once she'd zoned in on them, Rayne couldn't take her eyes off of them. As she wondered if the girl could possibly be a trucker, the girl looked up and saw Joe's truck and took off jogging toward it, a big smile on her face.

But Rayne still expected her to turn and go into the building. She was surprised when the girl hurried around to the driver's side and skidded to a sudden stop when she saw Rayne. She looked as startled as Rayne felt. And Rayne wondered if she'd been spotted watching her walk through the parking lot, staring at her boobs.

For a moment, they just stared at each other. The girl's face covered in surprise. Then she smiled.

"Hey!" she said. "You look lost."

Rayne's face burned with shame, and her mind flipped somersaults. She didn't exactly know why she hesitated to admit she was running an errand—late at night— for her husband. *Maybe because that makes him look like an asshat?* But she wasn't lost. "Umm, I just needed a quick dip—I mean drink. A soda, I mean," she stammered.

The girl raised her eyebrows at Rayne and smiled. She backed up a step as if to let Rayne open her door to get out and get her drink, but Rayne sat frozen in the car, not sure what to do.

"Want me to walk in with you?" the girl asked, and then laughed. "You look scared to death. Haven't you ever been in a truck stop before?"

Rayne shook her head no.

And she really hadn't. She'd picked Joe up at truck stops before, back when things were still good. If he was going to be close and had put too many miles on his log-book and knew he was going to have to park it overnight, she'd sometimes take half a day to drive to where he was. She'd pick him up and they'd go out to have a decent meal—Joe didn't want to eat in a truck stop when she was with him, he wanted something different.

Then they'd come back and play in his cab until they were both worn out and satisfied, and she'd spend the night with him. That was before. She tried to think back to when it had all changed, but she couldn't remember the turning point.

"Well, come on then." The girl waved her hand toward the building, jarring Rayne out of her stupor. "I'm thirsty, too. I'll walk in with you. My name's Storm."

"Storm? As in—"

"Yeah," Storm interrupted. "As in the weather kind of storm. My parents were hippies." She shrugged her shoulders and laughed again, drawing Rayne's eyes back to her breasts where they stayed for a long moment before traveling back up to Storm's face to see if she was serious. Storm's slight smile didn't waver, and her eyes blinked back at Rayne's, questioning. She *was* serious. What were the odds of a "Rayne" accidently bumping into a "Storm?"

Rayne was speechless as she continued to stare at Storm. Something about this girl scared the hell out of Rayne... scared her because she excited every fiber of her being.

The girl waited for Rayne to answer her or to get out of the car. When neither happened, she asked, "Are you sure you're here for a soda?"

"What else would I be here for?" Rayne answered quickly, without thinking. And then it dawned on her. This girl thought Rayne was trolling for sex. *Omigod. Did people actually do that here? HERE?! Was Storm a freakin' hooker?* Maybe *that's* why Joe won't give her any. If this is what he was finding at the truck stops, no wonder he didn't have anything left at home to give her. *That cheating piece of shit,* Rayne thought, as her mind filled with flashes of her husband with Storm.

"From the way you were eyeballing my tits, I'd say you're lonely," Storm answered.

Rayne looked away. She slammed her palms on the steering wheel, causing Storm to back up. "Son of a bitch!" Rayne screamed.

Storm jumped back a few steps. "Look. I'm sorry. I'll... um... Never mind." She turned to walk away.

"No! Not *you*. I'm not yelling at you. I'm sorry. Please, come back," Rayne said. She felt the tears coming. She didn't want to be alone. Storm was right. Rayne was lonely. And she'd still be lonely, even if she went straight home and crawled into bed with Joe. She couldn't deal with any more rejection from him right now.

"Are we cool then?" Storm asked as she headed back toward Rayne. "I was just trying to be nice, that's all. Really. You look kinda lost just sitting there in your truck."

And you're probably thinking I looked desperately horny if you watched me stare at your boobs for that long, Rayne thought to herself, but said, "Yeah. We're cool. I'm not lost. I actually live not far from here. I was running a quick errand when the sign caught my eye, and I don't know why... I... I just pulled in." Rayne looked up at her. "I saw you walking and wondered if you were a truck driver. You actually don't look like a truck driver at all," she finished, and then laughed, hoping Storm would volunteer her reason for being there, even if she was a hooker.

Storm stepped back up to Rayne's window and leaned over, resting her arms on the sill with her ass poked up in the air. With her this close, Rayne noticed her eyes were almond-shaped. They looked strangely exotic with her other conflicting features of a long, narrow nose and full lips, with long, cascading brown hair that fell in loose curls hanging just below her shoulders. Rayne breathed in the girl's scent that reminded her of something spicy and familiar at the same time—cinnamon.

Storm gave Rayne a perfect peek down her shirt, too. The way Storm's small breasts hung in their position reminded Rayne of peaches—round and juicy.

"Oh? And what does a trucker look like?" Storm asked, and then smiled, drawing Rayne's eyes back to her mouth.

Rayne couldn't help but notice her straight teeth, perfect and white, framed by a heart-shaped mouth. Unconscious of it, she licked her lips as she imagined what it would feel like to have that heart-shaped mouth pressed against hers. *Where the hell did that come from?* Rayne thought as she continued to stare at Storm's mouth. She felt her world tilt as she realized she was seriously lusting over a woman—*a woman? Wtf?*

Storm loudly cleared her throat.

Rayne looked up, and her face flamed again as she realized she was caught staring at Storm's lips. She was at a loss for words. Hell, she didn't even remember the question. Her face fell into a blank look. Storm giggled, and even her laugh was enticing... and contagious. Rayne laughed, too.

"I said, what do you think truckers look like?" Storm repeated.

"Oh! I'm sorry. I spaced out there for a minute. I know what truckers look like. My husband *is* a trucker," Rayne said. "And yeah, I know there's all types of truckers. I just meant that you look... well, *not* like a trucker."

Storm nodded her head in exaggerated slowness. "Ooooh...," she said, drawing out the word. "You're a *trucker's wife*. Wow. Now I see."

"See what?" asked Rayne.

Storm laughed. "There are only three reasons you'd be here. One, you're picking up your husband, which it's obvious you're not. Two, you're looking to see if your husband is here cheating on you, which obviously he must not be. Or three, you're lonely and looking for revenge."

"Revenge?"

"Yeah. You know, like a revenge fuck."

Rayne was taken aback, literally. She pulled her head back, distancing herself from Storm, who still leaned in the window, and gasped. "I have never cheated on my husband. *Ever.* We've been married eight years."

Storm shrugged. "Okay."

"No, seriously. That's not me. I'm not a cheater."

"Okay," Storm repeated and winked.

"I'm really *not* here for any of those reasons." Rayne ran her hands over her face and across the back of her hair. "Just a little trouble at home has my head screwed up. You know, I should go. My husband—the trucker—he's only in for one night. He leaves out tomorrow. Long haul. I need to run my errand and get home to him."

"Cool. Well, it was nice meeting you, Mrs. Trucker's Wife," Storm said and laughed.

"Oh shit. I never gave you my name! I'm sorry. It's Rayne." Rayne put her hand out the window, intent on being polite and shaking Storm's hand. "It was nice talking to you, too."

Storm giggled, probably thinking Rayne was being cheesy, but grabbed her hand and gave it a firm squeeze. They pumped once, up and down…and then—nothing. Neither of them let go. The feel of Storm's damp hand against her own instantly made Rayne's panties wet, and she didn't want to let go. Her face travelled down again to Storm's chest, and Rayne imagined what it might feel like to lick another woman's nipples, maybe even suck them. She looked up at Storm's face, which had changed expressions. Her eyes smoldered back down at Rayne, and her smile was gone, emphasizing the perfect heart-shape of her closed mouth.

What the hell is going on here? Rayne thought.

Storm broke the spell first. "Look, if you just need a friend, I'll get in and we can go somewhere and talk. I'm a good listener, and I just happen to understand truckers. Maybe I can help." She tilted her head at Rayne and smiled.

Rayne hesitated. She could just see her trying to explain this to Joe. *Yeah, honey, I ran into a Storm at the truck stop.* And could Rayne really tell her what was on her mind? It was so personal. Rayne chewed her bottom lip as she considered it. Maybe it was best to talk to a "new" friend; someone who didn't know her or Joe at all.

"I'd like that," Rayne admitted. "Get in."

Five

Storm jumped into the truck and Rayne backed it up. Then she realized she had no idea where to go. She looked over at Storm. "Ummm… do you have a preference where to go? Want to find a coffee shop… a diner or something? It's almost midnight, so not sure what might still be open…" Rayne rattled on nervously. She hoped Storm wouldn't suggest going into the truck stop. That would be awkward if she ran into anyone her husband knew.

"Just pull over in front of those big rigs back there on the party row," Storm said, pointing to the lot she had walked from. "No one will bother us over there and no one can see us from the road."

Rayne glanced that way. *Party row?* "Are you sure you want to just sit in the car? Don't you want to get something to drink… or eat?"

A slow smile spread over Storm's face. "I plan on eating. Just pull over there."

Rayne eyes widened and she sucked in her breath at Storm's innuendo. *Surely, that is not what she meant,* she thought. *Oh, hell no. That cannot possibly be what she meant.* Rayne's panties went from damp to soaking wet in seconds as her subconscious played images of Storm's full red lips against her most private parts. She suddenly realized what it was about Storm that scared her. Rayne wanted Storm… a woman. *When the hell did that happen? And... what the hell am I doing? She might be a hooker. A beautiful hooker, but a friggin' hooker!? I'm not paying for sex... AND I'm not having sex with a woman. I'm not—*

Storm interrupted her thoughts. "Right there." She pointed to a spot directly facing a long row of rigs. "That's perfect."

Rayne pulled into the spot she'd indicated and realized, almost disappointedly, that Storm's intentions must have been to only talk. Otherwise, she wouldn't have stopped her here in front of all these rigs. She leaned her head forward and looked at the trucks. Some had curtains drawn while others didn't, but she didn't see anyone. But still—anyone could easily look out and see them sitting right there in her car.

Luckily, her husband never came to this truck stop— as far as she knew—and Rayne didn't see his company logo on any of the rigs as she drove through the lot. Besides, if the trucks' drivers were this close to home, the rigs would be parked at the company lot, not here at a truck stop.

Rayne's vehicle filled with a loud silence. She stole a glance at Storm to see that she'd re-situated herself to lean against the passenger door, giving Rayne her full attention. *Like this isn't weird enough,* Rayne thought.

"So...," Rayne began, "I appreciate you offering to listen. My head's all screwed up. My husband and I have barely had sex in the past year. He doesn't, um... desire me anymore. I think he thinks... I'm fat and useless..." Those words stung even worse hearing them out loud. Rayne's eyes filled with tears.

Storm looked her over and Rayne burned under her scrutiny.

"You're definitely not fat. Let's get that out of the way up front. You're hot. You have a rockin' body full of curves, and beautiful long, blonde hair. The kind of thick hair guys like to wrap their fingers in. And you have a pretty face, too. There's *nothing* about you that's not extremely attractive."

Rayne looked away, embarrassed at her compliments. She hoped Storm didn't think she'd been fishing for them. But it was nice to hear someone say something good about her looks. She was starved for any kind of positive reinforcement.

"Seriously, I just think you need some attention."

When she looked back toward Storm, she found her leaned over moving toward her.

"What are you—"

Storm's mouth pressing against hers cut off Rayne's words. Within seconds, Storm had climbed on top of her and Rayne could feel the seat moving back. She had one hand on the seat control, her mouth pressed against hers, and the other hand squeezing Rayne's breast.

Rayne gasped in surprise, and Storm took that opportunity to taste all of her mouth, while grinding up against her. Rayne felt Storm's pelvic bone against her own, and without intending to, she spread her legs to give Storm better access. She wanted—no, needed—to feel that closer, deeper touch.

Shit! She didn't know which experience she wanted more of—the kiss, her breasts finally being rough-handled again, or something else to douse the fire that was spreading from within, making her feel as though her body was an inferno.

Rayne's mouth went slack, her back arched, and her lower body bucked up against Storm completely on its own, as if Rayne had lost all physical control.

"You like that, don'tcha?" Storm whispered. Rayne was frozen in shock. She couldn't answer, but her blood pulsed between her legs, begging for release.

"See. Here's what you need to do. You need to *tell* people what you want. If not your husband, then someone else." Storm breathed her hot breath into her ear as she continued to writhe and rub against Rayne. "Just tell me, Rayne."

Rayne didn't know what to say. She couldn't even ask her husband to have sex with her. She wasn't raised that way. She'd always waited for him to initiate it, but she'd told him in other ways—gave him signs. *What more does he need? A flashing sign over my head that says Screw Me?* No, he knew. He just didn't want her anymore. He made her feel unsexy... She hadn't considered until just this moment that she could actually get her needs met by someone else. Someone who obviously found her desirable. Maybe she didn't need it from him anymore. Or maybe she just didn't know *what* she wanted from him.

But this—she wanted this. *Oh, shit, how she wanted this.* And no one could be more surprised than her. She'd never in a million years dream of cheating on Joe before. But in her mind, through the years, if it had flashed up there even for a second, she never even contemplated getting it on with another *woman.* Guilt pinched her conscience as she realized it was still cheating, regardless of the gender. *Wasn't it?*

But... if Joe could be here and see this, she knew it would turn him on. He'd watched plenty of lesbian porn back in the day—they'd even watched it together. Maybe she could just be honest and tell him. Maybe he wouldn't see it as cheating if there wasn't another man involved. Maybe he'd still want a threesome with her and another woman. That could bring the spice back into their love life.

Pushing all thoughts of Joe out of her head, she tried to imagine herself set free—even for just a few moments—to erase all her inhibitions, and just let her body take over. Wild thoughts of reckless abandon flooded in, giving her hope of finally feeling intimacy again, even if with a stranger. She felt like someone else. Someone new. Someone rebellious.

She reached up and fiercely tangled her hands in Storm's hair and tried to pull her lips back on hers. But Storm resisted the pull, and instead sucked on Rayne's ear, sticking her tongue in and twirling it around as deep as it would go before sucking the wetness out again. It drove Rayne wild, and her body wiggled under Storm.

"You still haven't told me what you want me to do," Storm whispered, her mouth pressed against Rayne's ear. The hot breath from the words came as a sensual contrast to the cool air of a moment ago and nearly drove Rayne mad.

Rayne tried to form the words, but she just couldn't say out loud what her body screamed at her for. The constant rejection from her husband had crippled her confidence. Maybe she was useless—and not desirable. What if she asked and Storm refused? Or worse... laughed at her.

"I know you want me, Rayne. And you can do this. Let me help you out. I'll give you some choices," she whispered as her tongue darted in and out of Rayne's ear.

I can't believe this is really happening, Rayne thought. *This. Cannot. Be. Happening.*

"Aaaaa," she said, stretching out the letter in a long, breathy whisper. "I can just keep doing what I'm doing," Storm said. "We can just make out."

Omigod. This. Is. Happening.

"Beeeee," she said in a sexy, teasing tone. "I can reach my hand down between your legs and rub. Or—"

Oh shit. I think I know what you're going to say... please say it, Rayne chanted in her mind wordlessly as she held her breath.

"Or C! I can scoot down there and put my mouth against you until you beg me to stop," Storm finished, and as if trying to make her offer clear, she lapped at Rayne's ear—wet and loud—sending trails of pleasure darting through her body. Hearing her say those words nearly made Rayne come undone. She felt another wave of wetness flood her.

They bucked against each other, their heads a tangle of blonde and brown long hair, their sweat mingling, and their individual smells weaving together to make an intoxicating scent of chocolate and cinnamon.

"Before you answer me, I want you to look out the window. Look around," Storm whispered against her ear.

• • •

Six

Rayne's head jerked away from Storm as she quickly looked out the windows.

The line of trucks bearing silently down on them, which once looked sleepy and forgotten, were now alive with movement. While she couldn't see their faces—only that they were there—she was sure with the lighting, the drivers could see her and Storm perfectly. She was mortified and her body stiffened, ready to push Storm off of her and get the hell out of there.

"Wait! Rayne... No. I just wanted you to see—to show you that you aren't useless. You are desirable and sexy. If you weren't, they wouldn't bother to watch. Don't you see?" Storm whispered as she gently pushed Rayne's shoulders back down against the seat and licked her ear. "You have the power now. *You* are in control of *them*. Do you want to continue the show, or do you want me to get off—or both?" she said, and then laughed at her pun.

Rayne looked at the one driver who was close enough for her to see clearly. He was mesmerized, leaning up toward the front window watching... waiting for her to be taken by Storm. His eyes desired them, finding what they were doing sexy enough to hold their interest—probably jacking off. And there were others watching, all down the line. Suddenly, she did feel powerful and sexier than she ever had.

• • •

But she was married. And even if Joe might think this was hot, he probably would consider it cheating if he wasn't involved. She couldn't do it.

"Wait," she finally answered.

Storm backed off a little, but still hovered over Rayne. "You want to stop?"

Rayne shook her head, trying without success to veil her face with her hair, to try to hide her face from what she was about to admit.

"I don't *want* you to stop. But I love my husband. He might be all into this. But I don't want to do it behind his back. I'd rather he be a part of it—or have a chance to," she whispered shyly. "Sorry."

Storm hesitated a moment, and then smiled.

"S'kay," she said, and climbed off of Rayne. She slid back to her side of the truck and nodded her head. "You run your errand and just think about it. There's more you can do when your husband doesn't want you anymore than make out with another woman. There's hot guys everywhere that'd give you all the attention you want. Anytime. Anywhere. Watch this…"

She opened her door and stepped out. She walked to the front of the truck and leaned against the hood, facing the line of truckers. Rayne watched as her head swept slowly from right to left and then back again. All eyes were on her.

She watched as Storm pulled off her shirt and unhooked her bra, making a show of turning toward the drivers and spinning it on her finger before letting it fly off onto the pavement.

Rayne froze in place watching Storm reveal her skin bit by bit, right out in the open, in front of probably a dozen strangers. Storm turned around and faced Rayne again, her perky little breasts shining under the light.

Rayne moaned aloud. Storm picked up both of her breasts and squeezed, looking directly at her. Rayne's eyes fell to Storm's nipples—tiny and brownish, almost like two shiny pennies—and her mouth watered, and she moaned again, surprising herself.

Storm continued to stare at her as she unbuttoned her shorts and slowly slid them down over her slender, tan legs, delicately stepping out of them and tossing them onto her pile of clothes on the ground.

She then wore *only* a pair of tiny red panties.

Rayne held her breath. Storm first gave a lazy smile over her shoulder toward the drivers, than she looked back to Rayne, seeing she had her full attention, and slowly ran her tongue over her full heart-shaped lips. Rayne swallowed loudly, imagining that tongue and those lips on her where none had been for a very long time. She felt another surge of her juices fall and felt her own panties sopping wet against her.

Storm turned around and pointed at one truck. She crooked her finger, and Rayne gasped as she saw the trucker move fast to open his door and climb down.

Storm looked back to Rayne and said, "Omigod, girl! Just wait until you see this guy. He is *lickin-fuckin-licious*," Storm said, ending in a sing-song-voice. "And, most importantly, he's clean, too. Always."

Rayne's mouth dropped open. *Is this girl seriously going to have sex with a random trucker, out here in the open, where everyone can see? Can't she get arrested? What is this... wait—it's exhibition!*

Rayne had heard of people getting off on this. She had to admit to herself, it was hard to look away.

The trucker sauntered slowly from his rig toward Rayne's truck as Storm struck a sexy pose leaning against the grill, her arms spread wide across the hood as though lazily welcoming him. Her long dark hair fell in waves down her back and puddled behind her on the hood.

Rayne's eyes went back to the trucker, drinking him in from bottom to top. Probably early thirties, wearing plain dark Cowboy boots mostly covered by his long, tight faded jeans that hung low on his hips, a tight Abercrombie and

Fitch T-shirt, wavy brown hair, short everywhere but the top, where it fell in a sweep over one eye.

Thick eyebrows and dark lashes framed his eyes. Rayne couldn't see the color, but she didn't need to. If they had been canary-shit yellow they'd still be sexy with everything else he had going on. He had a strong chin—hell, he had a strong everything. Bulging muscles thumped against his fitted T-shirt, and emphasized his trim waist. She imagined a six-pack under there.

This guy was hot. He looked like a mix of college-boy, cowboy and trucker. *But does she actually know him?* Rayne wondered. *Or is this just some random guy she's picking up?*

As he approached, Rayne discreetly reached down and hit the lock buttons on her doors, although both windows were open, so it wasn't much protection. But she couldn't bring herself to roll up the windows. She wanted to hear what was happening, as much as she wanted to watch.

He walked straight to Storm and leaned into her, his hands landing on the hood of Rayne's truck, beside Storm. Rayne's eyes searched his hands for a ring. *No ring.* She breathed a sigh of relief. Silly, but it gave her hope that maybe the married truckers didn't do this kind of thing after all.

Storm leaned into him as though sharing a private joke, and Rayne couldn't hear what was said. He laughed a deep, rumbling laugh in response. Rayne could see him rubbing up against Storm, her bare breasts against his T-shirt.

Rayne blew a slow breath out, trying to control her own fantasies of this sexy creature in front of her. Then, his eyes on Storm, he unbuckled his belt, popped his button and unzipped his pants. Rayne's head angled to the right trying to get a better look, but he was too close to Storm. She'd just have to use her imagination.

He lifted Storm and sat her on the hood of the truck. Then he gently guided her panties off of her and down her legs. He tossed them onto the hood and his eyes met Rayne's. He winked. Rayne felt her face burn in shame. She looked away, to act as though she wasn't watching, but only for a second. Her eyes were drawn immediately back.

Rayne watched as he slid Storm toward him, her hands running up his muscled arms, over intricate tattoos that Rayne couldn't quite make out from this distance—but she could see they were well-done and just added to his undeniably hot body.

While Rayne watched, Storm made an exaggerated show of putting both of her hands between her legs and grabbing the inside of her own thighs. She pulled them apart, spreading her legs wide. She took the trucker's hand and gently guided it to her.

Rayne gasped. *No she didn't!*

She glanced up to the other drivers and saw wide-open eyes and some movement. The thought of them getting off on this increased her own flames. She couldn't blame them. Storm was a hot little number, and watching live sex was taboo, which made it even hotter.

Rayne wished she could slide her own panties off. But she wouldn't dare. Storm or the truckers might see her. Someone who knows Joe might see her. She sighed. For once she wished she could just do what she wanted and to hell with the consequences. But she couldn't. She wiggled in her seat, pushing down against the waves of want rolling through her.

As the trucker took his first thrust, Rayne sucked in her breath, almost feeling it right along with Storm. He held onto Storm and pumped in and out several times.

Storm grabbed a handful of his T-shirt, pulling him to her. "Harder," she demanded. "I like it rough. Take me harder."

He complied with full abandon, and as he did, Rayne couldn't stop herself anymore. She reached into her own panties and explored the folds and creases of her sex with one hand while using the other to grip the steering wheel. As she watched the couple on the hood of her truck getting busy, she found herself letting out short little moans.

Storm gracefully dropped back to lay flat against the hood and Rayne had a perfect view of her small breasts and hot little nipples. She had to get more room for herself. She lifted her bottom to slide her own pants off, praying no one could see. And she didn't stop there. Rayne hooked her fingers into her white panties and, while staring straight out the windshield, not wanting to miss a second of the show, she slowly pulled them off.

Her eyes felt dry from trying not to blink. She didn't want to miss a second of this. Both Storm and the trucker had rockin' bodies, and as he pumped into her, her perfect little breasts shook to and fro. The trucker's eyes were nearly closed and his forehead was beaded in sweat. The muscles in his arms bulged as he appeared to try to be restraining himself from letting completely loose and hurting Storm on the hard surface of the truck.

Rayne felt like she was going to explode. It was almost too much, but she held on. As her first experience with exhibition—Wait. Did this count if she wasn't actually involved in the act...but just watching it?—she wanted it to last at least as long as Storm lasted. This could be the fuel for her fantasies for the *next* eight lonely years.

She let her legs relax open, and began flicking and then rubbing the throbbing hot nub that was begging for attention. At each thrust the truck driver took into Storm, she slid a finger into herself, matching his rhythm with her own.

Rayne threw her head back onto the headrest and nearly screamed. It. Felt. That. Good. *Whoa. Slow down girl.* She took a deep breath and eased up a little.

The trucker stilled for a moment. *Oh no... don't stop.* Rayne thought. She moved her finger back out, circling her satiny folds then quickly pushed it back in deeper than it was before. The trucker grunted and started moving in Storm again, grunting and moving faster, more vigorous than before.

Rayne moved her hand faster too. She put in another finger, feeling like the trucker and Storm were about to wrap it up, and she wanted to join them—although by herself. She watched them with big eyes as she pumped her hand into herself back and forth. *Oh. Shit. This. Is. Un. Freaking. Real,* Rayne thought. *I'm actually getting off in a Trucker's lot. Joe would freak out.*

Rayne was so hot and wet that her hand slipped. She stilled for just a moment, afraid she might have hurt herself, but there was nothing but pleasure. She moaned—a good, long moan—and continued.

Storm suddenly went wild with the trucker. Her hips bucked up and down and she clutched at his shirt, dragging him to her and pushing him away, guiding his speed. She grunted loudly and then froze. But he wasn't finished, he gave her a two-second reprieve and started again, even faster and harder. Storm sucked in her breath and then licked her lips. She started bucking again too. They had found their rhythm, and they both moaned and moved feverishly, almost violently.

Rayne arched into the air, trying to keep ahold of a scream trying to squeeze out of her throat. She whimpered and panted and the waves rolled over and over her. Her hand stilled between her legs.

Storm stopped long enough to lock eyes with her. She looked almost savage, and a chill ran down Rayne's skin.

Storm smiled and throatily muttered, loud enough for Rayne to hear her, "Watch the Storm until the Rayne comes."

Rayne's mind processed the metaphor, and she realized at any other time, that line would've sounded cheesy, but not right now. Not right here. The look on Storm's face was nearly primal.

Not waiting for a response, Storm bucked against the trucker again, and this time Rayne saw his knees nearly buckle. He caught himself but threw his head back letting out a huge moan.

Storm grabbed his hand and brought it to her mouth, sucking two of his fingers until she too came, her moans and groans coming out around her mouthful of digits.

Rayne felt the blood rush through her as she felt the walls of her own sex squeeze around her fingers, clenching and unclenching. The final waves rolled through and she began to chant under her breath, "Oh shit, oh shit, oh SHIT!"

She rocked against her hand, her breasts rubbing against the steering wheel, as she rode the waves through to the end together with Storm and her sexy trucker, the crazy metaphors of their names rolling through Rayne's mind... Rain and Storm... a hot, wet, wild, dangerous and unpredictable summer rainstorm—*or Rayne-Storm.*

Rayne felt like she'd been ripped apart by the orgasm. She couldn't remember Joe ever bringing her this far, or maybe it was just too long ago to remember. She fell back against her seat, finally letting go of the steering wheel, limp with exhaustion.

With the help of the trucker, Storm rolled off the truck and stood on shaky legs. She threw her arms around his neck and hugged him, and her body shone in the dim light, glistening with sweat.

He patted her back, and then like a gentleman, reached for her panties, holding them up as she balanced herself hanging onto his arm and stepped into them. She grabbed the rest of her clothes, bundling them up close to her and gave him a peck on the cheek before turning toward Rayne. *She's getting back in my truck? Oh, shit.*

Rayne scrambled to pull her own panties on and then slide into her pants. She hit the unlock button and then waited for Storm to get in.

Storm didn't say a word. She just held onto her clothes and leaned her head back, limply resting against the cool leather seat.

Rayne unconsciously landed in the same pose, and they both lay with their heads back, lightly panting, and letting their hearts slow while their temperature came down. Rayne stared out the window at the faces still watching, but no longer ashamed to meet their eyes, and saw plenty of movement down the row of rigs. She didn't care. She'd never felt so relaxed and fulfilled. She closed her eyes, enjoying the euphoric feeling for a moment longer.

Honk!

Rayne and Storm both gave a little scream and jumped. Not knowing where exactly it came from—just that it was very loud echoing through the lot—they both frantically glanced around. Seeing they were still surrounded by just the big rigs, in their own little protective cocoon, it seemed, their eyes met and they burst into laughter. "Looks like that wasn't meant for us, huh?" Storm asked.

They both laughed again, covering their sudden embarrassment at thinking they'd been caught doing something naughty—*real* naughty.

Still breathing heavily, Storm didn't make a move to get dressed. Rayne lazily started the truck, turning on the air conditioning. The temperature in the car seemed to cool down rapidly, and she sighed in relief as she felt the sweat start to dry on her own body.

The space between them seemed to grow smaller as their hearts slowed down and their skin cooled. Soon Rayne felt her sudden reckless streak fade away, replaced by apprehension and modesty. Storm knew what she'd been doing in here while she was getting hammered by the truck driver; and she knew Rayne's eyes had been on her just as much as her male partner. *So. Embarrassing.* Her thoughts jumbled amongst themselves as she tried to come up with something—anything—to say.

• • •

"Thank you!" she finally blurted out. She wasn't thinking those words. Where the hell did that come from? She wished she could take them back as soon as they were out of her mouth. She felt stupid. Her face began to burn. *This. Is. Awkward.*

Storm shook her head. "No, thank *you*. And I hope you found what you were looking for here." She raised her eyebrows.

Rayne appreciated that she changed the subject. "I'm still not sure I was looking for anything. But what I meant was thanks for telling me I'm sexy and pretty. I actually feel that way now. You really helped my self-esteem. I'll be damned if I'm going to let my hubs feel like his issues are my fault anymore. Hell, maybe he is cheating on me—probably at the truck stops. If someone like you is here...there's probably one or two like you at all the truck stops. Right?"

Storm gave a small smile and looked away, focusing on gathering her clothes. She quickly dressed, letting the question hang out there, and Rayne felt uneasy in the silence. She looked away. *Oh shit, I hope I didn't offend her. It's not like I offered her money... yet.*

Finally, having gotten all of her clothes on, Storm turned back to Rayne, her smile having changed to sultry as she looked up and down Rayne's body, her eyes lingering on Rayne's breasts. She leaned back in the seat and dug into her pocket, pulling out a piece of paper. She slid it on the dashboard and reached for the door handle before finally answering her.

"I'm actually someone like you, Rayne. Nothing more. Nothing less. Just a lonely trucker's wife... but not lonely tonight."

She put one hand on the cheek of Rayne's astonished face and leaned in to gently kiss her on the lips. Then she got out of the car and walked away, quickly disappearing between the lines of rigs, leaving Rayne completely gobsmacked.

...and   inspired.

• • •
35

Seven

Rayne guiltily showered and crawled quietly into bed beside her husband. She hadn't wanted to wake him so she didn't bother to put pajamas on. The lamp was still shining a low light from his nightstand, and she knew the click of twisting the knob might wake him too, so she left it on.

He was sleeping soundly and obviously having a good dream—the blankets couldn't hide his hard-on poking up underneath.

I can definitely rule out equipment failure, she thought. *Nothing wrong with his tool.* She smiled when thoughts of her and Storm flashed in her mind. *But...I. Almost. Cheated. On. My. Husband.* The smile slid off her face and she worriedly bit her lip.

He had left the light on for her, and was here in bed—hard for her? He could've just taken care of himself and went to sleep satisfied, but obviously he *had* waited for her after all.

I don't deserve him. Her eyes filled with tears of regret for even considering cheating on him. He was a good man. A good husband. Even if a bit grumpy lately.

Moving her eyes from the tent-like shape above his waist, her eyes went to where the blanket ended just below his chest. His chest and arms were tan and still in great shape—not cut anymore with six-pack abs, but no beer belly

* * *

either. His dark hair was full and wavy, not a gray hair in sight. But he was still just thirty-four years old—six years older than her. Unlike her, he still looked much like he did when they married eight years ago. *Maybe better,* she thought. *And maybe I don't deserve him. But dammit, I've worked hard to keep myself looking good for him, too.*

Her face flushed when flickers of Storm's lips and tongue flew through her mind like a film on fast-forward. She couldn't stop the images. She didn't really want to stop them... she wanted to share them with Joe.

She felt remorseful and excited all at once. Maybe she'd discovered the answer to breaking down the wall that stood between them. Early in their marriage, Joe had fantasized about being with two women; he'd said so many times. But she had never taken him seriously. *Hopefully he was serious,* she thought.

Now she could tell him she might finally be interested. Then she'd explain what happened and see if he was still all about that kind of thing. She'd try anything to get the heat back into their marriage, and re-light that fire that had burnt out.

She just had to risk poking the bear first. Joe hated to be woken up when he had to leave early on a long-haul.

She looked at him sleeping so soundly and wondered who or what he was dreaming of. She shook off the little green monster of envy, realizing if someone had a right to jealousy right now, it would be him. At least he was only getting aroused in a dream. Rayne shook off a delicious shiver when her thoughts again went back to Storm getting screwed so thoroughly on the hood of Joe's truck. She had to share this with Joe. It was so freaking hot, there was no way he could get pissed off.

"Joe," she whispered. "Wake up."

Joe grunted and rolled over, taking his hard-on with him.

Rayne's lip poked out in disappointment, but she didn't give up. She reached under the blanket, then over his sleeping form and found him, still hard and hot to the touch. She stroked him, trying again to wake him up—this time without words.

Joe moaned and Rayne's hopes soared. Maybe she'd finally get him to give her some. She'd tell him what had her so hot and bothered that she dared to wake him. Rayne stroked him with more force, and gently brushed her lips across his back with butterfly kisses.

He jerked away, startling her. He clutched the sheet and blanket in one big hand and jumped out of bed, nearly tripping. He caught himself by grabbing the nightstand with his free hand. He looked around the room as if he thought someone else was there before realizing it was just Rayne.

He glared at her, his face showing anger along with the sleepy remains of his slumber. "What the hell are you doing, Rayne?"

Eight

Rayne sat up and gave him an indignant look before realizing she'd probably just startled him out of a deep sleep. She couldn't blame him for that, knowing he was *always* grumpy if woken up.

She softened her face and answered, "I'm trying to get a piece of that hard-on you're sporting there, big guy."

She hadn't bothered to get clothes on after her shower, and since Joe had snagged the covers and the sheets with him when he'd jumped up, she was left sitting there completely bare.

He stared at her wordlessly for a moment, so Rayne took that as encouragement. She leaned back on her pillow and slightly pulled up one leg, bending it at the knee; just enough to show him she was freshly-shaven. He blinked rapidly, apparently trying to shake off the sleep. Then she watched his eyes as they moved from her face down the length of her body.

"I'm wet, Joe. And *you* have a hard-on. Let's not waste it." She smiled at him and patted the bed, like she'd done a thousand times before—as close to initiating sex as she could get.

Joe slowly shook his head.

"Rayne, I've got to be up early. I don't have time for that," he quietly said.

Rayne's patience snapped. She jumped up and grabbed her robe off the hook, quickly wrapping it around herself. Joe stomped the few steps back to the bed and crawled in, pulling the covers tightly around him, but not even trying to spread the sheet and blanket to her side.

"What the hell is wrong with you? With us?" Rayne demanded. "I don't understand, Joe. You haven't wanted me for months. Is it me? *Please...* talk to me!"

"Dammit, Rayne. Just let me sleep," he muttered, and rolled over, giving her his back—again. But this time she saw him... *really* saw him.

She felt her eyes getting wet before a tear slid out. But not a tear of sadness—a tear of anger—of absolute-pissed-off-spitting-mad-fury. *That rat-bastard...*

As he laid his head back down on the pillow, his eyes already closed, she *saw*.

Someone had staked her claim on him. His neck showed the tell-tale sign of passion—from someone else's mouth. A perfect heart-shaped hickey marked her husband—and   broke   her   heart.

Nine

"So... you gonna talk? Or did you have something else in mind?" Storm sat with her head leaned against the passenger window, her body turned to face Rayne with her legs spread, one foot in the seat and one on the floor. She had one arm slung casually over the back of the seat—extremely comfortable in her own skin.

Rayne both loved and envied Storm's relaxed nature. As she took a long look at her, she noticed she was chewing gum. Her mouth moving in a lazy dance entrancing Rayne for a moment. *Those lips. Damn...* Rayne shook herself out of her trance and let her eyes travel down to Storm's exposed thighs, then quickly looked away. Her mouth was hard enough to avoid, but the pull of that tiny strip of denim that barely covered Storm's girly bits was damn near impossible to ignore. *Damn, this girl can rock a pair of jean shorts.*

Rayne sat very still, focusing her gaze through the window, with her hands gripping the steering wheel as though she was driving. But she wasn't. She blinked her eyes, and brought her focus down to her knuckles, white from gripping the wheel so tight. She had to keep it together, but also loosen up at the same time.

She took in a deep breath and let it out, and released her grip, letting her hands fall into her lap. Her eyes went back to the view of a stand of trees, mesmerized by the beams of morning sun filtering through them. They were parked at a dead-end dirt road, not far from the truck stop. It was early—early enough she could still hear a few random night bugs throwing out their last calls of the evening. The morning was much hotter than usual—in more ways than one. She second-guessed calling Storm. *Why the hell did I think she'd care about my shit at home?*

She wasn't sure she could talk about Joe anyway. She was doing her best to calm her mind, to not let Storm see a river of tears. She swallowed loudly around the huge lump in her throat, and pressed her lips firmly together. She shrugged.

"Talk to me, Rayne. You wouldn't have called if you didn't want to talk, right?"

When Rayne had woken earlier on the couch—having cried herself to sleep there—she'd found Joe had already left for his long-haul run. So she didn't get a chance to confront him, and it was *not* a conversation she wanted to have on the phone with him. She'd been wild with anger when her eyes first popped open—having gone through the grief phrase before she fell asleep. And like a tornado, she'd gone through the house breaking dishes, slamming doors and kicking furniture, until her anger fizzled back down to sadness again.

She'd slid down the wall in their bedroom, breathing hard, staring at his side of the bed where she'd last seen him lay... asking herself *why*, over and over. *Why would he do this to me? How could he do this to me?* When she'd caught her breath again, she'd screamed to the world that her husband was a rat bastard. Shrieked until the effort of her voice sharply prickled her throat, and she couldn't scream anymore. Then she'd sat there—limp, hoping the neighbors were still asleep and hadn't heard her.

Once she'd quieted down, her anger allowed the truth to finally break through. She'd realized she'd *almost* done it to him, too. Only once—the night before—but it would still have been cheating, even if it would have been with a woman... *wouldn't it?* That thought had reminded her of the piece of paper Storm had slid onto her dash.

She'd ran out of the house, straight to the car to look for it. At first, she had panicked, thinking Joe must've found it. It was gone from the dash. Then she had moved around to the passenger side and opened the door. The tiny piece of paper had fallen out, slowly drifting down to land at her feet; it must've slid off the dash while she was driving.

Rayne had stood for what seemed like eternity looking down at the scrap of paper that lay there, with the word "Storm" written in cursive, followed by a phone number. She'd drawn a cute lightning bolt through the "O" in Storm too. Rayne wondered whom the note had originally been meant for—and was surprised to feel a tinge of jealousy.

Her panties had gotten wet in the instant it had taken her brain to connect that swirly, girly penmanship to the picture Rayne held in her mind, of Storm's face, her hair, her lips. The images sped through her mind of her first sight of Storm's perfect little breasts to her heart-shaped mouth, shiny dark hair moving to and fro, and her long, but limber legs. The image ended with the sexy trucker, leaned over slamming into Storm's tiny, satiny-smooth snatch.

For just that moment, all she'd seen was Storm, and it had washed away all the painful of thoughts of her husband sleeping with another woman. But it was a short-lived respite. The hurt flooded back in, making her heart heavy as she'd carried the note into their empty house. She'd looked around and realized it was just a shell of house—not a home. No children, no laughter, no loving kind words or attention from her husband anymore. She'd felt the weight of eight years *wasted* bearing down on her and she'd had to leave.

The thought to *not* call Storm never crossed her mind. She'd immediately called and Storm had agreed to meet her back at The Quick Dip. From there, Storm had jumped in the car with her, and they'd driven just a few miles before they'd pulled off the main road and parked.

• • •

Storm loudly cleared her throat. Rayne glanced over to see her eyebrows raised at her. "Is this about your husband?" Storm gave her a questioning look, pausing again for a response. "Did he find out about last night?"

Rayne glanced over and finally met her eyes. *Damn, she has beautiful eyes too.* In the broad daylight, she could see what she'd missed last night. Storm's eyes suited her name, and were very unique for someone who obviously was of Asian descent—deep green with big specks of gold, framed by thick lashes. Her eyes were intriguing and intense. Only the almond-shape hinted at her parentage. *I wonder if it'd be rude to ask her ethnicity.*

She breathed in the scent of Storm. *Still spicy-ish.* The smell brought back the memory of the chocolate and cinnamon smells woven together last night, steamy and hot... and delicious. *Mmmm...* She continued to stare into Storm's eyes, lost in them and her fantasy, as she slowly ran her tongue over her own dry lips—the result of earlier that morning.

"Earth to Rayne." Storm clapped her hands in front of her, startling Rayne.

Rayne gave a little jump. "No. I mean yes... I mean..." she stammered, and looked back out the front window, not able to meet Storm's fiery green eyes. *Why did I call her? Like she's gonna give a flying shit about me and my husband. I just met her last night. I'm an idiot,* she thought. *I'm sure she's got her own drama. But too late now. She's here. I'm here.* Rayne shrugged to her own inner monologue, as though she was answering herself.

Storm pursed her lips together and tilted her head... waiting.

"He doesn't know about last night," Rayne whispered, her voice still hoarse from her earlier tantrum. "But it doesn't matter anyway. He's cheating on me. I saw a hickey on his neck last night. And then I went through his bag, and found condoms."

Rayne's voice cracked on the word condoms, but she sucked it up. She was done crying. She refused to let herself shed one more tear. "We don't use condoms. We've tried for years to have a kid."

"Oh. Shit," Storm whispered. "So sorry."

"Yeah." Rayne shrugged one shoulder, as if it was no big deal.

"Hey. Don't shrug it off. I'm glad you called. Sounds like you need a friend." Storm reached out and rubbed Rayne's arm.

Rayne's brain registered the trail of sparks that sent shivers down her back and caused a familiar slow, dull ache between her legs.

Storm continued with her hand on Rayne's arm, "You said last night you've been married eight years. How long do you think it's been going on?"

Rayne shrugged again. "I don't know. Things started changing about a year ago. He stopped wanting to be with me. He's prickly as a freaking hornet all the time, over the slightest things, and he seems to *want* to spend every day on the road. It's like he's avoiding me, even when he is home."

"Did you confront him about the hickey?"

"No. I was too shocked. When I got home last night, I tried to... um... sleep with him. Not sleep, but... you know..." Rayne felt her face heating up. *Dumbass, you just watched this woman get laid, up close and personal, and had her lips on yours not even twenty-four hours ago, and now you can't even talk about sex?! Wtf?*

"We didn't... umm... *do it*. We got into a fight, but I didn't see the hickey until after he laid back down. And I just... I...well, he needed his sleep. I was going to talk to him first thing this morning, but he'd already left when I woke up."

"Girl! Are you serious? He 'needed his sleep'?" Storm's voice was incredulous. Rayne looked over to see her holding her hands open in front of her, as though waiting for an explanation. "What the hell is that? You're worried about his *sleep*?!"

Rayne looked away again, ashamed of her own stupidity.

"I mean, like… really?" Storm continued, "Do you want some help carrying that cross?" she asked sarcastically.

Okay, now you're starting to piss me off. "Yeah. I know… it sounds like I'm a doormat. I'm not trying to be a martyr. But you don't understand my husband. Waking him up to accuse him of cheating on me wouldn't have gone well. Joe's easier to deal with after he's had a good night sleep," Rayne answered defensively.

Storm looked away from Rayne for the first time since they'd parked. She shook her head in disgust.

"Girl, you *seriously* needs to grow a set."

Rayne felt heat on her cheeks again. She ran her hands over her face and smoothed back her hair, and then answered in firm voice, "Yeah. I guess I do."

Storm took in a deep breath and let it out. "Well, what'cha   gonna   do   about   it?"

Ten

"I guess I'll have to wait until he gets home and talk to him." Rayne's voice sounded hollow again, even as she met Storm's eyes to try to seem decisive—strong.

"Oh, fuck that! I'll bet you've tried to *talk* to him before—many times. Am I right? How's that been working for ya?" Storm lifted her eyebrows and met Rayne's gaze head-on. "I'm just *saying*... isn't it time you *do* something? Something for *you*?"

Rayne hadn't thought about that. It hadn't occurred there was anything she could do. *Can I?* She felt the rage build within her again. A year's supply of built-up rage... from his avoidance of intimacy, to his lackluster efforts when it did happen... his inability to talk about what exactly the problem was, thus making her feel like *she* was the problem—and his anger. That's what pissed her off the most. For almost a year she'd been walking on pins and needles, never knowing what would set him off, spending every day either at work, or moping around the house waiting for him. *He's messing around on me. That's why he's been so snappy and stand-offish!*

That in itself would make someone jumpy and irritable around their wife; and explain why he never had sexual energy left over for her. And he'd let her carry the brunt of his guilt. He let her take responsibility for his bad moods. *That asshole.* She was tired of staying home and playing the good little wife. Tired of chasing her tail in hopes that Joe would want her again.

She looked at Storm with a determined look in her eye. "I'd like to find his sorry ass out on the road. Sneak up on him and catch him cheating." Just saying the word 'cheating' out loud reminded her of last night... being taken by Storm. The familiar wet, throbbing ache between her legs was begging for release again.

Storm tilted her head in thought. "What if you and I take a road trip together? We can head toward your hubs, but be open to some fun along the way. *Sexy* fun. I *know* the road, girlfriend. There's some amazing stuff I think you might be missing out on." Storm smiled and her eyes twinkled. "Seriously, you *need* fun right now. So you in?"

Rayne sighed. It did sound exciting, and she was tired of being ignored, and seriously fed up with feeling sexually frustrated. She didn't necessarily have to do anything she didn't want to. *So why not?* She was half-way through her summer break and couldn't think of one fun thing she'd done so far. *Heck yeah. I deserve some fun. To hell with Joe,* she thought angrily.

Rayne nodded slowly. Resolving to turn her hurt and pain into fuel to pursue something... something *different.* Something better than what she'd been living for the past year. She didn't know what she hoped to find, but she'd felt a recklessness blossom inside of her last night, when she'd done those *things* with Storm. She wanted to feel *more* of that. She wanted it to bloom and overtake every tiny part of her being, to patch over the spots of pain that Joe had left behind. Pain that had been growing for the past year, as it continued burning deeper and deeper, crushing her spirit— and smothering her soul. She wanted to feel happy again. Feel free. She wanted to just *feel.*

"Let's do it! Obviously he's doing more than working out on the road. So yeah, I'll go," Rayne answered enthusiastically. "Screw Joe. That rat bastard...," she finished in a less-enthusiastic whisper, her emotions taking dips and turns every few seconds. "He doesn't care how I feel, so screw *him!*" she said again, her voice hitched and she slammed her palms against the steering wheel.

"Feel this, Rayne." Storm leaned over and pulled Rayne toward her, using her hands tangled in her hair. She met her halfway and crushed her lips against Rayne's, forcing them open with her tongue—demanding... probing... promising.

Storm took Rayne's breath away as her body responded to the kiss. A low moan escaped, coming from deep in Rayne's throat. Their tongues slowed, twisting in a slow and seductive dance. Storm ended the kiss with her own breathy moan, timed to perfection with a panted whimper from Rayne.

Storm leaned back in her seat, her back still against the door. "How did that feel to you?"

Rayne blushed deeply. She swiped at a wisp of hair that had fallen in her face, while she tried to gather her thoughts. There was no denying her body's reaction to Storm, but she couldn't wrap her head around it.

"*Awww*mazing," she admitted, in a silly tone meant to deflect her modesty. "It felt amazing—and somehow it felt right... at the moment. But it's not me, and I'm not sure it's a good idea for us to do... *that*... again."

Rayne cringed before continuing, "I'm straight, Storm. Strictly-dickly. And I have a husband—at least for now. I'm not sure what's going to happen with that, but I don't think I'm ready to um... jump into any sort of... relationship..." she finished hesitantly.

Storm smiled and let an awkward pause sit between them. Rayne fidgeted, embarrassed at her belated attempt to lay ground rules. *Shit, she probably wants to get the hell away from me now. I guess I can forget the road trip.*

Then Storm laughed, long and loud. "For realsie? *Girl.* Don't even worry about that. I am soooo *not* looking for a relationship either. Just friends. With bennies. So let's hit the road. Like, today!" she said excitedly. "We can kill two birds with one stone. You know where your hub's is headed. We can listen to the chatter on the CB, and maybe get some help from the boys. If we miss him, we can always catch him on the flip-flop. Meanwhile, I'll show you the ropes on how to have some real fun. No strings attached."

"You really think another trucker would help us?"

Storm snickered. "Trust me, truckers are usually a helpful—and fun—group of good 'ole boys to girls like us," she said with a wink, as she smiled mischievously. "So how 'bout we go, and get geared up?"

THE TRUCKER'S WIFE

Episode Two

BRING ON THE RAYNE

One

The doorbell rang, and Rayne jumped. *Shit. Shit. Shit,* she thought. She'd spent the last hour pacing the floor, her mind playing hop-scotch as she waffled with herself as to whether or not to hit the road with an almost-stranger. A stranger that she'd almost had a *bi-curious* experience with. It'd been tempting, but Rayne was strictly-dickly. But she couldn't deny she'd gotten hot with Storm, and even hotter watching Storm with that sexy trucker.

Her bag was packed—with only the sexiest outfits she owned; which wasn't saying much. But once she'd slowed down to think about it, she wasn't sure this was such a good idea. Joe would be pissed if she just left with no explanation. *Maybe I should just call him? Tell him I met a friend, and I need to get out of the house… Or maybe I should just ask him if he's cheating on me?* She sucked in a deep breath and scrubbed her hands over her face, and then let it out.

Okay, first things first… just answer the door. Storm's probably thinking I'm avoiding her.

Rayne glanced out the window before opening the door. Storm—obviously having no patience for standing at the door waiting—was stretched out on the hood of her car, arms behind her head, sunglasses on. Her chocolaty-covered long hair lay in waves spread out under her head. She looked

sexy and relaxed. Hell, she looked asleep. And the car—
Omigod… the car.

Rayne had no idea what kind of car it was, but it was
definitely expensive. And sexy. *Damn, even her car looks like
rolling sex,* thought Rayne. *And her husband's a trucker? Guess he's
a higher paid driver than Joe.*

She opened the door and stepped out.

"Sorry. I was in the back of the house…" Rayne lied,
her words trailing off as she walked down the driveway and
around the car with big eyes. Her eyes got even wider when
she read "Jaguar" over the rear bumper. The body of the car
was stunning; it was a gorgeous coupe with a panoramic glass
roof.

Storm slowly sat up, pushing her sunglasses to the top
of her head, where they held her hair back. "Bout time,
hooker. I wondered if you were gonna hide in the house and
pretend you weren't here."

Rayne laughed nervously. She had thought about
doing just that. "Nice car," she said, hoping to change the
subject.

"You like it? It's a 2015 Jaguar F-Type S Coupe."

Rayne nodded her head, having no idea what that
meant, except money… lots of money; she was almost afraid
to touch it. Even the color of the car—red—screamed hot,
racy sex.

"So you coming, or not?"

Rayne glanced at Storm to see if she meant that as
sexy innuendo… but Storm had looked away and she
couldn't see her eyes.

Rayne looked back at the car, unknowingly chewing
her bottom lip, tugging at it with her teeth, as she thought
about it. She'd need to make it very clear to Storm, again, that
she wasn't interested in girl-on-girl sexy times… but she
could do that. They were both grown-ups, she felt sure Storm
would respect her boundaries.

The car itself looks like an adventure. A road trip... like Thelma and Louise, Rayne thought, and then gave a little laugh. Fun, excitement, freedom... she needed this. She didn't realize how much she wanted it until she saw Storm again—and her cool freakin' car.

An added bonus would be actually catching Joe in the act... if there was anything to catch. She knew she'd never do it alone. If she sat here, she'd just wait for him to come home and deny everything; then life would go on as it had... sad and wasted. Unwanted. Unsexed. Unfulfilled. While he was probably on the road, banging some whore every week. She had to know...

"I'm in," she answered.

"Then get your shit. Let's go." Storm pressed a button on her key fob and the hatchback lid floated up. She had left plenty of room for Rayne's things.

She turned and made her way to the driver's side, getting in and waiting.

Rayne rushed into the house, where she'd left her bags just inside the door. She grabbed them and locked the door, barely giving the house a last look as she ran back to the car, practically skipping as her excitement bubbled over.

Two

Rayne threw her bag in the back, and before she could raise a hand to close the hatch, it automatically closed on its own. She held her hands up in surrender... and made her way to the passenger door. The door handle was flush with the flank of the car, obviously retracted when not in use. Rayne bent down and peeked into the window.

"How do I get in?"

Storm laughed, then hit a button. The door handle poked out and Rayne grabbed it, and then climbed into the passenger seat. She still had a smile on her face when she adjusted herself in the seat and snapped her seat belt. She looked at Storm. "Ready for take-off," she joked.

But Storm didn't return the banter. She had gone serious, giving Rayne the suspicious eyeball. Obviously Storm had some concerns of her own to clear up first.

"So what're you going to do if we catch him and he *is* cheating?" Storm asked, and then crossed her arms against her chest. Rayne took a moment to think about her question, admiring the interior of the car.

Storm continued, "I don't want to be out on the road with you and have you go all Lorena Bobbitt on me. I'm not cool with that. I don't need any trouble."

Rayne rolled her eyes. "I'm not a violent person, Storm. I'll catch him in the act, and get proof that he's cheating on me first." She took in a big breath, and let it out, the thought of him cheating sending a dagger into her heart. "Then maybe I'll let *him* catch *me* so he can see how it feels. He deserves that and more for the last year of hell; not to mention the hickey."

Rayne cringed when she realized whatever she did or didn't do, there was probably a divorce coming. She felt her stomach flip as the realization sunk in. They'd watched many of their couple-friends go through nasty divorces over the years. *This could get ugly.* They didn't have much, at least as far she knew. Just the house. But all the money from both of their jobs went into one account, and since Joe brought home most of the money, he handled the bills. She had a debit card and a credit card, but rarely used either. She had no idea how much money—or debt—they even had. Joe handled everything. She might be walking away with nothing.

She shook her head. She wasn't letting that happen. He cheated. And maybe she *almost* did too—with Storm—but she'd stopped. She'd honored her marriage vows.

She was entitled to at least half of what they had. She'd worked just as hard as Joe had. She just happened to be in one of the most underpaid professions in the world, but she deserved her half. She'd just have to find a way to prove it.

"Yeah, I definitely need to sneak up and catch him in the act. And maybe have some fun on the way."

Storm nodded her head. "*That...* I can help with." She smiled and started the car, giving Rayne a wink before she poked the red start button and threw it into reverse. The tires screeching competed with the ferocious sound of the engine as she backed it out of the driveway too fast, causing Rayne to squeal. She felt the brakes bite and then Storm thrust them forward, throttling over the posted speed limit in her sleepy neighborhood within seconds. Rayne didn't feel a single bump in the road that she normally felt in her own car.

Damn, everything about this girl is fast and smooth, Rayne thought to herself.

She watched in astonishment as the motorized center air-vents rose slowly out of the dash like a something Rayne would expect to see in the Batmobile. She chuckled. Then she noticed the interior lighting change from one ambient color to another... she watched it slowly morph into different colors five times... *five different lighting colors in one car?*

She glanced at Storm who was smirking at her. "Pick a color. I've got Phosphor Blue, Pale Blue, White, Coral or Red. What's your mood say?"

Rayne smirked back. "Red of course; let's start with red."

Three

"Okay. So he left his morning. We know where he's headed, and we know how many hours a day he's allowed to drive before having to pull over. If we drive one or two more hours than him, we'll either catch him or pass him, right?" Storm asked.

Rayne shrugged. "I guess. I'm not sure how that works. Sometimes Joe fudges his log book. He might drive all night. Or he might follow the rules and pull over. We may never catch up, or we may pass him."

"*But!* I don't think we should catch him on the way. It's my experience, if a trucker's going to cheat, he's going to do it on the flip-flop, after he drops his first load."

Rayne visibly cringed.

"Oh, sorry. That sounded bad. You know what I meant."

A small smile tugged at Rayne's lips. Storm was witty, even if she hadn't meant to be.

Storm caught her small smile and went on. "So, if we drive faster than him, and cover more road, then we can still have a few hours each day to play." She looked at Rayne and winked. "Then we can follow him home and if he's up to no good, that's probably when we'd catch him. You agree?"

Rayne's thoughts swirled. She lost her smile thinking of Joe cheating… when, where and with whom? She couldn't even imagine it. She shrugged her shoulders again. She couldn't think straight to come up any other plan, not when her heart was flipping from breaking into a million pieces, to burning with jealous rage.

Storm saw her look of confusion. "Look, you just plug in the address into the GPS. I'll make sure we get there and get in position to see Joe leave. But from here to there, don't think about it anymore. Let me take you on a ride you'll never forget. Let go and live a little, *sista.*"

That brought the smile back to Rayne's face. She was glad Storm was taking charge. If she put too much thought into it, her mind would convince her the hickey she'd seen wasn't actually a hickey and she'd come up with another plausible excuse for the condoms. Soon, she'd be having Storm turn around and take her home before she ruined anything with Joe, and find a way to continue to blame herself for his shortcomings.

"You're driving. I'm just along for the ride," Rayne finally answered. She leaned up and typed the address into the GPS, and then felt the tension drop from her shoulders.

Four

Eight hours down the road:

"Okay, okay, *okay*. I get it. You're having second thoughts. But don't you owe it to yourself to see with your own eyes what your husband's up to, Rayne?" she said with a tinge of irritation in her voice. "It would be stupid to turn around now."

When Rayne didn't answer, Storm took her eyes off the road long enough to give her a quick glance. "I think maybe what you need is to forget your woes and get laid. It'd help to get you out of your funk."

Rayne rolled her eyes. Yeah, that's exactly what she needed. But she wanted that with her husband, not some stranger. Even if he was hot. Even if Joe was getting it from someone else. Until she knew without a shadow of a doubt he was cheating, she'd just have to tamper down her own desires—or just continue to handle it herself.

Watching Storm with that hot trucker last night didn't help much to ease the ache she felt between her own legs for very long. But what was really bothering Rayne was that she was feeling remorse about leaving without talking to Joe first. She was getting cold feet again about this trip—and maybe a little homesick.

After hours on the road and a failed attempt with Storm trying to teach her how to use the CB—which she was surprised to see tucked away in the glove department—Storm had showed a different side of herself; a little snarky and bitchy... and Rayne mentally gave in and said maybe they should just turn around and go home.

"The last thing you need is to go home. There's so much fun to be had... and don't you still want to find out what Joe's up to? This is the only way, unless you've got big bucks for a private investigator."

Rayne shrugged.

After eating up hundreds of miles of boring road, her anger at Joe had eased up, and the trip didn't seem like such an adventure anymore. Sadness and defeat were settling in, pushing out the fury she'd initially felt. She couldn't stay angry much longer without having Joe right in front of her flashing the hickey to remind her he cheated—or *may* have cheated. Her thoughts kept straying farther and farther away from the hickey and the condoms, and closer to what could she do to fix whatever was broken in their marriage.

She'd wanted to call him hours ago... just to hear his voice... maybe give him an opening to confess and beg for forgiveness, or better yet... to explain away the whole crazy scene. Make it disappear. Make her feel foolish. Anything to not have to accept her marriage was over.

But Storm had adamantly insisted Rayne should leave him on ignore or the whole plan could be ruined. She was very persuasive.

"Hand me that CB. Let's spice up the night," Storm said.

Rayne gladly handed it over to Storm, frustrated at her inability to figure out something so simple. Storm kept her eyes on the road, maintaining almost triple digit speed, and laughed as her hand wrapped around the mouthpiece.

"Okay, it's not that complicated. See, you press this to talk." Her finger hovered over the button on the side of the walkie-talkie-looking-thing. "When you're done, you say 'come-back' and then let go of the button. Then wait for someone to talk to you. Or you can just say 'over' if you're talking back and forth with someone. Main thing is to let go of the button when you finish talking to let someone else have their turn."

Rayne shook her head. She and Storm had been on the road all day, and the she was getting sleepy. Nothing exciting had happened as of yet, and her mind was shutting down, not processing the mechanics of the CB radio; and not really wanting to.

"*You* should be talking anyway. What if Joe's on that channel and listening? I don't want him to hear my voice over the air," she said to Storm, a little bit of snark sneaking into her own voice. Maybe being cooped up together in such a small car for nine days wasn't such a good idea under the circumstances.

"Oh, shit. I didn't even think about that. Okay, I'll do the talking. Listen and learn, young Grasshopper… Hey! I think I'll make that your handle!"

"Handle?"

"Yeah, everyone on the CB has a handle—kind of a nickname. I just use my real name since it sounds like a handle anyway, but yours can be anything," she said excitedly. "What about Grasshopper? I *am* teaching you the ways of the road…"

Rayne shook her head, scrunching her nose at the idea of it. "No! Do *not* call me Grasshopper. I don't *need* a handle and I don't *want* one. You can do all the talking."

She was getting very nervous. Rolling down the highway, feeling safe and inconspicuous in the cocoon of Storm's car was one thing… but Storm wanted to talk smack to the truckers on the CB—well, had actually wanted *Rayne* to do it, and at this late hour, all Rayne wanted to do was find a good, soft bed to stretch out and then curl up in. She was ready to get out of the car after driving most of the day.

Storm gave her a quick look, her face scrutinizing Rayne's, and then put her eyes back on the road and pressed the button.

"Anybody out there got their ears on? This is Storm. Come back," she said and then let go of the button.

"Hey Storm! You got Smokin' Okie. Missed you lately, girl. Where ya been hiding? Come on," a deep, rumbling voice rolled through the car and Storm glanced at Rayne and winked. Then she whispered—as if Smokin' Okie might hear—"This guy is so hot he can melt your panties just talking smut over the CB. In person, he's even better. *Smokin'* hot... and from Oklahoma. That's how he got his handle. He's a cowboy who slings a huge rope. I'm gonna see if we can hook up."

Rayne assumed she was talking about herself. She'd tried to make it clear to Storm she wasn't interested in getting busy, especially with a man—for that, her marriage would truly be over. She wasn't ready to face that just yet, and maybe not until she saw Joe cheating on her with her own two eyes.

Storm answered Okie, "I've been around. We caught some action at the Quick Dip last night. Wish you'd of been there. Where you headed? Over."

A short pause filled the air, and then he answered, "I'm not rolling at the moment. I'm sitting at the pickle park, ignoring the knocks on my door, and doodling in my comic book. Where you at? Over."

Rayne held her hands in the air as if to ask what the hell all that meant.

Storm laughed at Rayne's gesture and answered, "He's at a rest area that's normally frequented by lot lizards— prostitutes—and he's not interested. He's catching up his log book, probably for the next weigh station."

Storm pushed the button again, answering his question with a question, "What's your yardstick? I've got a friend I'd like you to meet. Over."

Rayne gasped. "**Storm!** Did you just ask him how big his... his... *cock*... was over the radio?" Rayne had trouble spitting out the word cock. It'd been a long time since she'd said that word aloud. She realized her language was slowly getting muddied by Storm's influence.

Storm threw her head back and laughed. "No, silly. Yardstick means mile-marker. I know he's around here somewhere if he's on his regular route. It's the same every week. But he could be behind us or ahead of us."

Smokin' Okie gave his yardstick/mile marker and Storm gave a disappointed sigh. "Sorry, Okie. You're in my back pocket. Over."

"S'kay, Storm. I'm not interested in commercial company anyway. I'm having shutter trouble tonight. Over."

Storm quickly interpreted for Rayne, "Commercial company means a prostitute...and he's tired—having trouble keeping his eyes open."

Then she answered Smokin' Okie, "You wouldn't have needed green stamps for this one. She's not commercial. Just a friend of mine—and she's hot." Storm slid a glance to Rayne and winked. "We're just looking for some fun to spice up our evening. Over."

Rayne could feel her face heat up. She wondered how many people just heard that and assumed Storm was talking about sex—*Was she talking about sex?* Rayne really didn't know at   this   point.

Five

"Wait a minute... was that you and your friend in the party row last night? I heard about y'all. Been some chatter on the radio from a few boys who said they saw the two hot girls at a truck stop making out and then one got out to step up the show. Heard it got pretty hot and heavy. Was that you, Storm? Come back."

Rayne felt like her eyes were going to pop out of her head. *Omigod. People are talking about us,* she thought in panic. The heat moved quickly from her neck to the tips of her ears as she blushed. *Shit! Shit! Shit!*

Storm smiled proudly. "Yep, that was us. Over."

Rayne cringed. *Nice, just go ahead and admit it to the world... For Cripes's sake...*

"Ha! You know after last night, you two earned yourselves a team-handle? I should'a known it was your crazy nympho ass. Over," he said, and then laughed while still holding down his button, loud and uninhibited, but sexy as hell.

When he released the button, and the air cleared, Storm asked, "Oh yeah? Spill it? Did they tag us the Bobsey Twins, or something even more original? Come back."

"The word on the air is 'RainStorm.' The radio chatter all day has been repeating it and you got all the boys worked up into quite a lather. They're all keeping an eye out for you in case y'all give any more shows. Over."

"You told that guy our names?" Rayne yelled in shock. "What the hell, Storm? Are you crazy?"

Rayne covered her face with her hands. There it was... her name... out *there*. Joe would know. He would hear all about the truck stop. She may as well kiss her marriage good-bye. And probably her half of any assets... she was screwed with a capital S, followed by a capital D for divorce. Her heart sunk.

Storm giggled and Rayne whipped her head around and glared at her. She had the urge to slap the shit-eating grin off Storm's face.

"Storm, this is *not* funny. You shouldn't have told that trucker our names last night. This could be a big problem for me."

"Oh, chill out! He already knew *my* name, I just told him yours. And you seriously think your hubs would connect 'rainstorm,' to his sweet 'lil teacher wife?" She paused, blinking her eyes several times at Rayne.

Rayne was speechless. Shame doused her ability to think about anything other than Joe possibly knowing she'd kissed a girl—a woman—and watched that woman having sex right in front of her, with a random trucker on the hood of *his* truck! *Did he know?* She took in a deep breath and held it.

Storm's gaze went back out the front window. "I think you give him too much fucking credit. And if he does figure it out, so what? He cheated first, right? All we have to do is find out who with. The road's not that long, and people do talk—obviously." She smirked again and waved the radio in the air, proving her point. "May as well just let loose and have all the fun you want now."

Rayne slowly let the breath she'd been holding out, and leaned her head against the window of her door. Maybe Storm was right. The damage *was* done. *Wasn't it?* He cheated... there was a hickey and condoms to prove that. So yeah, she kissed a girl. *And I liked it.* And now, here she was, out on a road-trip with an almost complete stranger, trying to follow him and catch him with his pants down. *What's the use?*

Thoughts of who he might be screwing ripped through her head for the millionth time... someone younger? Someone skinnier? Someone prettier? After all she'd done for him?! After *years* of loyalty as his wife, staying home alone and lonely while he was out on the road, never having any fun and pulling non-stop duty as a full-time teacher, as well as his house-keeper, shit-stain scrubber, laundry-girl, personal shopper and his freaking cook? *What the hell for?* It was all a waste. All those years. *Gone.* How could she have been so stupid?

She snapped out of her own thoughts in time to hear Okie respond to something Storm had said, "Okay. You pull over at the next eat 'em up and meet you there. I'll be parked in the Party Row. I'll be moving on in just a few minutes and I'll throw 'er in boogie. You'll probably still beat me by half an hour, at least. Over."

Storm practically danced in her seat, still pushing the car over triple digits while setting up her rendezvous over the CB. Her face beamed. "See ya there, Smokin' Okie. Don't rush. I don't want you feedin' the bears. You still driving the same K-whopper? Come back."

"Yep. Everything's the same, and don't worry... I've been starvin' the bears for going on five years. Not about to feed 'em now. You girls be careful too. Keep the shiny side up, ya hear? Over."

"10-4," Storm answered and handed the CB to Rayne. "Put that back, would ya?"

Six

"Translation?" Rayne asked, with her eyebrows raised, although Storm couldn't see them. She was busy watching her red Jag eat up the road at 100 mph. Rayne was trying to keep the snark out of her voice and off of her face, but her eyebrows weren't cooperating.

Storm laughed. "Let's see... eat 'em up is the next truck stop. That's where we're meeting him. The Party Row means the last row in the lot—where all the fun happens. Feeding the bears means paying a speeding ticket, starving them means he's going to drive the speed limit... did I miss anything?"

Rayne pointed at the speedometer. "I'm assuming it's all they can eat with you?"

Storm gave her saucy look. "Gurrrl... there ain't a Smokey out here who's ever followed through in giving me a ticket. They know my car... if they've got the time... I make it worth their while to give me a pass."

Wow, Rayne thought. *I think I'm out of my league here. Screwing cops? That's got to be illegal, not to mention slutty. Very. Slutty.* For the millionth time, she doubted how wise it was to jump into a road-trip with a near complete stranger.

She sighed and then thought back over the rest of Storm's CB chatter. "Um... boogie? K-Whopper? And I can figure out what keep the shiny side up means. We have friends that ride motorcycles."

"Boogie means put the truck in top gear... he's gonna hurry, but not speed. K-Whopper is a Kenworth truck. Just making sure he hadn't changed trucks since the last time I saw him. And let me tell ya, the last time I saw him... Omigod, girl. This is another guy that is *lickin-fuckin-licious*," Storm said, ending in a sing-song-voice. "And, most importantly, he's clean, too. Always."

Rayne rolled her eyes before answering. "Yeah... That'd be important, Storm. Especially since it sounds like you intend to have sex with him."

Storm's voice rolled with laughter. "Girl, I intend for *us* to have sex with him! You're not going to be able to say no to this delicious piece of man-candy. You'll see," she said smugly.

Rayne bit her tongue. She wasn't having this debate with Storm again. She had no plans to cheat on Joe. At least not until she had no doubt he was cheating on her; and maybe not even then. She might experiment a little... she wasn't sure how. But she just might be willing to let her hair down a tad.

She'd tried to explain her reasoning to Storm several times. Although it didn't make sense to Storm, some sex seemed not as bad as other sex. Not that she was agreeing to do anything, but if she did... she had her limits.

Sex with a woman... Joe *might* forgive. Exhibition and showing her 'girls' to some horny guys... *maybe*. But having intercourse with another man? *Hell no*. She'd have no chance whatsoever for Joe to ever forgive her. She wasn't ready to buy a ticket to see-you-in-freaking-court-land just yet. But yeah, she'd love to just let loose and get some satisfaction. Maybe just once...

As her conscious warred with her libido within her head, Storm flipped on a cd, blasting Kid Rock full throttle.

Rayne let her mind fill with the angsty rockers' words and tried to forget about Joe for a while.

Seven

Storm pulled into the truck stop and headed to the back row. Rayne's stomach gurgled as they passed the building. She could use some good home-cooking right now... if that's what they called it.

Storm unexpectedly slammed on the brakes. Rayne threw her hands up, pushing against the dash before the seat belt bit into her. "What the hell?" she yelled and looked at Storm.

But no answers came out of Storm's mouth. As Rayne stared at her, her slack open mouth transformed into a proud smile. She pointed toward the trucks.

Rayne looked all around... seeing nothing or no one unusual; just a line of rigs, like at every other truck stop they'd stopped at. "What? Is it Joe? Is he here?" she asked in a panic, looking back to Storm.

"Don't you see what's written on the windows? Look!"

Rayne squinted her eyes; and then her hand flew up to her mouth as she gasped. A half dozen scattered rigs had writing on the front windows... written in white—soap maybe?

The words said: "Looking for a RainStorm!" and "Dry spell here: need RainStorm!" and other twists on their handle.

Rayne was speechless for a moment. Then she found her words. "Son of a bitch! This. Is. Not. Good."

Storm looked like she was biting back of fit of laughter. She was clearly amused—or proud. Then she gave up and doubled over, snorting in laughter. Realizing she was the only one laughing, she choked back her giggles and looked at Rayne. She tilted her head, studying her for a moment and then reached out to grab Rayne's hand.

"Rayne, they didn't even spell your name right. No one will know it's you, girl."

Rayne grumbled back, "How'd they know we were coming here? How could they possibly know we were coming *here*... tonight?"

Her chest seized up in a panic. *Had all this been a set-up?* She'd been having weird feelings about Storm all day; maybe she wasn't who she thought she was. And now this? Someone had to have set this up. Her head whipped around to Storm.

"Did you do this, Storm? Did you freaking *tell* people we'd come here and... I don't know... *screw* them? Perform? Geez, I don't even know what they're asking for..." her voice trailed off as she looked back to the rigs.

"Girl! *Shit!* Kill the voices in your head! Geesh. They've probably just been reading the mail. They were most likely already here and heard we were coming. That's all."

Rayne's eyebrows scrunched together and her eyes got wide. "Reading the mail? What freaking mail?"

Storm giggled again, and caught it before it came out in full-blown laughter.

"Listening to the CB chatter, silly. Sandbagging... reading the mail... that's trucker talk for someone who's listening but not talking. We chattered on the CB all day. And we didn't try to hide anything when we were talking to Smokin' Okie," she explained. "It was all said in plain English... er... plain trucker slang anyway."

Rayne gave a quick but firm shake to her head.

"Not 'we,'" Storm. *YOU*. You said all that on the CB. This is your gig... not mine. I don't want any part of it. I'm not getting out of this freaking car."

Storm reached into the backseat and pulled out her make-up bag. She began touching up her face and smoothing her long chocolate-colored waves. She finished and dropped her bag in Rayne's lap.

"Suit yourself." She shrugged. "Sounds like stage fright to me. I get it. I was just trying to show you a good time. But at least come inside the truck stop for a minute to stretch your legs and get something to eat and drink. Okie will be here in a little while and you can come back and lock yourself in the car, if you want. But you gotta eat."

Rayne's stomach rumbled its agreement, but her mind fumed.

Stage fright? What the hell? Was this some sort of game to Storm? She didn't sign up to be some freak show for truckers. Just because she'd made the mistake the first night she'd met Storm, and been a small part of her little exhibition show didn't mean she was open for business now.

She was a teacher for Pete's sake... not a hooker. She'd had two goals when she agreed to this trip. Find out if Joe's screwing around, and try to make a friend in Storm and have a good time. *Road trip good time.* Girl's trip. She mentally slapped herself for being so naïve. It was time to figure out a way to get home. But she did need to eat. *Dammit.*

Rayne blew out a frustrated breath, and then roughly jerked the bag out of her lap and unzipped it. She dug through, pulling out Storm's lipstick and compact. She dabbed some color on her lips, and added a swipe of eyeliner and shadow to her eyes, and then swatted her nose with the powder puff. She tossed Storm's bag back to her, and yanked the rear view mirror over as far as it would reach—almost hoping it would break—and finger-combed the tangles from her own blonde waves. If Storm didn't always look and smell so yummy-delicious, she wouldn't even have bothered. But

Rayne didn't want to look like a tired old hag next to her, so she did what she could.

She snatched at the door handle and pushed her door open. She got out, stomping toward the truck stop, shaking her ass with attitude, and hoping Storm was right behind her. Regardless of her fake bravado, she really didn't want to walk in there alone.

Eight

Okay, so food calms me down, Rayne thought as the waitress walked away to put their order in. Rayne mentally chanted *hurry up, hurry up, hurry up.*

She'd almost forgotten she'd been mad at Storm by now, after looking over the menu and smelling the burgers on the grill, knowing soon she'd feel full and satisfied—at least in the food department.

She'd expected to walk in to a bunch of horny truckers sitting around ogling them, but surprisingly, only a few tables had customers. And the ones that did, barely gave them a passing glance. Rayne had visibly relaxed and sighed with relief when they'd slid into the booth, practically unnoticed. The drivers with the writing on the windows must be waiting in their rigs, hoping for a chance encounter. *Yeah, right,* Rayne thought. *Not happening again, guys.*

She'd let the silence sit heavy between them until after they'd ordered, busy with her own thoughts. But now she looked up to see Storm's eyes were glassy with tears; not yet running over.

"Storm, are you crying?" Rayne asked sympathetically, with wide open eyes. "What's wrong?"

Storm gave a quick shake of her head, and then turned and faced the window.

"What is it? What did I do?" Rayne asked.

A shudder went through Storm and then she cleared her throat. She picked up a napkin and dotted the tears out of her eyes.

"It's nothing." Storm shrugged. "I just wanted us to have fun on this trip. I know it's some heavy shit, with your husband and all, but I haven't had a girlfriend go on a road-trip with me for years and I'm messing it all up, aren't I?"

Rayne sighed, scrunching her eyebrows together in thought. *How do I say this without first pissing her off so bad she won't take me home, and second, not sounding like a needy fangirl?*

She sucked in a huge breath, and then let it out before she tried to explain. "Storm. I know your intentions are good. But we've been gone almost three days and all you seem to think about is sex. That's cool. I think about it a lot too. But I kinda expected a little more fun outside of the sex department... kinda like Thelma and Louise-ish? If I remember the movie right? They had fun, didn't they?"

She raised her eyebrows, waiting for Storm to crack up at her nerdiness, and reached across the table, taking Storm's hand.

No response.

She continued. "I guess... when I first met you, I was blown away by your free spirit. I think you're so cool. I'd *love* to be like you; I really would. Just to be able to throw caution to the wind and just do whatever the hell I want. But that's not me. I've got responsibilities; a career, a husband—for the moment. But that doesn't mean we can't have fun. I mean, I don't want to have to drive off a cliff or anything, but can't we find some other cool things to do out on the road?"

Storm's lip quivered, but then instantly turned into a huge toothy smile. Her eyes twinkled at Rayne as though she'd just told a joke.

Rayne stared hard at her. *Okay...That was freaking weird,* she thought. *Bipolar much?* She wasn't sure if she was just tired and homesick, or if Storm was seriously starting to show her true stripes.

• • •

"Cool. Then you're not mad?" Storm replied, all smiles. She squeezed Rayne's hand, and flicked her head, tossing her long dark hair over her shoulder.

Rayne pulled her hand back, and gathered her own hair together, pulling it over one shoulder just as the waitress had returned and was sliding their food in front of them.

"Nope. Not mad. Let's just eat," Rayne said in a dry voice, staring at her food, and realizing not once had Storm mentioned her own husband. It struck Rayne as odd, and even odder that it was the first time Rayne had realized it. She'd been so selfishly caught up in her own drama with Joe, that it never entered her mind to ask Storm about her own marriage and if her husband knew what she was up to.

Oh well, now's not the time.

Rayne picked up the big burger, and held it vertically to let the grease drip onto the plate before biting into it. Cheese, mayo, pickles, chili, lettuce... her mouth was watering. She dug in.

Nine

With her belly almost full, and the mood shifted back to good again between them, Rayne was now just playing with the leftovers of her food. She picked up a French fry and stuck it in her mouth, sucking the salt off of it as she listened to Storm tell another funny story about yet another trucker. She told good stories. Rayne wasn't sure if they were true, but she'd made her laugh several times and it felt good for them to be "okay" again.

As she slowly pulled the now naked fry from her lips, she heard a deep, rumbling voice beside her. "I like the way your mouth looks around that French fry, girl."

Wtf? Is that a reference to SlingBlade? Rayne's head whipped up expecting to see some moron trying to be funny, but her face instantly heated when her eyes met his... *gotta be Smokin' Okie.*

His eyes were smolderingly dark and sensual and staring right back into her own, locked in. Rayne's neck stretched as she strained to see them better. What had her captivated were the deep gray iris' with tiny flecks of gold smattered throughout, shuttered by thick, dark eyelashes and full eyebrows. He looked a lot like Joe... only better.

Rayne had never seen such beautiful eyes on a man— ever. Hypnotic, piercing...she couldn't look away as he studied her own eyes just as intently.

Although she wasn't uncomfortable in the least, in the back of her mind she was prompting Storm to say something—anything. Introduce them... *whathehellever*... just break their eye contact somehow. Rayne Could. Not. Look. Away.

She felt captive, mesmerized by him. Trapped in their own little world of just him and her...strangers.

"Smokie!" Storm squealed and jumped out of the booth, wrapping her arms around him and giving him a full open mouth kiss.

Finally. Crap! What the hell just happened there? Rayne thought as their stare was broken and she checked out the rest of him.

His square chin supported a gentle smile, the ends of his mouth barely turned up, but enough to show one dimple in in right cheek, almost buried under the stubbly dark shadow that looked a few days old, matching the dark frame of his eyes.

"May I?" he waved a hand toward the booth asking if he can sit. *Who does that? May I? For realsie?* Rayne thought. *A gentleman-trucker-cowboy. Can we clone him?*

He slid into the booth beside Storm, but not before Rayne saw his tight, black jeans—and who the hell wore *black* jeans nowadays anyway? But she couldn't deny he made them look good, and if the package outlined there wasn't hard, Rayne would eat the shiny black boots he was wearing. Huge pectoral muscles thumped his fitted black T-shirt, and pulled her attention to his trim waist. She could almost see a six-pack under there. This guy was too good to be true.

He laughed his deep, rumbling laugh at something Storm said—Rayne's brain was on mute, she could hear nothing but his laugh, and her own lusty thoughts for this creature in front of her—he lifted his cowboy hat from his head, and placed it on the table, and then ran his large hand through his thick raven-black hair, his fingers rumpling it into an even sexier rippled mess. Her eyes followed the hand back up his muscled arm to the undeniably hot tribal tattoo that wrapped around it.

The air around them tickled Rayne's nose as Storm and Okie start right in catching up. It no longer smells like burgers and fries and a greasy truck stop.

It was ripe with a strong sexual vibe and Rayne can almost smell it in the air. It triggered a pulsing throb down south of her beltline, so she crossed her legs and took a long, cool sip of her drink from her straw, watching the two talk. Well, watching *him*. While they talked. And her mind fantasized.

"—you coming?" Storm asked again, quite loud.

Rayne snapped out of her fantasy, finally able to stop staring at Okie as she jerked her head around to look to see who was listening.

"*What?*" she whispered loudly back to Storm.

"I said, Okie wants to show us his 'truck,' are you coming?"

Rayne shrugged her shoulders, trying to look undecided. *But um… yeah… hell yeah, she was coming. Almost literally.*

Smokin' Okie stood and Rayne watched as he put his hat back on. He gave Rayne a nod and held out his hand to her. She looked at it. *What? What does he want?*

"Can I help you up, Miss Rayne?"

Oh, hell yeah. This guy was almost too good to be true… Rayne's heart swooned.

Ten

Rayne was truly mind-screwed. Her body felt like a raging inferno—burning like fire—and quivering with desire, with only one thing that would quench it... The long, hard piece of man-candy she was staring at front and center, ready for her.

She hadn't been this close to another naked man, other than her husband, since college. She licked her lips, wanting to reach out with her tongue and touch him; taste him...

How had she strayed so far? She would've never pictured herself sitting another man's rig, in this blow-her-mind, sopping-wet-panty position two days ago... She cringed as one last glimpse of her husband's face floated through her mind, and then *poof*, it was gone... and it was *game on*...

Goosebumps scattered across her skin as he slowly stripped her from the waist up. Her breasts bounced as they rolled out of the bottom of the tight shirt she was wearing—surprising him with no bra—and her nipples reacted to the cold rush of air, hardening into sharp points.

"Mmmm," he said, licking his lips as he devoured her tits with his eyes.

He leaned back and pulled his own black T-shirt off; and it wasn't bluffing about what was beneath. Where it had been pulled taut across his chest now revealed chiseled muscles, smooth except for the happy trail that runs around his belly-button up between the middle of his pectorals.

His jeans were slung low, hanging on his hip bones, and deliciously sexy. On the bed in the cab sleeper, he had to stand on his knees which caused the waistline to tug even lower, pulled at by his pant legs dragging behind him. His feet were bare, and even those were sensual; manly, but clean and well-groomed.

The man even smelled unbelievably delectable. Clean, with a light sent of sandalwood and leather. The smell of him filled up the cab and tickled her nose.

"How you want to play this?" his sensual voice rumbled as he stared at her erect nipples. "You want it slow and easy... or do you want it rough?"

She shivered. *Anticipation from knowing she's in control either way?* She looked at him with trust in her eyes; he'd given her no reason not to.

"I want it *rough*. I want it *hard*. And I want it *fast*," she answered without even a blush. "That work for you, cowboy?"

He nodded his head.

"Yes, ma'am. I aim to please." His eyes went even darker. *Smoldering.* Then he moved quickly. Like a rattlesnake. She gasped as he kneeled and grabbed the top of her shorts, yanking them down around her hips and pulling them off, flinging them behind him—so fast she fell backward against the mattress, barely catching herself on her elbows.

Without any hesitation, he roughly pulled her thighs apart and dropped between her legs, holding one large hand on her flat belly as though to firmly hold her still and hovering his mouth just over the apex of her thighs, breathing out heavy warm air against her already-wet red panties. The dark spot grew bigger.

She sighed loudly and threw her head back.

His fingers circled around the wet spot on her panties—not slowly or gently—purposely driving her wild.

• • •

She arched her hips and moaned, wanting more. His hands reach behind him, pulling up her legs and grabbing ahold of her ankles. He continued to breathe against the silky cloth over her mound while he ran his hand up her ankles, and then massaged her calves for a brief moment before sliding them up her thighs. He squeezed her thighs hard, and then pushed them higher into the air, giving her feet a chance to dig in and hold her legs up.

He hooked a finger in each side of her panties and rolled them up her thighs, over her knees and down toward her feet, finally freeing her of them and tossing them onto the quickly-growing pile of clothes.

He wiggled out of his own jeans, leaving him in a pair of snug black boxer briefs which did nothing to hide the size of his package. He pulled off his briefs quickly, exposing all of himself. He didn't even glance at himself.

Humble, thought Rayne. Especially in light of the fact that his cock was beautiful. Straight, unblemished and huge with a matching set of large heavy balls.

She licked her lips as she watched him and then said, "Talk dirty to me, too."

He ran his hand up and down his shaft as he answered her.

"Yes, ma'am. That automatically comes along with the hard, rough and fast fuck package. And I fully intended to tell you how beautiful your wet little pussy is before I slam my cock, *balls deep* into it. I want to hear you *scream* while you wriggle beneath me taking my weight along with every... inch... I've... got..."

She moaned again and her eyes were swimming with desire as she reached out and cupped his balls, giving them a steady squeeze. His eyes closed for just a moment, enjoying the pleasure/pain and then he opened them and looked around. His pupils were dilated, giving him a savage look.

He reached into the corner and found where he'd hidden a condom. He ripped it open with his teeth and quickly slid it onto his hard, long shaft and then slammed his body down, landing between her still-spread-wide-open legs and crashing onto her with almost feral aggression.

A huge breath of air was forced out of her mouth, but she recovered quickly, reaching behind him with both arms to pull him further onto her, further *into* her.

One hand reached for her hair and he tangled a long lock of it around his fist, giving it a tug while he drove himself straight into her with a loud rumble reverberating through his throat. She emitted a high-pitched yelp before her body responded and stretched to accommodate him.

"Oh hell yeah. You feel so *tight* around me. I can feel you pulsating, baby. You like it like this?"

His other hand squeezed a tit forcefully, kneading the flesh between his fingers, and then pulling back and flicking her nipple with his thumb and forefinger. She moaned.

"You love it, dontcha? You love it rough like this."

She arched her back for more, unable to answer him, although it didn't sound like a question anyway. More of a statement.

Her breathing was coming out louder with each breath—almost panting—and she finally yelled out as he went deeper and deeper, teasing her sensitive clit with every in and out movement. He slammed into her over and over, seemingly thrusting harder each time.

She took it all, yelling and moaning through her loud breaths, wanting even more as their bodies rocked the cab.

"You're dripping wet. You like to bring out the bad boy in me, don't you?" he asked as he pounded against her, his ass going higher in the air at every withdrawal before quickly thrusting back into her. "Say it. Tell me..." he said between thrusts.

"Yes. I like it!" she worked out in a hoarse voice, thick with passion.

He let go of her breast to get closer, and his chest moved closer to her face, his head now much higher than hers. His chest was right in front of her mouth. She waited for him to thrust and the space between them to close, and then latched on to his nipple. He threw his head back and howled in surprise as she bit him and then sucked it.

His hips moved faster as she latched on.

"*Mmmm. Mmmm. Mmmm*," she moaned in tempo with each thrust, with her mouth full.

"Yeah. Suck it harder," he whispered loudly.

She sucked hard, holding her mouth in place by wrapping her arms around his back tightly and fisting her hands together. He slammed into her harder... and they worked themselves into frenzy, finally moving together in unrestrained harmony. She wrapped her legs around him as he moaned long and loud.

"Girl, I feel you squeezing around my cock. You almost there?" he asked as he continued the same pace and tried to look down at her face.

She didn't answer—she couldn't.

She let go of him, falling onto the mattress, and flung her head to the side. She let out a loud, almost primal scream and used her back to lift her hips higher and higher, to meet each thrust, bucking like a wild, young, unbroken bronco.

"Girl, you ready to come? Speak up... I can't hold on much longer," he yelled as he continued to sink balls deep into her, over and over again.

His hair was wet and messy, and his brow glimmered with a sheen of sweat. A vein in his neck pulsed. He looked like he was going to explode—barely hanging on.

Her toes curled and she clamped her legs tightly against him as she screamed, "Now! I'm coming *now*... oh oh yes oh damn... don't stop," she yelled as her body convulsed with an intense orgasm that ripped through her. She continued to buck, devouring his cock inch by inch as it repeatedly slid—quickly and easily—into her dripping wet snatch.

• • •

He couldn't hold back any longer. He slammed into her harder than ever, grunting loudly and desperately. His body twitched as she huffed underneath him, her eyes closed and her mouth open, sucking in air rapidly.

After a moment of catching their breath, with him holding his weight off of her as much as he could using his elbows, he rolled to the side. Their sweaty, slick skin immediately met the cool air in the absence of their combined heat, and goosebumps appeared in ripples.

He pulled himself up on an elbow, looking down at her, and then ran his big finger down her cheek, catching the stray wet strands of hair, and pulling them off of her face.

He was a beautiful man to look at, and thoughtful too, in addition to being as panty-melting as Storm had promised earlier.

"You okay, darlin'?" he asked her as he gently tapped her chin with his forefinger. "I didn't hurt you, did I?"

She let out a huge sigh before answering.

"Yeah, you did. Thank you," she answered in a raspy, satisfied voice, and then closed her eyes again, savoring the afterglow.

He kissed her on her forehead and smiled down at her.

Eleven

He'd barely caught his breathe before he was back up on his knees, head nearly touching the top of the cab as he worked his way toward the passenger chair that Rayne was sitting in.

She'd been quiet as a mouse—a heavy breathing mouse—as she'd watched them. At first guiltily embarrassed, she had tried to look away. Look at the rig's cab... look out the window... look at *anything* other than the sweat-glistening bodies of Storm and Smokin' Okie writhing and twisting, bucking and moaning... drawing her eyes back to them again and again.

She couldn't stop watching, and they didn't seem to mind, so eventually she'd told herself to think of it as not reality—it was just like a porn flick—like she and Joe used to watch together... but live, and so much hotter.

As Smokin' Okie reached her, his smoldering eyes took in her flush, her heaving breasts and the strained look she knew she painted all over her face. He tilted his head and looked into her big blue eyes, and then ran a gentle hand down her hair, careful to avoid her breasts. *Still a gentleman. Damn, this guy is almost perfect.*

Rayne wished she too could give him permission to not be such a gentleman. To just take what he wanted, roughly, like he had with Storm.

• • •

As his hand caressed her hair, his finger moved down to trace around her ear and then lower to her neck and over to shoulder; and then he stopped. Her body protested, and her back involuntarily arched. A shiver ran down her spine at the promise of his touch so close to her breasts. Her nipples felt like they were stretching to meet the heat of his hand—but they weren't even close. She closed her eyes and took a deep breath, trying to slow her heart beat down and cool off.

"You sure you don't want a ride too, Miss Rayne?" he asked in a slow drawl, with a twinkle in his eye, and one dark, perfect eyebrow arched. *He knew.* He knew she was dying for it. This was a man who knew women, and what they wanted very well, and he knew how to give it to them.

Clenching her thighs together and hugging a pillow to herself, she was literally rocking in her seat, trying to quench the screaming, aching need.

She hesitated too long. Just as he held out an open hand to assist her out of the chair and onto the bed, she answered, "No. This was Storm's gig. Not mine.

"Maybe next time, Cowboy..." Her hot core throbbed painfully in tempo with each breath she took, begging for release—begging for her to change her mind.

Rayne unfolded herself from the passenger seat, tossed the crushed pillow onto to his oversize bed, and reached for the door handle as he backed up.

She looked over her shoulder as she hesitated again... Maybe just this once—this one guy; one romp in a truck... Would Joe find out? *And so what if he did?* the rebellious part of her thought.

Smokin' Okie saw her hesitation, watching as she chewed her lower lip in thought. His eyes traveled from her face to her big tits, then down to her shapely legs. He crooked his finger in a "come here" gesture. Rayne let her eyes drop below his waist, seeing he was still hard and ready to go.

She wanted nothing more than to crawl under him, legs spread wide... and get the pounding she'd just watched Storm take.

But she slowly shook her head and watched him back up, his eyes showing a mixture of respect and regret. Then he gave up and flopped down next to Storm, who was finally speechless—*thank Gawd for that*—in her carnal bliss. He threw his arm around Storm, rolling her over for more... and Rayne crawled out of the rig, back to the safety of the car.

• • •

THE TRUCKER'S WIFE

Episode Three

RIDING THE STORM OUT

One

"Storm, I'm beat. Let's pull over early tonight and catch up on some sleep."

She hoped Storm wouldn't point out that it wasn't 'tonight' yet. It was only the middle of the afternoon. But damn... she needed *out* of this freaking car. She was fighting sleep hard. And getting a little stir-crazy cooped up with her secret that she hadn't told Storm yet. She needed to stretch her legs. She needed to move. Before she exploded.

The stress of the previous night and the mind-numbing war her conscious had fought with her libido was partly to blame too. Not to mention having to wait for Storm, curled up in the front seat of the car... waiting... and waiting... and waiting. Until Storm finally crawled out of the rig earlier this morning, looking like she'd been rode hard and put up wet. *Oh wait. She had.*

Rayne had wanted to give in to what her body begged her to do too with Okie. She wanted to be wild and free like Storm; just wallow in her desires and pleasures and not give a shit what anyone thought about it.

But she hadn't been able to. She just couldn't do that to Joe.

Instead she'd crawled down from the rig and had tried to sleep in the car, while Storm finished her sexy times with her hot trucker. And then, Storm had selfishly fallen asleep in Smokin' Okie's rig, leaving Rayne uncomfortable and fighting to get some sleep in the damn car all night—which had never happened. She'd slept in fits and starts, probably not more than an hour total.

She'd finally given up trying to sleep.

She was so freaking bored, so she'd dug her phone out from where she'd buried it in her bag. She knew she'd subconsciously buried the phone out of sight and out of mind so that she wouldn't be tempted to call Joe or take his calls—not that he ever called her when he was out on the road much anymore. But just in case… she'd turned it off and let it fall to the bottom of her purse.

She'd been surprised to see Joe *had* tried to call. Twice. The second time he'd left a message. The message was two days old. He'd left it the same morning he'd left, which was the same day she'd left with Storm.

But he hadn't known she wasn't home. And obviously he hadn't known she'd seen the hickey or the condoms. At least his message didn't sound like he'd known.

His sad voice rolled through her head for the thousandth time as she remembered his words she had memorized:

"Rayne, I'm *sorry*! I know I said some mean things last night. And I swear to you, I didn't mean them. You *did* look sexy in that nightgown. It's not you… It's me. I just couldn't look at you right then. I've been trying not to… well, I've just… I've been…"

There was a pause.

She could hear him take a deep breath and blow it out before he continued, "Dammit, I don't want to say it on a stupid voicemail. I've got something to tell you. It's been killing me keeping this secret from you for almost a year now. Stressing me out, and making me crazy, girl! I swear, I never meant to hurt you. All I was—"

His voice cut off, interrupted by a loud noise. Rayne's heart had nearly done a flip. In milliseconds her brain told her he still loved her... *he was saying sorry!* Maybe this could all be worked out... her heartbeat immediately sped up fueled by hope.

But the sound that cut Joe off sounded like a door being opened. A second later, Rayne's hopes were dashed when a different voice—a female voice—had said, "Oops. Sorry! I didn't know you weren't dressed yet! I'll give you some privacy!" Then she'd heard the sound again, as though the same door was closing.

The message had ended there. Joe had disconnected the call. Her heart had fallen. *Lurched.* She'd felt like a fifty-pound hammer had come down on it and she'd wanted to vomit. She replayed it over, and over, and over... trying to recognize the mysterious woman's voice.

She'd listened so many times her phone had finally died. A heavy sadness had come over her.

It was final then.

The hickeys, the condoms and now *this.* She felt empty. Depleted of everything. She hadn't even had the energy to find her charger to plug in her phone.

She didn't even want to call him back. Cuss him out. Demand to know who... she'd just sat there with her phone clutched to her still rapidly beating heart—her now aching heart—and tears streaming down her face, until the sun had peeped up over the horizon and the door to Smokin' Joe's rig had opened. She'd been relieved to see Storm crawl out.

She'd crammed her phone back into her bag, wiped her face clean of all emotion and kept Joe's message to herself. This was too personal to share with Storm.

It didn't change anything. She still wanted to see with her own eyes. She wanted to catch him. Scratch his eyes out. *Beat the other woman down like a boss.* Cry. Rant. Rave. Burn him with the heat of a thousand suns.

But she also wanted to be wrong.

Somehow... completely, totally wrong. About everything. She wanted her husband back. She wanted him to tell her something that made all this make sense, made it all a huge misunderstanding. Something they could move past and laugh about years from now. She wanted him to still love her. Love her like he used to.

Her emotions were battered. Her head was warring with her heart, and she couldn't wait to get back on the road and crawl up Joe's ass.

But Storm had insisted on going straight to a hotel, just for a private room to shower. *Wtf? Why couldn't she use the damn truck stop showers so they could get on the road?*

Rayne had mumbled and muttered, but was actually secretly happy once they got in to the room and she saw the comfy queen size bed. She needed to sleep. Only sleep would stop the ear worm of Joe's message winding through her head. She'd crawled into the bed after Storm locked herself in the bathroom, snuggling deep to escape the sliver of sunlight sneaking through the drapes, which was trying to convince her it wasn't *time* to sleep!

Rayne finally persuaded her confused mind it was okay to go to sleep in the freaking morning, and just as she'd drifted off, with a pillow over her face, buried under the silky sheets and comforting weight of the bedspread, Storm had shook her awake. Pushing her to hurry, hurry, hurry and get up! They had miles to make up, she'd said.

Rayne had wanted to kill her.

Since then, they'd been on the road all freaking day with only one short stop for lunch, and they were hopefully catching up to stay on Joe's trail.

Rayne rubbed her eyes and shifted again in her seat, trying to stay awake. She felt like a bobble-head. She kept drifting off and smacking the window. Storm giggled each time and Rayne fought back the urge to slap the shit out of her.

Her eyeballs were burning and her neck felt like it just couldn't hold her heavy head upright anymore.

"*Storm!* Did you hear me? I asked if you want to stop early. I can't stay awake much longer," Rayne said, speaking louder to get Storm's attention over the blast of Miranda Lambert screaming from the radio.

"Just go ahead and sleep in the car. We need to keep rolling," Storm answered, and then went back to singing something about rusty kitchen scissors and hiding her crazy.

Yeah. That'd be good, Storm. You do that well. Hide your crazy, that is. Rayne thought. *And suuuure… I'll just sleep in the car—Again. Thank you very fucking much.*

Rayne sighed. She looked in the back seat and grabbed a little neck pillow Storm kept back there, balling it up and stuffing it between her head and the window.

She lay back and closed her eyes.

Actually it was more comfortable with the car moving. Or maybe she was just thoroughly exhausted.

She relaxed and concentrated on the smooth ride and the feel of the engine thrumming under her ass. The car, the ambient light, Storm's spicy-cinnamon scent beside her and the constant vibration soon had forgetting about Joe, and instead lulled her into thinking of her missed opportunity with Smokin' Okie which led her thinking to other thoughts.

Dirty, nasty thoughts.

Two

As she was pulled under by sleep, images snuck into her subconscious, taking her hidden desires and weaving them into dreams—erotic dreams, filled with visions of gorgeous truck drivers on the road that found her irresistibly sexy. They wickedly snatched up her skirt and leaned her against the front grill of their rigs, taking turns pounding into her from behind as she clung to anything she could grab on to; heaving, breathing hard and coming, over and over again.

In one snippet of a dream, the night was dark, but the lights of the rig were brightly lit, providing just enough light to see her and the man behind her—and what they were doing.

She felt eyes all over her and the shadowy man. She stole a glance over her shoulder and saw dozens of trucker drivers watching... enjoying the show, touching themselves.

In the back of the crowd she saw a flash of Joe's face. He too, seemed to be watching his wife be taken by random truck drivers, one after the other. It looked as if he was fine with it. His handsome face shone brightly among the crowd of dark, blank faces. He wasn't smiling, but he wasn't making any move to stop them—to stop her. He just stood there, hands in pockets, watching with a thoughtful expression.

Rayne wasn't sure what to think about that... *Does he like it? He's not mad?* Seeing him watch her being taken like this turned her on even more, and she arched her back and moaned.

Still not hearing any protest from Joe, she screamed out the word, "Harder," between the thrusts that had her entire body slamming into the truck, only her hands gripping the grill guard in front of her face kept her from slamming her head. *Would Joe stop her now?*

The shadowed man behind her stopped abruptly, leaving her hanging without release, the thin thatch of curls wet and dripping, covering her throbbing and pulsing—

Three

Wait. What? Rayne rubbed her eyes.

Confused, she shook her head and realized she'd been sleeping. The car had stopped, interrupting her dream... and what *was* she dreaming about? It was quickly slipping away.

She sat her seat up—when had she lowered her seat?—and looked at Storm, who was leaned up against her own door, legs crossed, patiently waiting for Rayne to wake up. Storm had a devious look on her face. Rayne felt cold air from the vent hit her in the apex of her thighs, and realized she was dripping wet... now she remembered her dream. It flashed through her mind on super-speed. She'd *almost* gotten off—finally.

She shook her head to clear away the last remnants of the dream, and ignored the insistent throbbing between her legs.

She squinted at the clock on the dash. Her eyes blinked and then widened as she realized she'd slept four hours. She glanced out the window. The sky was dark. *Wow. I must've really been worn out from my melt-down.*

"Where are we?" Rayne rubbed her hands down her hair, trying to smooth it. *I must look terrible.* Then she looked around to see where the flashing strobe-like lights were coming from. They were parked in front of a building with a blinking sign that said, "The Trucker's Club – Adults Only."

"Welp, we're back on track. Right on Joe's trail! Thought we'd stop in here before calling it a night. We need to be sure he's not in here first. If not, there's usually plenty of interesting things go on up in this place—and they have good food."

Rayne hesitated. She looked at the lot holding a line of big rigs. She didn't see Joe's. And she was hungry... starving, actually.

"His truck's not here. I'll go in and eat, but then let's grab a room and get a real bed. I'm not sure I feel like hanging out tonight. I'm still tired."

"Look, I know these people. It's cool. No one's going to bother you if you don't want them to. I got your back." Storm raised a fist.

Rayne weakly raised hers and gave a pitiful show of a fist-bump. She was still shaking off her sleep.

Storm jerked her head toward the door to the building. "Let's go in. You can freshen up in the bathroom."

"Pop the hatch for me?" Rayne asked.

Storm popped the hatch open and Rayne dug through her bags until she found her small make-up kit and her car charger for her phone. She jammed the make-up bag into her oversized purse and yelled, "Done." The hatch slowly lowered back in to place.

She crawled into the car and plugged in her phone, pushing it as far under the front seat as she could so it wouldn't tempt someone to break in and grab it. And then she walked to the front of the car where Storm was waiting with a large bag slung over her own shoulder, but she looked fresh as a daisy—a spicy-smelling daisy. *How does she do that after all day on the road?* Rayne wondered. *I probably look and smell like shit.* She tried to pat down the flyaways in her wavy hair as she followed Storm through the front door, questioning her decision to come on this trip again. She felt her heart beat faster in trepidation as all eyes turned toward them.

"Storm!" someone yelled out. That was followed by a rousing echo of "Storm" several times mixed in with "Where ya been, girl?" and "We missed you's." She was obviously well-known and liked here.

"Been on the road," she answered loudly to everyone. "This is my new friend, Rayne." Several deep voices laughed. Rayne assumed they thought Storm was making up her name... *Storm, bringing in a rain... ummm... cliché.* She wished she could melt into the floor like a puddle. She could feel the burning stares all over her body as Storm stepped aside, revealing Rayne standing behind her. Rayne gave a small smile and a wave. She'd have preferred Storm wait to make introductions until after she'd freshened up. Oh well.

A tall, blond man with heavy-lidded eyes sauntered up to Rayne, looking her over from head to toe. He had bedroom eyes. Brown, lazy, I-wanna-fuck-you-eyes. Rayne checked him out the same way he did her. His black shirt fit tight against his lean chest, cinched in at the waist, tucked into a pair of faded blue-jeans with rips at the knees. His legs were long and muscular, crowding the jeans that covered the tops of black leather biker boots. *Hmmm,* Rayne thought, *truck driver or biker?*

"You've got that just-got-out-of-bed sexy look going on, dontcha' girl?" he leaned and whispered into her ear, with a sexy, southern drawl. "I like it. Whatcha' call that? Beach-hair or something, right? With the messy waves? *Mmmm.* And your name's Rain? Like r-a-i-n? I'll be damned. *Rain* with the sexy *Beach-hair...* you're just what I'd expect a Storm to drag in."

Rayne had to laugh at that. She wasn't expecting his come-on to actually be clever. Or was it just cheesy? Rayne wasn't sure. Her mind was still foggy and not quite awake. She didn't think the man was expecting answers, and she certainly wasn't going to correct his spelling... she couldn't believe Storm used her real name anyway. What if Joe heard about her coming in? Can't be that many Rayne's out there hanging out at Trucker's Clubs...?

Storm grabbed her hand and pulled her to the bar. Blond Sexy followed them. He offered to buy them a drink and Storm accepted for the both of them. Rayne raised her eyebrows... she hadn't eaten all day. She really just wanted some food and more sleep. A motel room. A bed. But she didn't want to be a party-pooper their first night out, so when the beers and shots arrived, she pulled up her big-girl panties and clinked shot glasses before swallowing hers in one gulp, then chasing it down with the beer.

It burned going down her throat. It had been a long time since Rayne had drank alcohol—other than wine—and she'd forgotten the burn, following by the warm sensation that crawled up from her belly, immediately relaxing her a notch. When he asked if they wanted another, she nodded her head. Two turned to three and Rayne also finished her beer.

Soon she felt like she was on the outside watching as Storm and the sexy blond guy bantered back and forth. She could barely make out some of the words around the noise of the club, but she did hear Storm ask if he'd heard of Joe. He hadn't.

The rest of the conversation was lost in a hullabaloo of loud laughter, clashing billiard balls, glasses and bottles chinking together with her own thoughts rattling through her head about Joe. She tried to nod her head when someone spoke at her, hoping she was nodding to the right things.

She wasn't drunk, but she was feeling relaxed and enjoying the scenery. With Storm and Blond Sexy talking, she had plenty of time to look around. After doing a quick scan for Joe, in case his truck was out back, she was surprised to see most of the truck drivers sitting, or standing around the pool table, or belly-up to the bar were *hawt*. Or maybe that was her beer goggles speaking...

Soon, Storm grabbed her hand and led her to the back of the building, with Blond Sexy following behind them. They went through one door, then down a hallway and turned a corner. The door at the end had a tiny window covered in metal, from the inside. Storm rapped her knuckles on the door. The little window slid open, showing a beefy-looking guy peering through at them. His face was tough and stern until he saw Storm. Then it broke into a big grin. He didn't even speak before slamming the window shut and opening the door wide.

He threw his arms around Storm, lifting her into the air and twirling her around. "Where you been, girl?" he asked.

Storm kissed him on both of his cheeks, and then shrugged. "Around. Been looking for a trucker named Joe. Any Joe's been fucking around in here lately?"

The bouncer shook his head and then looked around Storm and saw Blond Sexy and Rayne. His eyebrows raised when his eyes rested on her. He turned back to Storm and asked, "Who's the chick?"

"She's my friend. Her name's Rayne."

"Hmmm," he murmured, nodding his head in approval. "Watching or riding?"

Storm stole a glance at Rayne and then answered for her, "I think this time... just watching. If she wants to change up, I'm good for the difference. But *I'm* riding and he's with me." Storm poked her thumb toward Blond Sexy who nodded at the bouncer.

The bouncer laughed. "Yeah, Storm. I kinda figured that."

She reached into her bag and pulled out a roll of cash. She peeled off several bills and handed it to the bouncer. He smiled and waved them in, and then locked the door behind them.

Four

Rayne eyes tried to adjust to the flashing white-strobe light. It blinked on and off, giving fragmented snapshots of the room.

It was clean, and classy-looking in an old café sort of style, surrounded in booth-style benches. Classic sexy Marilyn Monroe pictures were nicely framed and hung over every bench-seat. There were over a dozen people sitting around, all wearing the same silky robes... *this is odd*, Rayne thought.

The seats were vinyl, wrapping nearly all the way around four walls. Instead of the booths facing tables, as if in a restaurant, they were all facing the center of the room. There was a very small table, but it was between each booth seat—which held seating for at least three, four if squeezed— and on the tiny tables were baskets.

The baskets held a variety of things: condoms, lubricant, wet-wipes, paper towels, and sex toys and hand sanitizer. Over the baskets were extra robes hanging from hooks, the hem nearly reaching the table. It looked like a cult of some kind with everyone wearing the same thing.

Most eyes—those that weren't involved in heavy making-out sessions—were on Rayne and Storm as they walked in. Storm snatched two robes and grabbed Rayne's hand, strutting as she pulled her to the far corner, where a double stainless-steel sink was mounted in a cabinet, beside two dressing rooms, like those seen in department stores.

They both stepped into one dressing room together, and before Storm had the door completely shut Rayne was in her face. "What the hell is this, Storm?"

Storm's eyebrows furrowed. "It's the *back-room.* Haven't you ever been in a 'back-room' before? Anywhere?"

Rayne shook her head. She honestly had no idea what Storm was talking about. Joe had never brought her anywhere like this before, and never mentioned 'back-rooms' to her—ever. "No," she blurted out. "I have no idea what's going on."

Storm's furrowed eyebrows raised at that. "Ummm… didn't you see what was in the middle of the room?"

"No. That flickering light is hard to see with, and I was looking at the booth-seats, and the baskets, and…and… the *people* sticking their tongues down each other's throats in front of everybody… what did I miss?"

Storm laughed. "You'll see. Let's just change into these robes. Then we'll go out and take a seat by ourselves. I promise, no one will bother you. If they do, they get bounced quickly. Just relax and consider it a *show.* I paid for you to watch. That's all you have to do… *Watch.* M'kay?"

She put her hands on Rayne's shoulders, brushing her long blonde hair over her back and looked into her big blue eyes. Rayne was almost hypnotized looking back into Storm's sexy almond-shaped brown eyes… "You said you wanted to see new things… live a little. This is seeing. It's living. You can set your own boundaries, but you've got to have an open mind. Trust me on this."

Five

Rayne nearly laughed when she had turned her back to Storm to strip and put the robe on, rolling her clothes tightly and stuffing them in her bag, and then turned around to find Storm standing there in chains and black leather.

Not that she didn't look hot; she *did*. She was still pulling on a pair of black vinyl boots that finished off her little black outfit that stopped just under her small but perky breasts, not only completely exposing them, but pushing them up as though they were flowing out the top—making them look much bigger than the last time Rayne had seen them. The brown nipples were in stark contrast with the black suit.

Her laughter dried up as her eyes stopped at Storm's nipples… and she had to swallow hard past her dry throat. She felt her core clench, and there was an immediate warm wetness. Rayne considered putting her panties back on before going out there, but it was too late.

Storm winked at her, and then put her robe on over her naughty little outfit. She took Rayne's hand and pulled her out of the dressing room.

They dropped onto the first open bench-seat and shoved their bags underneath it. Rayne took her time settling in and crossing and uncrossing her legs, feeling naked and exposed—jittery and nervous.

She tucked the edges of the robe around her, and tightened the gap that was threatening to show her big breasts to the room.

Then she heard Blond Sexy's voice. "Pet, you're just in time. It's our turn."

Rayne's head shot up. *Is he talking to me?* she thought in a panic. But he wasn't. It was Storm that stood up and walked to the middle of the room to where he was standing beside a machine—something she'd never seen before. It was a saddle-shaped thing set up on a stage. Blond Sexy was holding a penis-shaped attachment in his hand, and when Storm nodded, he equipped the black-saddled thing with it.

Storm stopped just in front of him and lowered her head, looking at the floor, and standing very still. *What the hell is she doing?*

Blond Sexy untied her robe and then roughly jerked it off her shoulders, throwing it to the floor in one swipe. Rayne jumped up in disbelief, ready to intervene until she saw Storm slightly turn her head and give her a quick sly wink.

Rayne sat back down, but her hackles were up. She flinched again as Blond Sexy flicked at Storm with two fingers, and the crotch of her outfit flung open, exposing her tiny shaved mound to the entire room.

Rayne held her breath as she felt her face redden for her friend. Her mind started mentally flipping through her bag—even as she kept her eyes glued to the scene unfolding in front of her—as she tried to figure out what, if anything in there could be used as a weapon, if need be.

Blond Sexy was also dressed in a sexy leather outfit. His included a collar around his neck. Unspoken words passed between he and Storm and he nodded. He then unfastened the collar and placed it around Storm's neck, tightening it to fit her snug, but not too snug. He attached a thin leash to it, which he let just hang—for now.

Then he picked up a leather crop that Rayne hadn't noticed before. He used the crop to lift Storm's face just enough to see her eyes through her long, chocolate-colored hair. "You'd like to ride the Sybian, Pet?" he asked.

"Yes, Master." Storm's normal feisty attitude was gone—*poof*. Like night and day. Rayne was flabbergasted at the change in her. She wondered if possibly Blond Sexy had spiked her drink with something. She was getting very concerned. This was not the take-charge firecracker she'd met last night at the truck stop...

"You have to pay to ride, Pet." Blond Sexy lifted the crop and rubbed it down Storm's cheek. She leaned into the caress. "Now turn around and bend over," he barked.

"Yes, Master," she said as she whipped around and grabbed the edge of the stage where the saddle-shaped thing was mounted. As she stared at the penis attachment, Rayne saw her lick her lips and heard her moan. And then Storm flinched as the crop whipped out against her exposed ass, cracking against her smooth ass-cheek.

Rayne tensed again, ready to jump up and stop it, until she saw Storm's eyes flutter and her mouth drop open, emitting a long, low moan. Not pain-filled—pleasure.

She bucked again as the crop hit her once more... than again. This time coming down with a much louder slap, causing Storm to moan even louder. Rayne realized this was obviously Storm's thing—she liked it—so she too began to relax and watch intently. She was surprised to realize she was clenching and aching with each flick of the crop too.

Finally, Rayne heard Blond Sexy say, "Mount."

"Yes, Master," Storm answered. She didn't hesitate to throw a leg over and slide up next to the attached dildo... but she didn't quite touch it. She dropped her head and waited for further instruction.

Rayne looked around the room. There were over a dozen people besides the bouncer, herself, Storm and Blond Sexy—now known as "Master." They were all either watching Storm intently, some with the hands in their robes... or they were quietly screwing, both parties facing forward so neither missed the show.

Rayne bit her lip and stretched, leaving her arms behind her head and leaning back on them...anything to keep from touching herself in front of everybody. It was throbbing in a repetitive pulsing rhythm now, and completely drenched. It begged to be touched.

"Slide on, Pet." Blond Sexy slapped the dildo with his crop, indicating his exact instructions. He picked up a small black box. Rayne leaned forward trying to see exactly what it was.

Storm grabbed the dildo and held it while she lifted herself up and slowly slid onto it. She closed her eyes and breathed in deeply, moving halfway down it and then back up again. She moaned and began to slide down again—

—The crop shot out and snapped her nipple. Storm jumped and her eyes snapped open, flashing with pain. She froze with just the tip of the attachment still in her.

"Sorry, Master."

"Don't move until I tell you, Pet."

Nice reminder, **after** *you popped her, asshole,* thought Rayne. A leather crop on a nipple? That had to hurt. Rayne cringed, but Storm didn't seem bothered by it at all; actually the opposite. Rayne could see her juices dripping down the dildo, and watched her chest heave with pent-up passion. It almost hurt to watch and Rayne hoped for release for Storm more than for herself by now.

Blond Sexy pointed the little black box at the machine and it began to vibrate. Storm gritted her teeth against the movement. It was plain to see it was an effort not to move. Her Master turned it up little by little, while Storm barely held on, her legs trembling with effort not to slide down.

Finally, he said, "Ride, Pet."

Storm slid down the shaft of the fake cock, taking it all. He turned the controls up. Storm began by rolling and rocking her hips, and then going into an up and down movement, and then repeating as though it were a dance she was very familiar with.

Her head was thrown back in ecstasy and she was moaning long and loud now. Her master had unsnapped the front of his leather outfit and was using the same up and down method on his own shaft, in rhythm with Storm, as he watched her.

Rayne crossed her legs, squeezing her thighs together, trying to get some sort of relief. Her movement caught Storm's eye. Storm studied her a moment and then jerked her head at Rayne to join her. Rayne saw pleading in her eyes.

But she shook her head no. How could she possibly have sex—of any sort—in this room so close to strangers? No way... and she'd already said, *no sex with Storm*. She wasn't gay, or "bi"... and as tempting as it was, she needed to keep the line drawn between them if they were going to be on the road for nine nights together.

Blond Sexy turned the machine up another notch and it appeared Storm was riding a bucking bronco. She squealed as she caught the edges of the saddle with her fingertips and held on tight. Storm's juices were all over the machine, and Rayne longed to be on it too. To finally feel fulfilled—to have a good, long orgasm, even if it was by a machine. The thick pulse of her snatch quickened.

Rayne heard herself moan as it took every bit of self-control not to reach her hands into her robe and take care of matters herself.

She looked around, trying not to stare, but curious what everyone else was doing. She was the only one not getting off. She looked back to Storm and their eyes met. Rayne saw the longing in Storms eyes again—and sympathy?

She reached behind her and patted the machine. Rayne raised her eyebrows and lifted her shoulders. What was that supposed to mean? Did she want Rayne to climb up behind her? Ride it with her?

Storm answered her unspoken question by patting it again and jerking her head over her shoulder, as though to say, "Get on!"

Six

Rayne took one more look around.

She'd never seen any of these people before, in her entire life. She'd probably never see them again—she couldn't stop herself. She stood up and let her robe drop around her feet and she walked to the center of the room. She heard everyone quiet around her but she kept her eyes on Storm.

She climbed up behind Storm, expecting the 'master' to flick Storm with his crop. But he just looked at them with a big smile on his face. He gave them his nod of approval and dropped his leather crop.

Rayne nudged her hips across the smooth black leather saddle an inch at a time—hard to do while it was moving so fast—until she was backed right up to Storm's ass.

The machine slowed, but the vibration and the close proximity to Storm nearly made Rayne come right away. She held it back. She wanted an opportunity to ride, and riding after an orgasm seemed like it would probably be torture; *although Storm might enjoy that*, she thought.

Rayne needed something to hold onto. She couldn't get a grip on the leather seat in her position behind Storm. She put her arms around Storm, her hands accidently landing on Storm's breasts—with those perfect little copper pennies.

She quickly let go—but nearly fell off and grabbed for them again, telling herself it didn't mean anything. They could ride together as two girls having fun, right? Storm didn't seem to mind.

She closed her eyes, feeling the thrum and buck of the saddle under her as she rode barebacked—in the truest form. She felt the softness of Storm's breasts in her hands and she hung on, and visions of them rolled through her head.

Her hips moved in rhythm with the machine, and although she didn't have an attachment inside her, just the smooth leather bucking up against her, the feeling of skin on skin as she pressed against Storm, and the memory of Storm's perfect, brown nipples that she was now holding in her hands brought her close to coming.

She bit her lip, trying to prolong it.

Rayne hands loosened, her fingers searched for the copper-tinted buds—quickly finding them and rolling them through her fingers, and then pinching them.

Storm reacted with a loud humming that Rayne could feel vibrate through her back against her own breasts. Their sweat mingled together as their bodies bucked up and down and side to side on the machine, plastered together with heat and sweat.

Blond Sexy turned the machine up and Storm reached back, searching. First her fingers brushed the small thatch of Rayne's naturally blonde curly hair on her mound, sending shocks of more pleasure rocketing through her—she was embarrassed at how starved for human touch of any kind she was.

Then Storm's finger landed on her clit. She barely touched it, but it was enough to nearly send Rayne over the edge.

She didn't think she could hang on any longer, she felt herself lose control... she began a slow shudder. Her toes curled and her legs tightened against the black bucking-machine as the first wave hit. Her legs gripped just under Storm's, they were fit together, like a puzzle... skin to skin.

Rayne had forgotten how good it felt to just *feel* her skin against someone else's…

There was no doubt that Storm felt Rayne's grip on the machine change, as their legs were pressed together. Rayne felt and heard Storm let go too. They rocked together, both moaning and yelling out. Rayne dropped her head onto Storm's shoulder, feeling as though she couldn't hold it up under the pressure of the orgasm.

She tasted her salty skin and unconsciously sucked at it, her mouth fastened tightly and not letting go. She pinched Storm's nipples hard then, twisting and tugging on them, and Storm forced her fingers deeper into Rayne, wiggling against the roll of the moving saddle and the onslaught of the orgasmic waves rushing through her, soaking them both.

Rayne could feel the cool air hit the wet cheeks of her ass and knew Storm probably felt it too—their combined juices mixing together. The strong smell of their heated, wet sex was intoxicating.

Her eyes closed in pleasure and she was able to forget there was a roomful of eyes on her. She forgot her empty life and her cheating husband, and for a little while, forgot the lonely feel of emptiness deep inside her.

She dropped her hands and gripped Storm's thighs, squeezing hard as the biggest wave surged through her, driving her into a frenzy of desire. She moved against the flow of the saddle, pushing down when it bucked up, trying to finally appease the aching, throbbing need she'd ignored for so long.

They were both breathing hard as they came together, and as they came down from their orgasms, Blond Sexy adjusted the machine slower and slower until it ground to a full halt. The blood rushed through Rayne's ears and it was blessed silence beyond it.

Storm slumped over, going limp and resting her arms on the front of the saddle, and her head fell onto her arms in exhaustion.

Rayne leaned over Storm's glistening back, shining with their combined sweat, and placed her head on her arms too.

The ladies sat motionless, other than random quivers, catching their breath and waiting for their legs to stop trembling.

With her eyes closed, Rayne realized she felt light-headed, as if she were a feather, slowing floating back to earth... it was an amazing feeling that she'd missed for a long time. As she cooled down, she inhaled; Storm still smelled of cinnamon and spice, under the tantalizing scent of sex and sweat.

And then she felt a twinge of guilt. But the satisfied feeling between her thighs quickly overrode it. Besides, this wasn't really cheating. At least it wouldn't be in Joe's mind, unless there was a man involved, and no man had touched Rayne—yet.

If Joe was here, and could see her on this machine, alone or with a woman... maybe he would have found her sexy and desirable again. *He'd have loved it—at least the old Joe would've*...she thought to herself before climbing down.

Seven

Storm slid the key card into the door, and the girls stumbled into the hotel room with their bags. They both tossed them onto a separate bed, marking their spots, and then made a bee-line toward the bathroom, bumping into each other in their hurry.

Storm laughed. "You can go first. I'll wait," she offered.

"No, you go. I need to check my phone anyway. Just don't be too long. My body is definitely not used to... well, it's screaming for sleep."

Storm sauntered off into the bathroom, shaking her hips on the way, and left the door open. Rayne's eyes were still glued to her as she stripped off her shirt, leaving her naked from the waist up. She was facing the tub as she unbuttoned and unzipped her shorts and pulled them down her tan legs, kicking them off to the corner.

She slowly pulled her panties down, and using one foot, she daintily dropped them on top of the shorts and shirt. She bent over the tub, taking an usually long time adjusting the water temperature.

Rayne sucked in a deep breath... she had a birds-eye view of Storm from behind.

She was surprised she still had the energy to be turned on—and shocked at her body's resistance to her mind—she *wasn't* into girls. *What the hell?* Obviously, her libido disagreed. Or maybe it'd just been so starved for sexual attention for so long, it was grabbing onto anything willing and available.

Storm turned on the shower head, and climbed in, pulling the curtain shut behind her. Rayne realized her hand was rubbing herself... she moved over to the bed and sat down, trying to clear her mind, but it wasn't going away. She needed to come again; an almost painful need.

She dropped backward onto the bed, leaving her feet on the floor and reached into her shorts, finding her little nub that had come back to life in the past twenty-four hours. It was swollen and throbbing, but her body wanted more than just a rub down.

She lifted her ass and jerked her shorts down to her knees, and then reached back between her legs with both hands. One hand rubbing her nerve-filled nub, the other slipping inside her.

She lifted her feet onto the bed, frantically rubbing herself as thoughts of Blond Sexy's large package flashed through her mind.

She wished—for the first time in years—that she wasn't married. She pictured Blond Sexy coming up behind her and shoving himself into her balls-deep while he grabbed her hair, pulling her head back. She envisioned Storm sucking on her breasts while Blond Sexy took her from behind; she could almost feel her hand tangling in Storm's long, dark hair, pushing her face into her breasts as Storm licked and sucked on her nipples.

Her body clenched as she came. The fantasy turned hazy and disappeared as the sound of running water overtook it. Rayne brought her fingers out, rubbing her juices up her mound and onto her stomach.

She stood up and pulled her shorts back on, shaking her head—her screwed up head that she couldn't control anymore. Maybe she needed to ask Storm to just take her home. She felt like she was a hair away from just letting go...

doing something that she couldn't come back from; something that would forever ruin her chances of fixing this shit with Joe. *As if it could be fixed. Yeah right.*

Rayne grabbed her phone, swiping to see if she had any more messages from Joe. There were three missed calls. All from Joe. No texts.

Her heart began to pound as she punched in her number to listen to the voicemails...

"Rayne, just calling to see if you got my message and check in. Call me back," the first message said. Rayne raised her eyebrows. Joe had pretty much stopped calling to "check in" months ago. That was unusual. Probably wanted to stick his toe in and see how much she'd figured out.

She hit delete and played the next one.

"Rayne, I need to talk to you. Call me back."

Hmmm... That one sounded like he was getting a little pissy. He wasn't used to *not* having Rayne at his beck and call every minute of the day. She was sure two unanswered calls had him in a tail-spin.

Although she didn't feel good about letting him worry... he deserved it. And more. Finally, *he* wants to talk? Now that it's probably too late? He's never wanted to talk before. Treated her as if she was invisible... just a room-mate. Or a house-keeper.

She mentally shook off the rage that was threatening to overcome her. If she let it in, she'd end up calling Joe and showing her hand, and give him a chance to make his excuses. A chance to hide the truth. She needed to not tip him off. She needed to see the truth with her own eyes.

She rolled her shoulders and decided no. She absolutely would not call him back. She hit delete and played the next one.

"Rayne, since it's not like you to not answer your phone or call me back, I got worried and called Susan... next door? She said you aren't home. It's eleven o'fucking clock! She saw you get into a red sports car. Where are you and who are you with?! I need to know you're okay. Call me back. Right. Fucking. Now!"

Rayne gasped and her hand flew to cover her mouth. Never, in all their years of marriage had she done anything like this. And Joe was pissed. He didn't use the f-word very often either—and he'd said it twice!

She felt a shiver go down her spine at his wrath, knowing she would have to deal with it now—but wait. *Hell no.* She didn't *have* to deal with it anymore. He cheated. Screw him.

She wasn't going to call him back. Let *him* feel rejected... like he'd made her feel. Let *him* wonder what she was up to... like she'd had to wonder. Let him walk a mile in her shoes. And maybe she'd walk a mile in his.

She turned her phone off and dropped it into her bag. Then she stripped off her clothes and walked into the bathroom.

"Any hot water left in here?" she asked Storm, before pulling back the curtain and stepping in.

THE TRUCKER'S WIFE

Episode Four

RAYNE AND STORM
BRING THUNDER

One

"You finally ready to shove your sweet little teacher life into the closet and have some real fun now?" Storm asked with one eyebrow arched. She smiled slyly at Rayne, and licked her lips. She smelled of cinnamon. "I want to see you swing those curves on the dance floor."

Storm's chocolaty-colored long hair cascaded down her back in long, loose curls—an hour to put in, and they'd probably fall back into her normal waves after the first dance in the sexual steam of the dance club. Either way, Storm always looked beautiful, even in the morning when she awoke with her hair tangled and flat.

She was rocking the tight little mini-skirt she had on with her tall, strappy black heels. The skirt was denim— probably only hung down a total of three inches from Storm's panties, and the top she wore was clingy, sparkling and ivory-colored. Even outside in the light of the moon and with the limited parking lot lights, Rayne could see right through it; once inside where there were sure to be blue lights on the dance floor, her copper-colored nipples and perfect, perky little tits would give a show to everyone.

She's a hot little number… that's for sure. Fresh and feisty, too, Rayne thought. Without a doubt, if she walked in there with Storm, all eyes would be on them. Male or female.

* * *

They'd spent the day shopping and pampering. Manicures and pedicures, and even a quick trip to the salon where they enjoyed massaging chairs while having their hair washed and styled. It was all Storm's treat.

Rayne had at first refused, but Storm was adamant she could afford it and wanted to take a few hours to do 'girly-fun-stuff' together. So Rayne had given in and enjoyed it, even while harboring some doubt as to why would an almost-complete stranger want to drop this much cash on someone else.

Was it Storm's way of trying to make her feel better? She hadn't told Storm about Joe's calls, but she was sure Storm could tell her mood had changed. Her lip poked out was an obvious clue.

So why throw money at her instead of just a hug and an ear? Did the girl not have any close female friends...ever? The irony of Storm, was that she didn't seem capable of touchy-feely in the way of comforting a friend... but she had no problem touching Rayne any other time.

She mentally tried to shrug those thoughts away; but she was still uncertain about Storm. The snarky little attitude that had been sneaking into their conversations the past few days, and her constant need to be chasing sex had almost caused Rayne to put an end to their road trip this morning. Rayne's patience had run out and she just wanted to go *home*. She didn't need Storm—or this trip—she had finally decided. She could just go home, wait for Joe and straighten this shit out with him, before she did something even more stupid than just taking off on a road-trip without telling her husband. Or taking his calls. Or explaining.

She cringed when she thought about how pissed Joe probably was by now. Not one word back from her yet. Every time she decided to just call him, even if it was to lie and give a lame story about where she was—pretend she still didn't know what he was up to—Storm talked her out of it.

She'd finally just turned her phone off so she couldn't see him calling or texting... but she'd planned on calling him this morning just to let him know she was okay, and she was on her way home, if she could ever get a minute without Storm crawling up her ass.

But then Storm had dropped a bomb on her. One that finally had shattered the tiny shard of hope Rayne had left. She had no reason now to hold out. Why should she care? Finally, she was free to do whatever she wanted—or whoever. If she wanted. And right now, that sounded pretty damn good.

As she thought about her response, she realized her lips—slick with cherry-flavored lip-gloss—were again pressed together and poked out, in a insolent pout—at least that's how Joe always used to describe them when she was super-pissed and had her chin set so hard.

She looked down at herself... she did look sexy as hell in the dress Storm had bought her earlier. A $300 dollar dress that blew Rayne's mind. First, her entire seasonal wardrobe usually cost about that much from TJ Maxx. Second, the fabric of the dress actually changed colors, depending on the light. It was like an iridescent kaleidoscope—and Storm had bought her shoes that matched too!

This dress is too damn kewl to NOT walk into this club and show it off, she thought.

The little rainbow-like shimmery dress was tight and clingy. It pushed up her heavy girls, forcing them to spill out the top. Plenty for the guys to look at... It was cut mid-thigh to show some skin, and Rayne was glad she'd always made a point to work out her legs. She could admit to herself that her legs looked damn good. They weren't stick-thin—nowhere close—but they were tone, defined and tan... She'd never had any complaints from Joe about her legs at least.

Her long blonde hair smelled heavenly and was just hanging loose, the way she preferred it. But it was soft, shiny, thick and clean. When she moved, it brushed across her exposed back, or over the top of her tits, tickling her skin and sending a little spark of pleasure down her spine. *Pitiful.* Getting her kicks on her own hair touching her own skin… Really? *Really?* That was seriously attention-starved and screwed up.

So hell yeah. She was ready.

She just needed to shake off the mad still clinging to her face and loosen up before walking in there. She was still pissed about what Storm had found out earlier. She hadn't been able to shake it for more than a few minutes all day, even while Storm was spoiling her on their 'girl's day out,' and *ewwing* and *ahhing* over all the sexy new things she was adamant Rayne needed now.

She took a deep breath.

Storm moved closer to Rayne, looking into her big blue eyes from her own. Rayne returned her look. It was hard not to be drawn into Storm's eyes; the deep green irises with spatters of gold flecks begged to be stared at. Her long eyelashes shuttered them, making you work to get past and find what was so mesmerizing, besides the fact that they were exotically almond-shaped.

"Earth to Rayne… Stop staring at my eyes, bitch, and answer me! You ready to get your groove on, party girl?" She did a silly neck roll and finger-snap, with her snapping hands finishing their dance to land on her hips.

Rayne laughed at Storm's ghetto impression as well as at herself. How embarrassing… she wondered how long she'd just stood there, probably looking like a female RainMan studying Storm's eyes—again.

"Come *on*, hooker!" Storm said, "We'll have a great time here. I promised to give you liquor and laughs, dirty dancing and dick-heavy dudes! We're here. You still want all that?"

Rayne wanted to be *wild*. She wanted to do something she'd never done before… to feel something deep… maybe numb her pain with a different kind of pain. She wanted to set her spirit free and do *what-the-fuck-ever* for once in her life. She was ready to kick her lame-ass housewife slash teacher-persona to the curb. Why not? Joe obviously didn't care.

She nodded at Storm and tilted her head to the side…and then to the other side, matching Storm's ghetto-play, with her own hands on her hips, as she answered in her best snarky voice, "Bring it, bitch."

Two

Earlier that morning…

"So… Storm," Rayne said cautiously, while watching out the window as the trees blurred by. "What's the plan?"

After scaring the crap out of Storm by crawling into the shower with her last night, resulting in a water fight reminiscent of her slumber party days. They had laughed like crazy loons, and then quickly—and innocently—washed and crawled into bed.

Storm had gone right to sleep. But Rayne had been unable to. She had quietly lay there listening to the sounds of Storm's slumber while going over what had happened so far on this trip.

First, Storm had gotten busy on the hood of Joe's truck with a random trucker, whom she'd *also* told Rayne's name to. *Then* she'd gotten snarky with her about how to use the CB. *Then*, shockingly, they'd been christened a team name—RainStorm— that Joe might or might not wonder about. *What if he figured it out?*

Then she had *almost* participated in a threesome.

And the back room—that was the worst—and it was in front of strangers. The screamin' saddle. If she could have one take-back on the whole trip, it would be that.

A lot of crazy shit had happened so far. Shit that never happened in Rayne's typically boring life. She'd thought she wanted to spice it up, but maybe it was getting too hot for her to handle after all.

Regrets rushed through her mind. *What am I? A freakin' bitch in heat? A slut? Gay?!* She was disgusted with herself. Embarrassed. This wasn't her. This wasn't 'Joe's wife.'

She knew all of it was her own fault, she was a big girl… but it felt like Storm was rubbing off on her a little. Influencing her to be something she wasn't. And she realized it was starting to feel like every little thing about Storm was bugging her, too.

Maybe it really was time to go home and just wait for Joe. *Alone.*

She'd finally drifted off to sleep with that decision firm in her mind. She was going home. She'd deal with Joe on her own turf and stay out of trouble until then.

But she'd woken to Storm all bright-eyed and chirpy, dressed and packed—and she even had Rayne's stuff packed up too, leaving out only a fresh outfit and her make-up bag.

Rayne had tried to stall, asking for coffee and breakfast before they left—no use getting on the road going the wrong way—but Storm had smiled and said, "It's already in the car, hot and steamy and waiting for you, love! Let's go!"

So here they were again, rolling down the highway in the wrong direction; opposite from home… kicking herself for not putting an end to this charade.

"The plan is still *the plan*," Storm answered with a tinge of snark. "We've got to be right at your husband's back door. If we don't see him on the road, we'll find him at his company warehouse, watch him re-load and follow him. I'm sure we can catch him dipping into the sugar on the flip-flop to his Home 20."

Rayne rolled her eyes. She *soooo* didn't want to give Storm the satisfaction of asking, but… "Translation again,

Storm. We're not on the CB. Can't you speak plain English please?"

Storm sighed.

"Back door means we're behind him. Flip-Flop is his return trip. Home 20 means exactly that… a driver's *home location*. And I assume you know what 'dipping in the sugar' means? That's not trucker slang."

Rayne nodded, and then shrugged, not knowing or caring if Storm saw her.

But she did.

"What? Why are you *shrugging*? Wasn't that the plan all along?"

Rayne cleared her throat. Maybe now was a good time to *change* the plan.

"Yeah, I guess it was. I just didn't know it would be like this," she answered.

"Like what? Are you *bored*?" Storm asked. "For fucks sake, I've tried to show you a good time along the way. You had fun on the saddle. And I did present you the finest piece of fuckable, willing man-candy on a freakin' plate and you still wouldn't take even take a nibble… what *do* you want, Rayne?"

Rayne looked back out the window, watching the sunlight flash between the trees as they sped by… like her thoughts—too fast to grab hold of anything and make sense of it or get a clear picture.

The silence stretched awkwardly between them.

"*Oh*… wait a minute. I remember. You said you were expecting some Thelma and Louise-ish bullshit." She laughed sarcastically and Rayne snapped her eyes back to her. *I'm about a cunt hair from having to tell this snarky bitch off and walking to the nearest bus stop*, she thought.

"No, no, no… I'm not being facetious. Really," Storm said, and laughed. "I just wanted to remind you of what you said. But think about it, Rayne. That movie came out when you were like… what? Five years old or something?

I don't know when you last saw it, but I think you're forgetting most of the movie. It wasn't all kicks and giggles on their road trip. It was *tense*. It was *drama*... and it *didn't* end well for them."

Rayne struggled to find her memories of the movie... Thelma and Louise singing happily together in a convertible with the wind blowing through their hair, the girls slamming back shots and dancing in a club... Brad Pitt... That was all she could come up with. *Was there more?*

"They had fun! They... they *danced*... they... they..." she answered defensively, but her words trailed off as other parts of the movie flooded into her mind... everything else she could remember was related to sex, crime or running from the law. *Okay, bad movie reference. I don't think I want to put those thoughts into Storm's head*, she thought.

Too late...

"Nope! Their little road trip consisted of an *attempted rape* on the back of a car, picking up a *sexy hitchhiker* for Thelma, and her nearly climbing the wall as she was being professionally nailed by him, *armed robbery* and a *double suicide*."

She gave a firm nod of her head, with a cheeky smile.

"Now, if that's what you want, I can find you a sexy hitchhiker and you can *finally* get a little bit of action, but I'm out when it comes to going to jail or driving off a cliff into the wild blue yonder—I love myself too much for that." She turned toward Rayne and winked.

Rayne folded her arms across her chest. "No. I *don't* want a dirty hitchhiker. Thanks for the thought though," she answered sarcastically. *Son of a dick, everything's got to come back to sex for Storm. Can't she just have a little no-sex fun... is that even possible for her?*

Storm laughed, throwing her head back in abandon. "*Gurrl!* You are so worried about getting crotch-critters or something else that you're setting your sights too low. I've been out here a *looong* time, and I've yet to get the crotch-rot." She giggled again, and Rayne felt pressure building in her chest. She was feeling trapped, confused, and wanting more than anything to reverse time and never have climbed into this damn Jaguar. She needed to change the subject before she exploded.

"What's *your* husband think about what you're doing?" Rayne asked unexpectedly, stopping the giggles from Storm so fast it was as though she'd stuffed a sock in her mouth.

Storm's smile disappeared instantly, and she gripped the steering wheel tighter, her knuckles turning white.

"What he don't know won't hurt him," she snapped while looking straight out the windshield, her eyes lasered in on the road.

Oh... touched a nerve. Maybe there's something to this, Rayne thought. *Maybe it's time I get her to lay her own shit bare.*

"How could he *not* know? You seem pretty well-known and... um... *popular*... with the truckers. And you said he *is* a trucker... so how could he not be hearing about you? Or even hearing you talk on the CB radio sometimes?" Rayne asked with one eyebrow arched.

Silence filled the car again for a moment, and Rayne felt their speed pick up. She looked at the speedometer and saw the needle sneaking toward 100mph. She unconsciously put her hand on her seat belt, making sure it was in place.

And then Storm answered in a very serious voice while keeping her eyes focused straight ahead on the highway. "Look, Rayne. You came to *me* when you thought your husband was cheating on you. I *offered* to take you on this road-trip to find out. You *wanted* to come. This isn't about me and *my* husband. Let's talk about what I found out about yours today."

Three

All thoughts of Storm and her situation flew out the window. Rayne's heart skipped a beat and all she could think about was Joe.

"What? What'd you find out?" Rayne demanded.

Storm smirked.

"Seriously, did you find out something about Joe?" Rayne's voice had increased in volume, unintentionally, as her patience dropped to negative-zero. "Tell me right fucking now!"

"Whoa! I will tell you... *damn*," Storm answered, blinking her eyes innocently and trying to look hurt. "This morning while you were still asleep, I came out and chattered a bit on the CB. I found someone who saw Joe in his rig, out on the Ho Chi Minh Trail. Several times. Always with the same crackerhead riding shotgun."

Rayne's eyebrows scrunched together. "Hocheemen Trail? What is that? A park or something?"

Storm laughed. "No. Not *hocheemen*... Ho - Chi - Minh – Trail. That's what truckers call California Highway 152. They usually try to avoid it if possible, because it gets bogged down with accidents. Slows them down."

Rayne felt like she couldn't breathe. Joe was actually seen with another woman in his truck? Now she knew... Emotions passed through her mind as fast as the cars flashed by in the granny lane beside them. Disbelief, sadness, anguish and then rage. *Now this shit was real. Very real.*

Her eyes filled with tears, and she felt heat pinching her cheeks—on fire. She wanted to punch something. She drew in a deep breath, trying to calm herself.

"Who is it... the *crackerhead*... do you know?" she asked in a shaky voice.

Storm glanced over and met Rayne's eyes for a split-second, and then she looked back out the front window. She also took in a deep breath before answering.

"Her handle is Blindside. Her real name's Stacy."

"*Blindside?!* How stupidly appropriate is that?" Rayne yelled as she angrily swiped at the wetness under her eyes. "What's she look like?" she whispered with a thick voice; she could feel more tears sneaking up and the familiar lump trying to form in her throat. She knew she was seconds away from a don't-fuck-with-me-I'm-super-pissed-cry.

Storm shrugged her shoulders as though she didn't know.

Wait, was that a flash of arrogance in that swarmy shrug? Rayne wondered. She shook her head to herself and realized her temper was probably only playing with her imagination.

"Dammit!" Rayne yelled as she slapped her hands against the dash. "Stop the car, Storm! I need to get out. *Right. Now.*"

Storm jerked the wheel to the right, swerving from the hammer lane to the granny lane and into the emergency lane in one fast swoop. The car bumped along the rough pavement as she slowed it down gradually, not wanting to come to a skidding stop and kick up loose rock.

When they had stopped moving, Rayne jumped out and stomped toward the back of the car. Passing traffic blew past her—too close—blowing her long blonde hair into tangles. She jerked away from the highway and stumbled down the embankment, headed for the trees. Just a few steps into the sparsely wooded area, she threw herself against one, wrapping her arms around one large trunk and pressing her cheek hard against the roughness.

Her body shook as she finally let it go… starting with a primal scream—all but drowned out by the heavy traffic—and ending with sobs.

She heard Storm following, right on her ass, and soon felt her hand on her shoulder. She slapped the hand away. Right now she felt murderous, as though venom had replaced the blood in her veins. She stepped away from the tree trunk, grabbing sticks and hurling them as far and as hard as she could. Several hit nearby trees, the splinters and shards flying back at them.

Storm hurriedly backed up a few steps and cleared her throat.

"Look. I'm not so good at the 'console-your-bestie' thing. I haven't had much practice with people of the same sex—I don't have a lot of female friends. But I *am* sorry you're crying," Storm offered in an almost pleading desperate voice.

Rayne scoffed and threw a lethal glance at Storm over her shoulder. *Sorry I'm crying? What the hell? How about sorry my husband's a cheating rat bastard?* As she stared at Storm's hands tugging nervously at her hair, Rayne dropped her head with a tormented sigh.

Rayne felt her anger subside just a little. This wasn't Storm's fault. *Hell, if it wasn't for her, I'd probably never really know the truth. And I definitely need her now,* Rayne thought, as the rage started to clear out of her mind and thoughts of vengeance slid into their place.

"It's okay, Storm," she muttered, her voice hoarse from crying and screaming. She pulled her shirt up and wiped her eyes, exposing the bottoms of her heavy breasts—no bra again today. "I'm done crying. Let's just get back in the car and keep to the plan. I want to meet this 'Blindside" bitch. Up close and personal."

Storm's eyes widened as Rayne stomped past her with a deadly look in her eyes. Rayne accidently (?) shoulder-checked her as she passed, causing Storm to stumble back a step.

Four

"You tell me. What cha' want to do tonight? Anything you want, Rayne," Storm offered as she eased back onto the interstate.

Rayne thought about it, anger still clouding her mind.

"What I want to do is fight and forget him," she answered. She still felt adrenaline rushing through her at the thought of that crackerhead, "*Blindside*," screwing her man. Or even just riding in his rig. She closed her eyes and breathed deeply. Who was she kidding? She'd never been in a fight in her life.

"How about dancing? You said you wanted to dance. There's a club a few hours up the interstate. We can go dancing. *Party!* Get a room and get back on the road first thing tomorrow," Storm offered in a hopeful voice.

"I don't much feel like dancing anymore, Storm," she mumbled. "And I have *nothing* to wear to a club."

Storm smacked the steering wheel in delight. "That just means we get to go shopping first! That'll put you in the mood to go dancing."

Rayne rolled her eyes. "Storm, I don't have the money to go shopping. Especially now. I don't even have the money for a freakin' lawyer."

● ● ●

"Don't need money for that if you catch him cheating," Storm said and reached over, patting Rayne's leg. "The judge will make him pay for both attorneys."

Rayne shrugged. She didn't even want to think that far ahead. She was still trying to wrap her mind around the fact that yes, her husband had another woman, and no, he didn't want her anymore. That freakin' hurt. A lot.

"Doesn't matter. This shopping trips on me. I can afford it," Storm said. "That's where we're going." She nodded her head to seal the deal, giving Rayne no room to argue.

Rayne just wanted peace—escape—from her thoughts. She leaned her seat back and turned toward her door, letting the sun stream in on her face. She was mentally exhausted. Crying always did that to her. She let the warmth of the sun and the feel of the road draw her into sleep.

Five

Later that night:

Rayne realized Storm wasn't dancing beside her anymore.

She kept dancing, but looked around until she found her, leaning against the bar with a guy on each side of her, their hands roving all over her body while they whispered in her ear. Or tongued her ear. Rayne wasn't sure from this distance, but what she could see was Storm's guys both had similar tattoos and leather vests too, like the man currently rubbing up against her out on the dance floor, his hard package pressing against her, flirting with her ass.

Rayne had drank a little too much. She was slowly crossing her boundaries that she'd promised herself she'd stay within until she could get home. But the booze that she'd hoped would settle her nerves about Joe, was blurring her lines in the sand. And right now, she just didn't care.

Storm was ignoring the two guys all over her—but not stopping them—while she held up her phone, pointed at Rayne. *What the hell? Do I have a phone call? On Storm's phone?* she thought, feeling a stab of panic and guilt simultaneously.

Then she saw a little flash and realized Storm was just taking pictures. Rayne shot her a sexy smile and threw an arm up over her shoulder, running her hand down the bristly face of the hot biker moving slowly behind her. She'd have to tell

Storm to send her that picture later... something to remember this night.

The biker's arms came around Storm and she ran her hands up and down the intricate tattoos. He felt so good behind her, although he wasn't much of a dancer; he just swayed side to side—barely moving—while Rayne danced all over him, and let him touch her and squeeze her. It felt slutty. And dangerous. And *good*.

She worked herself on him, the pulsing lights and thumping music feeding her confidence. She shook her ass and gyrated around his thick, muscular leg, ending up behind him again. The back of his leather vest was stamped with an interesting picture of lighting and clouds, etched around the word, "Thunder." She wondered if that was his name, and giggled.

Then she laughed. Hard. And continued to laugh until she had to stop dancing and was nearly bent half over in laughter. The biker turned around and caught her just as she began to lean sideways.

"Hey. You need to sit down or something?" he asked, while holding her shoulders firmly, but gently.

Rayne laughed even harder and sunk down to the floor, holding her stomach.

"Yeah, you need to sit for a minute," he answered himself, "but not out here." He reached down and pulled her up, and then half-carried her to a booth that was already full of young guys, all probably just barely over 21.

"Move," he said. They scattered like chickens without a moment's hesitation, and he slid Rayne into the booth, scooting her over and sliding in beside her.

He gave her a concerned look, leaning over to look at her face and said, "You need some water. I'll be right back." He had a rough kindness in his voice.

While he was gone, Rayne was able to put an end to her laughing fit. She wiped her eyes, using a napkin left

THE TRUCKER'S WIFE

behind by the young crowd of boys and tried to smooth
down her hair before her biker got back—if he came back.

She felt stupid for not being able to stop laughing.
She realized she was on emotion overload. She'd ruined the
dancing and maybe embarrassed him. Now he thought she
was drunk... *really drunk*. But she wasn't. Not really. She'd
only had a few beers, and two shots of vodka—a lemon shot
they'd called it. And she and Storm had both eaten before
drinking. The laughing—bordering on hysteria—sobered her
up quickly.

Maybe it was a good thing she'd lost her shit. One of
them needed to be able to drive, and it sure wasn't going to
be Storm. She'd put back twice as much as Rayne had and she
was smaller.

She'd just explain to the sexy biker about her laughing
melt-down... if he came back.

● ● ●
138

Six

The tattooed biker startled Rayne as he appeared from behind and slid a sealed bottle of water in front of her. It seemed he'd been gone a long time, and she was beginning to think he wasn't coming back. The bar must be busy.

"Thanks," she said.

"You're welcome, ma'am. Mind if I sit?"

Ma'am? For realsie? She raised her eyebrows at his politeness, and patted the seat beside her. Then she scooted to the farthest end and turned to lean her back against the wall, so that she could get a better look at him.

Sitting still without the movement and lights of the dance floor, she was surprised to see he was a little older than she'd thought. His silvery-blond hair wasn't short, but not necessarily long either. It hung in a long, blunt fringe over his ears and off to the side of his face, covering one eye—the other eye was a piercing cool gray in color—his hair wasn't scruffy in a need-a-haircut kinda way; it looked as though it had been purposely cut that way. His square jaw, covered in a light-colored five-o'clock shadow, supported plump lips. He smelled of leather, and Rayne imagined he probably drove a motorcycle.

She also imagined the thrum of the engine under her. She could feel her own engine revving as she checked him out.

His rugged, manly, inked-up biker look conflicted with his broodingly sexy grown-up-boy-next-door qualities. He could easily pass for the 40-year old version of hundreds of college boys she'd drooled over on campus when she should have been studying years ago.

"You seem to be doing much better now. You don't look as drunk as you did out on the dance floor," he said, and then smiled. "Had me worried there for a minute."

Rayne blinked her eyes a few times and cleared her throat, realizing she must've been staring for quite a while. "Sorry. I'm not drunk. I do have a buzz, but it was your vest that sent me into a fit of giggles. I apologize."

The biker dropped his head and looked down at his vest. Then he looked up and slowly shrugged his shoulders, as though asking her what was so funny about it. His smile was gone, and his face was blank.

"My name is Rayne," she explained quickly, not wanting to offend him. "And my friend that I'm with... her name is Storm."

"And?" he asked, with his brows furrowed.

Rayne laughed again, this time a forced laugh of embarrassment.

"It's the back of your vest that tickled my funny bone... It says Thunder. So, you know... Rayne, Storm...Thunder? I just thought that was really funny, is all."

He squinted for a moment, and then laughed, long and loud. A second later he wrapped his strong arm around Rayne and pulled her closer.

"Well, darling', it sounds like we're all meant to be together then."

Rayne found herself pulled up against him with his lips pressed to hers. In a flash, he'd managed to push the table away from them with his long legs and pick her up while kissing her, settling her on his lap. Her short dress didn't allow for her legs to straddle him without riding up, so she felt cooler air hit her panties as the hem scrunched all the way up around her hips.

His hands ran up her thighs and found a resting spot on each side of her ass, squeezing again and again through the bunched up dress, as his tongue parted her lips. She moaned lightly into his mouth. She could feel him harden under her, and she pushed against it, wanting—needing—to feel it deeper.

This was the first man she'd felt against her, up close and personal, since before she'd married Joe. She was turned on not only by him, but because he was obviously—if his ramrod hardness could be used to measure—turned on by her.

She chased the thoughts of Joe out of her mind and grinded harder against the biker as his tongue thrust against hers greedily. She felt him grow bigger and harder. He was huge and her mind imagined what he must look like under those jeans.

This is what I she want, she told herself. To let go, to be wanted again. Like Storm. *Just go with it. It's not like we're screwing or anything. We're right here in public.*

Wait. We're right here in public! She pulled her mouth away long enough to take a quick look around. At least a dozen eyes were on her—all dudes. From the look on their faces, they liked what they were seeing.

Between the alcohol and her anger at Joe, she didn't care. Actually, it turned her on more to be watched. She wondered if she was an exhibitionist and just now discovering it.

He pulled her mouth back to his and her legs began to quiver as he kissed her deeply. She moved in a rhythm on his lap, rubbing his hardness against her wet panties. As she moved, she felt his hands push her dress up even more.

She realized anyone looking might thing she was riding him bare-assed, as her panties were just a tiny piece of flimsy fabric held together by two strings on each side. The strings were probably still covered by the bottom of her dress, but she could feel the air hit her naked ass cheeks.

She didn't care. Let them look. Let them think she was naked under that dress. That made it even hotter. She felt hot and wet and was throbbing with need.

The music roared in her ears, drowning out her moan. She breathed it into his mouth. She felt like she'd caught fire. She pulled her mouth away and grabbed his hair in both hands, shoving his face down onto her breasts, which were spilling out the top of her dress. *Oh shit. I'm going to explode,* she thought. *I wish he could get to more of my breasts, suck them... pinch them... something...*

The music in the bar continued to thrum through her body as his hands moved to her breasts, pushing up on the bottoms as he buried his face even deeper. She felt his tongue lick long and hot through the cleavage. Not exactly what she was thinking, but hell yeah... it felt good. He lapped at the space between, teasing her breasts with unspoken promises— while she moved faster and faster on his lap, feeling the hard bulge in his jeans finally make contact with her swollen nub.

She shortened her movements to feel more of that, and she felt like she was in a frenzy, rubbing herself on him in a back and forth motion so fast the lights seemed to be bouncing around them. She should stop. She couldn't stop...

A moment later his mouth latched onto the top of one breast, and one of his hands moved down. He roughly slid her panties out of the way, without interrupting her rocking motion, and touched her, moving down... coming dangerously close to the core of her heat.

The tip of one finger reached into her panties and made contact for just a second, but that's all it took. She lost herself. Bucking and moving, his hand couldn't get to her. But she imagined it *in* her, and her hips thrust faster as his mouth sucked harder and harder on her breast, almost painfully.

She felt her body start to quiver as though it was anticipating something huge. And it was. An orgasm began to slowly emerge, clenching and unclenching tightly.

She froze—the anticipation so much that it *made* her stop moving. As if she might lose it if she so much as breathed. She was so close... but he didn't stop sucking her breast. She didn't know where his hand was now, but she didn't need it. One touch of skin against her—that's all it had taken. Her body was so starved for sexual attention.

As she held herself up, inches off away from his lap, with her head thrown back, he had given up trying to get into her panties, and finished her with just soft kisses across the top of her breasts—releasing an orgasm that ripped through her full throttle.

Rayne knew her mouth was open. She knew she had just made some sort of primal noise, but it was lost in the music and the sounds in the bar, even to her own ears.

Seven

"Thunder, I've got to go find my friend," Rayne said, trying to hide her embarrassment as she climbed off of his lap and wiggled around trying to get her dress pulled back into place.

She looked around with big eyes. Now that the moment was over, it didn't seem quite so awesome to be watched—at least not when she couldn't make a quick getaway. Her face burned with shame. She wished she could crawl under the table and hide from the watching eyes.

The gaggle of young guys that had vacated their table earlier were all watching… as well as half the bar; *guys and girls*. She saw several guys slumped low in their seat and rolled her eyes as she wondered if they realized everyone could easily see their hands on their laps under the tables.

She shook her head and climbed over Thunder to get out. "I'm going to the ladies room, and then I've got to find her."

He grabbed her arm before she could get away.

"Sure. Just one thing. My name's not Thunder. I'm just a son of Thunder."

Rayne looked at him in confusion. "Your vest says… Wait. What?"

• • •
144

He smirked at her and gave a little shake of his head. "Not from around these parts, are ya, honey? Thunder is the name of our gang. My name's Seeder."

"Gang? As in a biker gang?" Rayne asked incredulously. She just thought he was a guy on a motorcycle. Not a gang member. Since when did biker gangs hang out at dance clubs? Didn't they have their own place? What the hell? And Seeder? What kind of name was that?

He nodded his head as he stuck a hand down his jeans and adjusted himself. Rayne was embarrassed to see his hard-on hadn't subsided at all, if anything, it looked even bigger than it had felt through the jeans. She felt like a slutty tease. She'd gotten off but left him suffering. But he'd started it. He's the one that had put her on his lap. Still, she felt her face flush even more. She needed to get *away*.

With his smile gone, and his hair definitely messed up now, he suddenly looked dangerous to Rayne. Or maybe that was due to the fact she'd just found out he was not just a biker… he was a *gang member*.

Regardless, she answered his nod with one of her own and hurried off, needing to find her bag and clean herself up. Then find Storm. Or maybe not in that order…

She worked her way through a crowd, most of whom were smiling at her in a creepy way… or winking at her. At least the men were. The women looked at her in disgust. She ignored them and pushed her way to the last place at the bar where she'd seen Storm standing with the two guys—both who had worn similar vests to *Seeder's*—*Omigod, how could I have been so stupid*, she thought.

She looked all around and didn't see Storm or the guys. Then she looked under the barstool that was currently filled with another ass, and there she saw her big bag… with a set of short little legs using it as a foot-rest. *Shit!* Storm had just bought her the bag today and it was her first ever REAL—not knockoff—Louis Vuitton bag. *Bitch!*

She snatched it out from under the little feet, angrily swiping at it to clean it off, and stood to meet the eyes of the owner. Ready to give her a piece of her mind.

Geesh, she looks twelve years old, Rayne thought. *Nevermind.*

Rayne rolled her eyes at the wide-eyed young girl and walked toward the flashing signs of the bathrooms, continuing to look for Storm while she went.

She didn't see her. But she really needed to wipe herself down. She felt cold, wet and nasty. She'd just have to find Storm when she finished freshening up. Or maybe Storm was in the bathroom. That would be awesome. Because she was ready to go. A biker was one thing… she'd love to feel a Harley vibrating between her legs, but a biker gang? *Uh…no thanks.*

Eight

Rayne felt better after a quick wipe-down at the sink. She tried to tell herself she couldn't care less what the other ladies standing there with shocked faces thought of her hiking up her dress, shimmying out of her panties and using paper towels to wash herself down. She was never going to see these women again, and if they'd been out *there*, they'd already seen her do worse. But she was embarrassed. However, she'd choose cleanliness over modesty any day.

She patted herself dry with another handful of paper towels, and then tossed them into the trash. She reached down and plucked her thong panties off the floor with one finger and tossed them too. They were drenched. *Disgusting*.

She pulled down her three-hundred dollar dress, wiggling it over her hips into place, and flicked her long hair over her shoulder. She shook her hips at herself in the mirror—fake bravado—and then ran her hands down over her hair, knowing they were watching every move she made.

She turned and gave them a saucy wink to further camouflage her modesty, then swung the door open, shaking her ass on her way out with a little bit of attitude.

Nine

Rayne closed her eyes and let out the breath she was holding when the door to the ladies room swung closed. *How freakin' humiliating!*

She wanted to find Storm and get the hell outta here.

When she opened her eyes, she jumped. Seeder stood directly in front of her. *Shit.* She hoped he'd have given up on her by now and left.

"You took long enough," he grumbled.

Rayne tilted her head, studying him. What did he want from her? Surely, he didn't think there was going to be more?

"Let's get out of this place," he said and jerked his head toward the door.

Rayne shook her head while answering, "I can't. I came with a friend. I have to leave with her. I just need to find her first."

"Are you talking about the spicy little number that was all over my brothers?"

Rayne raised her eyebrows. "Your brothers?"

"Yeah. The guys with the matching leather vests. They're in my club. Sons of Thunder."

"Oh, so not *related-brothers...* just fellow gang members... Okaaay..." Rayne answered, cringing inside. *Yep, Three biker-gang-dudes. Triple shit.*

"Yeah. They did have on vests, now that you mention it. Are they still with her?" She craned her neck to look around Seeder, hoping to see their heads. Those guys were tall—and big—they should be easier to spot in a crowd than Storm.

Seeder laughed.

"*She's* with *them*. They all left here half hour ago on the bikes. She wanted to ride on BackFire's bike, and see the club house."

Rayne stopped breathing for a second. *Backfire?* Her mouth dropped open and her eyes were wide. Her mouth finally caught up with her brain. "Are you freakin' kidding me? She was *drunk*!" Rayne yelled. "She can't hold onto a motorcycle like that." She took off pushing her way through the crowd to the door, hoping to find the bikes all still there, and maybe Storm hanging out in the parking lot.

Rayne shoved the heavy door to the club open and rushed out, with Seeder swaggering behind her. The cooler, cleaner air washed over her. But so did dread. The parking lot was quiet, not a person to be seen. And right up front, near the door was only one motorcycle. She assumed that one belonged to Seeder.

Oh, shit.

Ten

Rayne's foot hovered over the brake as she took a sharp turn at forty miles per hour, trying to stay close—but not too close—to Seeder as she followed him to the clubhouse.

In any other situation, she'd be thrilled to finally be driving Storm's red Jaguar F-Type coupe. But not right now. Her jaw hurt from clenching her teeth; her mechanism for dealing with the emotions that were flipping from concern to anger for Storm. *What the hell was she thinking? Riding on a motorcycle after drinking? Leaving me alone? Taking off with two gang members?!*

Rayne swore to herself, once she found Storm safe and sound, she was gonna kill the bitch.

She saw Seeder's blinker begin to blink, and then he threw up his left arm, indicating he was going to turn. Rayne slowed the Jag down in a hurry. If Storm was okay, she'd be pissed if Rayne ended up slewing biker-guts all over the front bumper of her beloved car.

Rayne pulled to a stop behind him as he got off the bike and unlocked the chain wrapped around the metal gate. The chain unwound itself and fell to the ground, under the gate. She watched as he bent over and picked it up and tossed it to the side before pulling the gate to the open position.

That chain was huge. It must've weighed a hundred pounds, yet Seeder tossed it aside as though it were light as a feather.

He hopped on his bike, and rolled it through, parking it off to the side to let Rayne by. He waved her through and pointed to a squatty, creepy concrete building with few windows—and the windows it did have were blacked out. *I guess that means park there?* With the almost dozen motorcycles that were lined up out front? *Shit.* Rayne began to tremble. *Omigod. I sooo don't want to go into this joint,* she thought. *I'm gonna wring Storm's neck once I save her ass.*

'Thunder Towing' was crudely painted across the front of the building. Messy, unprofessional and shitty writing. Rayne let out a mocking *humph* at their sign. *I'll just bet they're a tow service.* She'd watched Sons of Anarchy. She knew what kind of businesses biker gangs got into... and she knew they usually had a 'cover' business to hide their real money-makers. She looked around and there wasn't even one tow truck anywhere she could see.

Dumbasses, she thought. *Could at least try to look the part.*

Seeder rolled in beside her and parked his bike, and then got off and walked around to offer his hand to Rayne, to help her out of the car.

Rayne scornfully ignored it, pulling herself up and out, slamming the car door, and stomped past him. She wasn't going to be taken in by his gentleman bullshit. She just wanted to get Storm and get the hell out.

Loud rock music blared from the building and Rayne almost didn't hear Seeder when he yelled.

"Whoa there, little lady!" he called out just before she reached the door.

Rayne whipped her head around, shooting him a scathing look. "What?"

His eyebrows were raised as he slowly shook his head from side to side. "You don't want to just stomp into a biker club house unannounced or without one of us in front of you. That shit won't fly," he warned loudly, having to force his voice over the music.

Rayne sighed. Then she let her hand drop off the doorknob and stepped back, crossing her arms in irritation as she waited for Seeder to get his sorry ass in gear and open the damn door. Her head began to ache in rhythm with the loud thumping music. *Hurry the hell up, asshole,* she thought as he walked as slow as molasses around his bike and toward the gate. *Damn. Now he's got to shut the gate.*

He took forever winding the chain back around the metal and then snapping the heavy lock in place...irritating Rayne even more. He finished and turned around, smirking at her before he slowly sauntered over. *Finally!* He put his right arm around Rayne and his hand landed on her ass, which he gave a squeeze before sliding it up her back to rest lazily on her shoulder.

Rayne gritted her teeth, grinding them together. Just as she was about to shake his arm off, he pulled the door to the club house open. She forgot all about his arm as her eyes took in the staggering scene.

Eleven

The music poured out the door as Rayne stood in shock. She felt Seeder push/pull her in with him and she stumbled a little, her eyes still frozen on Storm. Seeder steadied her and then yelled into her ear, "Want a drink, Sweet Thing?"

Rayne jumped a little, he'd startled her back into reality.

"My name's Rayne. And no. *Hell no!* We're leaving," she said and marched toward the pool table where Storm was giving a scandalous dance dressed only in her birthday suit.

She stopped short, mesmerized by Storm. Although she was obviously drunk, she still danced like a professional—somewhere between a ballerina and a very, *very* good stripper.

Rayne's feet stopped a few feet before the table Storm was dancing on, behind the other bikers, and she stared in awe at Storm's beautiful, lithe body, writhing and winding to the music while her hands seductively slid over herself, slowly sliding from the apex of her thighs up over her flat belly and then to her small but sensual breasts.

Storm seemed lost in her own little world; her almond-shaped eyes were half-closed and her long dark hair hung in damp waves as she moved. Her dancing was stunning. It was graceful—it was freaking amazing. Rayne watched as she seemed to float in the air, unaware or unashamed that she was completely naked. She appeared to be dancing for herself and no one else. Her eyes didn't look at anyone.

She did a little twirl and then suddenly seemed aware of her audience. She made her way back to the edge of the table where she gracefully bent over in front of one of the many bikers surrounding her and swayed her narrow, tan hips in his face—looking at him from over her shoulder—moving in perfect rhythm to the music.

The biker leaned in and licked Storm, a huge, wet swipe of his tongue from bottom to top. She continued to sway to the music in front of him as he grabbed her hips to try to hold her there as long as possible. His head moved as he wet her again and again with his wet tongue. His hips moved against the table, and Rayne could see him pressing him hardened bulge against the wood-grained edge each time his tongue slipped in and out.

Storm's head swayed to and fro with the music and when the tempo picked up, that was her cue to start dancing again. She pulled away from the biker and danced to the middle of the pool table again only to stay there less than a minute before choosing another biker to bend over in front of. This biker took his turn with his hand, instead of his mouth. Rayne watched as he slid two fingers into Storm.

Storm's hips froze for a second, and then thrust back and forth, meeting the movement of the biker's hand and losing her rhythm with the music for a moment as she gave in to her body's wants. When the tempo changed, she darted away again, performing her suggestive, yet bizarrely beautiful dance in the middle of the table where they bikers couldn't easily reach her; they were loving the tease. *For now anyway,* Rayne thought.

Rayne could see Storm's sex was swollen with desire and dripping wet. Her nipples were harder than she'd ever seen them and her eyes were nearly glazed over.

Storm was loving this. Her and almost a dozen bikers. *What the hell was wrong with this chick?* Rayne cringed. She was embarrassed to be a part of this, and it could end badly. For both of them. She looked around and realized they were the only two women in there... and with Seeder... she stopped to count heads. A full dozen bikers. *Oh, shit.*

"You want to dance up there with her, Sweet Thing?" Seeder whispered loudly in her ear. "Or do you want your own table?"

Rayne felt a chill go down her back. *No freaking way I'm getting up and dancing for a bunch of bikers. Not gonna happen. I haven't totally lost my mind...*

Seeder squeezed her shoulders a little too forcefully. "Up and at 'em, Sweet Thing! Dance with your friend!"

If he calls me Sweet Thing again, I swear I'm going to cut off his dick and stick it in his mouth, Rayne thought. But she smiled sweetly and whispered loudly into his ear.

"I need to get my bag out of the car. This dress is too tight to move... like that..." she pointed to Storm. "And I'm a little shy to go bare-assed just yet. But I picked up a sexy little thing today at a lingerie shop—a *very* little something— that I think you and the boys are gonna like. You mind if I go get it?"

"Damn, girl. I don't mind at all. The more skin, the better. And I prefer vanilla to spice anyway..." He winked suggestively.

"Hurry back, Sweet Thing. I might just take a *dash* of spice until you're ready." He mockingly held his thumb and pointy finger up. "You can use the can to change in. It's over there." He pointed to a narrow door that had the word, "Pisser," scribbled across it in black ink.

Rayne nodded and forced another fake smile to her face. Then she squeezed his arm and returned his wink. *Like hell I will,* she thought, as she answered aloud, "Okay. Give me ten minutes, big guy. I'll be right back."

Twelve

Rayne threw herself into the car and locked the door. Her chest heaved in and out in panic as she looked for the start button, missing it several times before she finally hit it.

She put the car in reverse and kicked up gravel as the car flew backward and then she turned the wheel, headed for the entrance.

"Oh, bloody hell!" she screamed as she faced the locked gate. "Son of a dick!"

Her heart was thumping and she was breathing hard and fast. It beat harder as she realized she couldn't get out; they were locked in. Unless they left on foot, and that didn't seem to be a good idea with a dozen motorcycles to give chase.

She jerked the car into reverse again and threw more gravel up as she sped in the opposite direction, around the building, looking for a place to hide.

She pulled in behind a dumpster at the back of the lot. It didn't cover all of the car, so she pulled past it and turned around, then slid in again facing the building so she could see if someone was coming at her. *This'll have to do,* she thought, as she fumbled to get the CB radio out of the glove box.

She dropped the handset, then scooped it back up and pressed the button. She yelled into the mike, "Hey. Anybody got your ears on?" she asked hesitantly, feeling silly.

She let go of the button and waited.

"You got BigTop here, honey. What's your handle? Come back," a cranky voice answered.

"I'm Rayne... Storm," she answered, realizing no one would recognize just Rayne. "*We're* RainStorm. We need some help... Come back."

She tapped the nails of her other hand nervously against the steering wheel, looking around the dark parking lot. She wasn't sure if Seeder would walk around here looking for her, or how much time she had. She needed to get Storm out of there before she got hurt, and she sure couldn't take on a dozen bikers.

"Whatcha need, honey?" BigTop answered in a patronizing tone. "Come back."

"We're at... umm... a clubhouse. It's a biker gang. Their name's Thunder. And Storm's drunk... She's...dancing right now—naked. They want me to dance too and there's no other women here. I need some help getting us outta here before they expect... um... something more than dancing." Rayne answered, her words coming out fast but haltingly as she tried to convey the urgency without telling too much. She was afraid the cops might be listening. And what if they came and the bikers accused Storm of being a hooker?

"—Oh. Come back," she added quickly.

"What's your yardstick? Come back," said BigTop.

Rayne's eyes darted around the car. Yardstick? What did Storm say that meant? She couldn't remember...

"Where ya *at*, girl? Come back." Apparently the trucker could tell Rayne was not familiar with the CB or the language yet, and she could hear frustration in his voice.

Storm panicked again. She'd followed Seeder but she had no idea how to tell anyone where she was. She didn't even know what exit they'd got off to go to the night club, and during the roundabout drive from the night club to the bikers club, she'd kept her eyes on the back of the motorcycle, hoping not to hit it and didn't pay attention to where he'd led her.

She pressed the mike button. *"I don't know!"* she said, almost in hysterics.

There was a pause. Rayne looked at the handheld to be sure she had let go of the button; she had. She held her breath as she waited for another response.

A different voice came across the radio then. A soothing, calm voice that was familiar. "I got this, BigTop. Hold tight, RainStorm. I know that club, and I'm right at your back door. Give me ten minutes. Over and out."

Over and out? Does that mean I'm not supposed to talk anymore? Did he say that because one of the bikers might have a CB? Do motorcycles have CB's? Crap. Maybe they have a CB radio in the clubhouse? Her mind raced and she practically broke the handset shoving it back into the glove box after she turned the CB off. She wasn't saying another word.

She looked around the lot. No one had come for her yet. How long had it been? Four minutes? Five? Rayne had lost track of time. She just hoped Storm was still dancing. She pulled back out from the cover of the dumpster and headed to the front of the building.

She slowly parked and stared at the door. She dreaded going back in there. But she couldn't just leave Storm. She'd wait for help for five minutes... ten at the most. If the music stopped, she'd run in.

Thirteen

Rayne had reluctantly given up on the truckers and was climbing out of the car to go back in, ready to try to talk their way out, or meet their fate, when the lights of a big rig turning into the driveway nearly blinded her.

She threw a hand up to shield her eyes and her mouth dropped open as she watched an 18-wheeler rig tear through the gate as though it were silly string, sending the metal pieces flying and the metal chain snapping to the ground.

The sound of the rig smothered the heavy rock music coming from the biker club. *Wait—not rig... rigs!* Another one made the turn right behind the first one. The two rigs flooded the grungy parking lot with their lights. *Angels,* Rayne thought. *Blinded by the light of angels.* Her eyes watered up in relief.

She looked beyond the second rig, hoping to see more following, but there were only the two. She hoped these were team-drivers at least. Four against twelve seemed a long shot, but it was better than two against twelve.

She stepped back toward the line of bikes guarding the front of the building as the rigs made big swings, one at a time, to park their trucks lengthwise across the span of the building—and further, effectively blocking all the bikes from leaving as well. The rigs were pointed in opposite directions.

* * *

She alternated watching one cab, and then the other, waiting for her rescuers to get out while nervously stealing glances at the door to the club over her shoulder.

Finally, she watched the back of one driver climbing down. The running lights of the rig gave her just enough light to see first the cowboy boots, then the tight black jeans hugging a lusciously-curved ass, and then the black T-shirt bulging with muscles. A cowboy hat bobbed down the steps, jumping onto the gravel and turning around. She exhaled a breath she hadn't realized she was holding.

Smokin' Okie swung a shotgun over his shoulder— the scary end pointing behind him—as he nonchalantly sauntered over to Rayne. She felt her panties go moist and remembered Storm's 'panty-melting' comment about Okie. She was right. Rayne ran to meet him halfway.

She hugged him, nearly knocking the gun off of his shoulder. He hugged her back with one arm. Then he stepped back and looked her over. He licked his lips. Rayne knew she must look terrible by now and cringed at his appraisal.

"Rayne! Looking fine, girl. You girls are lucky I had a blown tire this morning. I'd have been far ahead of you, but I had to do a flip-flop and hang around until it got fixed, and then decided to catch up on my comic book and fell asleep. Now where is that crazy-assed friend of yours?" he asked in a deep, rumbling voice.

His eyes darted around, taking in everything and looking for trouble. She couldn't see the gray of his eyes or the gold flecks that she knew were there; they looked almost black in this light, but they were still smolderingly gorgeous.

Rayne felt her belly flip with desire and remorse... she kind of regretted missing her opportunity with him, especially after hearing the message Joe had left with the mysterious female interrupter.

"Thanks for coming, Okie. She's in there. Dancing naked on a pool table! There's eleven—no...twelve...bikers in there... *touching her.* I swear I think she's about to be split like a pig on a roast by those guys."

She took in a deep breath and let it out, continuing with her story with barely a pause, "We were at a dance club and she took off on the back of one of these guys' bikes. I followed her here... and... and... I just need help getting her out!" Rayne's words came out all at once, in a rush. Her hands were waving around, giving chaotic emphasis to her words in her excitement.

Footsteps crunched gravel behind her and she gasped and whipped around, expecting to see a biker sneaking up behind her. Her eyes were wide open.

Definitely not a biker... the rotund—but very tall—trucker held up big, beefy hands, as though in surrender and laughed a deep, rolling belly-laugh. His head was shaved bald, and he was wearing a plaid flannel shirt, unbuttoned and worn like a jacket over a stained T-shirt.

"Easy girl!" he said. "I'm with Okie. My name's Pork Chop. Just happened to have my ears on when I heard your call on the CB. I was one exit up, so I told Okie I'd help him out."

Rayne looked the man over. Even in the near-dark, she could see his round, sweaty face turn red. He looked down and kicked at the gravel with his shoe. She raised her eyebrows and crossed her arms.

He looked back up and turned even redder. "Okay," he admitted. "I might have wanted to get a peek at the famous RainStorm we've all been hearing about too. But I mean you no harm, girl. I'm really here to help."

He looked embarrassed until Rayne laughed, and then he joined her, his big belly shaking under his stained T-shirt. His legs looked like tree trunks and his arms were huge. He was just a big country boy. She decided she liked him. Plus, any friend of Okie's was a friend of hers, and right now, she could use all the friends she could get.

"Anyone else coming?" she asked, looking back toward the broken gate.

Okie shook his head. "Nope. Just us."

"Two of you? Against a dozen bikers?" she asked in disbelief.

Pork Chop reached behind him with both arms and when they came back around, he was holding a gun in each; they looked like toys in his big mitts. Rayne backed up a step, right into Okie.

"Don't spook, girl. We got this. Y'all be fine," Okie said in her ear.

"Yep. I got one bullet for each biker plus an extra, Just in case I miss. And that's in just one of these Glock 40's. Thirteen more in the other. Let's go chase the Storm," Pork Chop joked and headed toward the door.

Rayne looked at Okie's gun with hesitation,

"Mine holds five shells. It's plenty. Let's roll." He followed Pork Chop, with Rayne hesitantly bringing up the rear.

Fourteen

Schklikt, klikt.

Rayne jumped at the loud sound of the double-barrel shotgun being racked right beside her in Smokie's hands.

PorkChop hadn't hesitated in kicking the door open and walking in with both guns on the ready. He walked twenty-feet in and pointed at the chaos.

Okie was right beside him in only a moment, his gun ready too, and Rayne stepped up beside him. The three of them faced the room.

The sound of the shotgun carried over the music and Rayne saw a biker behind the bar look at them with huge eyes, and then duck. A moment later the music was killed and the only thing that could be heard was fucking and sucking.

Storm was laid out, still completely nude, across a small table on her stomach with her legs spread wide. One tatted-up biker was behind her, his pants and briefs pulled down, pumping in and out of her.

Another was next to Storm's face… getting head. She had her face turned sideways resting on the table and was using one arm to hang on to the edge of the table and the other to hold the guy she was sucking. Her eyes were closed.

The remaining other bikers were standing around, some of them rubbing their own bulges, while waiting their turn; others had their hands on Storm, squeezing her breasts

163

or her ass, whatever they could catch hold of in her frenzied movement. Rayne could see red marks all over her skin—obviously from where they'd touched and squeezed her.

Rayne felt fear run through her, followed by rage. It was too late. *Oh, shit. I shoulda come back in before now…Omigod, Omigod, Omigod! Freaking animals!*

Her hand flew up and covered her mouth in disbelief. She must've screamed, because as she lurched forward to try to singlehandedly pull the bikers off of her friend, Okie gently stopped her with the butt of his gun.

"Just wait a minute, darling," he loudly whispered. And then he whistled, loud and long… and the pandemonium in the room froze as all eyes looked to him and Pork Chop. Then to her. Then back to the truckers and their guns.

Storm's eyes popped up and pulled her mouth away from the biker. "Okie! What the hell? How'd you get here?" she asked, her voice showing no signs of being drunk. "Get in line, dude!"

She wiggled her hips, which still had a biker buried within, in invitation.

Rayne felt like ice water had been dumped on her as she realized Storm was stone-cold sober. All this worry for nothing. *Omigod, what a slut.*

Rayne's face scrunched up and her lips squeezed together, frowning in disappointment—and revulsion, as she stared at Storm.

Rayne felt like an idiot.

Okie shook his head at Storm and then glanced at Rayne, then back to the Storm and the bikers.

"Get up, Storm. Your friend here called for help. Party's over. Get your clothes on. Come on, hurry up," he ordered and jerked his head toward the door while holding the shotgun up, the business end pointed at the group.

Rayne watched as Seeder, who'd been standing beside Storm waiting his turn, made his way toward them.

"Stop right there, son," said Okie in a strong, calm voice.

Seeder held his hands in the air. "Whoa! We don't need any trouble here. Nobody needs any help." His eyes looked at Rayne in disapproval, then back to Okie.

"If Sweet Thing there doesn't want to join the party, she's welcome to go. But you can't take this one." He pointed his thumb back at Storm. "She's made a lot of promises she's yet to keep. We'll need her here awhile yet. You *truckers* can kindly get the fuck out of our club house, and find your own party girls. I believe your girls hang out in the lizard lot?"

Rayne snapped out of her stupor and screamed at him, "Keep your dirty hands off of her!" She didn't care if Storm wanted this or not, she was putting a stop to it. This wasn't right, and Rayne would make Storm see that.

Okie bumped up against her shoulder. "Wait," he said to Rayne.

To Seeder, the biker, he said, "We're not here to take anything of yours. We 'truckers' take care of our own; and she's one of us. We also don't take what's *not* freely given." He jerked his head toward Storm and raised his eyebrows in question at her.

The biker behind Storm was patiently waiting, still inside her, with his eyes pointed at the ceiling. He was biting his lip. He finally turned his head to their little trio and gave them a look of pure arrogant loathing.

One look at his face and Rayne realized this had to be the boss. Or the leader of the pack... what-the-hell-ever they called the big dog in charge. Rayne stepped back half a step from his glare.

"Welcome to *my* club, *truckers*. Now either join in, sit your ass down and watch the show, or get the hell out. Nobody's *taking* anything. This bitch is giving it away—for free. Just ask her," he spit out between gritted teeth. "And hurry the hell up. I aim to finish this load."

Storm perked up. "Yep! Free for all! Line up, guys for a fuck or a suck. Okie, you too. *Especially* you, baby," she said. She began sucking again, keeping her eyes open.

She looked right at Rayne, blinking innocently while the aggressive biker behind her resumed slamming into her harder and harder. Then her eyes closed as she moaned around the mouthful she had.

No shame. No pride. Rayne shook her head at her. *Damn. She really is crazy. She's truly psychotic,* she thought. Then she turned to Okie. "I can't leave her here, Okie. I'm going to have to stay in case anarchy breaks out among these horny, drunk assholes. She could still get hurt. I'm so sorry I bothered you for help."

She looked down at the floor, awash in her own shame for bringing Okie and his friend on a wild goose chase. Shame for Storm and her behavior. She hoped Okie and Pork Chop realized she wasn't *that* kind of girl just because she was travelling with Storm.

She began to tremble as she realized they would probably leave and she'd be here to face this all on her own. There was no way she was willingly joining in... But she couldn't leave Storm alone with these guys either. And what if they just decided to take what they wanted after Okie and Pork Chop left? A shiver ran down Rayne's back.

Everyone was full-throttle, back to their orgy... as though Rayne, Okie and Pork Chop weren't even standing there. A moment later, the music came back on. Pork Chop looked at the bar and then back to Rayne and Okie. He shrugged his shoulders. "I can stand to have a beer. I'll wait with you, Rayne," he offered.

Okie put a reassuring hand on Rayne's shoulder. "I'm not going anywhere either," he yelled over the music. And then he and Pork Chop headed to the bar, looking over their shoulders to be sure Rayne followed closely behind them.

"Damn shame what happened to her. I heard she didn't used to be like this..." Pork Chop said loudly, his voice

• • •
166

carrying over the music to Rayne's ears, although he was talking to Okie. She couldn't hear Okie's response, but she saw him sadly shake his head.

Rayne wondered what they were talking about, and meant to ask... as soon it was quiet enough to hear each other talk without screaming.

Fifteen

Rayne felt a whimper escape her throat and was glad for the music that hid it. The close proximity to Smokin' Okie while watching Storm with the bikers had unexpectedly aroused her. She wiggled uncomfortably on the barstool as she watched Storm's final suck and fuck team.

She'd been horrified, but surprised at Storm's energy and spirit. Twelve bikers meant six blows and six rides. And they rode her hard, on both ends. As the last two bikers moved in when their buddies moved out—without even a thank you very much, ma'am, or a wet wipe for that matter—Rayne sighed in relief.

It was sexual torture watching, but she couldn't look away. She glanced over her shoulder to see Pork Chop stealing a glance too. Mainly he'd stayed locked in conversation with Okie whose back had stayed turned away from the show and eyes on the beer he was sipping. But Pork Chop's gaze had been caught on the mirror in front of them several times. Sometimes just to check on Storm when things got louder, sometimes because he obviously couldn't look away.

Rayne couldn't blame him. What red-blooded man wouldn't look? Well, Okie wasn't… and she did wonder about that. But she ignored her curiosity.

She watched as the last biker situated his enormous package between Storm's legs, and then slid in with one big thrust. Storm was on her back now, and her body trembled, but she still stayed focused enough to wrap her hand around the thick length of another biker and slide him into her mouth, sucking greedily as the biker leaned his head back and closed his eyes. His hands dug into Storm's long hair, twisting and tangling it as she slid him back out of her wet mouth and twirled her tongue around and around, and then slid it back in between her lips.

Rayne let out another soft whimper as she watched the biker in front of Storm ram himself—of considerable length, too—in and out, holding onto her small tits, squeezing and kneading them in his hands. She really looked like she was loving every minute of this. Rayne resented her free spirit and lack of honor. Well, sort of.

"Saved the best for last, baby," he said. Rayne barely made out his words over the loud music. "Hang on tight."

Rayne could feel her own sex throbbing and pulsing. She worried about standing up. She'd thrown her panties away back at the dance club and she felt sure she was sitting on a wet spot now… and it was only getting wetter. Her dress was probably ruined. She'd be embarrassed in front of Okie and Pork Chop, and hoped the low lighting of the clubhouse would camouflage the spot.

But still, she couldn't look away. She licked her lips as the biker ran his palms down from Storm's tits to her small hips. He held on firmly and increased his pace, going faster, his muscles tensing up as he swiveled his hips a little. She could see the sweat beading up on his forehead, as though he was holding back, trying to make it last. He pushed deeper and deeper until he was balls deep on each thrust.

Damn, he's huge. Where in the hell is she putting all of him? Storm was a small-framed girl, with narrow hips. Rayne couldn't believe her eyes, but the long shaft was completely disappearing with each thrust. Rayne felt another wave of longing roll through her.

She felt the aching emptiness of her own sex and longed to feel what Storm was feeling right now. Filled up. Hot flesh on flesh. Ecstasy.

What did that mean that she was enjoying this? Was this all Storm's influence, or had there always been something deep inside her, longing to get out... longing to be promiscuous. *Promiscuous hell... this is all-out sluttyness. Wrong. Wanton, whorish behavior!* Rayne wouldn't be surprised to see a stack of money showing up when it was all over.

Wait. Maybe she is a whore? A trucker's wife didn't have the kind of money to throw around that Storm did. This could explain a lot.

But at this moment, paid whore or not... she still begrudged Storm and her ability to not give a shit what anyone thought; just to take what she wanted and *enjoy* it, without worrying about any consequences. Not a care in the world. Must be nice.

She also admired Storm's coordination as she continued to work on the other biker, stroking him repeatedly and then shoving him into her mouth and sucking while being slammed by the biker between her legs.

Storm leaned into the guy as far as she could, pushing him to the back of her throat. That biker seemed to be in heaven as his eyes continued to look up at the ceiling and his lips moved very fast, as though in chant, or song... or something, while his hands stayed in her hair. Rayne would give almost anything to have someone—anyone—feel that kind of desire toward her.

The biker between Storm's legs paused mid-stroke and then leaned forward, reaching for Storm's nipples. He pinched them, and then flicked them back and forth, apparently more for his own amusement than Storm's pleasure. His hips began to move so fast in and out they were almost a blur. He was soon going like an animal and Storm's reaction to it was to suck harder, much to the delight of the other biker.

Rayne almost came undone when Storm finally arched her back, and screamed out a wild, passionate howl. She writhed and shook, and both of the bikers moaned too, in unison.

Rayne wiggled and writhed on her bar stool right along with them... so close to release—yet so far.

The biker at Storm's head backed away, buttoning up before nearly falling into a nearby chair. Storm braced herself on the table with both hands as the biker between her legs finished, her knuckles turning white from the pressure. He took his last few thrusts, shuddering at last and then falling still on top of her.

Damn, that was hot. Rayne as she wiped her own forehead and then twirled around on the bar stool, facing the same way as Okie.

"Can I get a bottle of cold water for the road, please?" she asked the biker standing behind the bar.

And maybe two bottles... One to sit on, one to drink.

THE TRUCKER'S WIFE

Episode Five

THE CALM AFTER
THE STORM

One

"You're a fucking quitter!" Storm screamed.

Quitter? Rayne paused a moment and thought. She shook her head and rolled her eyes at Storm's crazy tantrum and continued to pack her things, giving her back to Storm's words. She wasn't going to ask. She didn't even want to know.

A blur flew past her head and she jumped as a bottle of perfume crashed into the mirror over the built-in desk and a million wet spider-web cracks spread out over the glass, as the expensive scent of Storm filled the room.

"What's your problem?" she screamed at Storm, with big eyes, startled by the sudden violence.

After Storm's performance at the biker club last night, Okie and Pork Chop had helped Storm to her car, which Rayne had drove—much slower this time—and Okie had led them to a nice hotel. He'd parked his rig and went in and booked a room, after Rayne embarrassingly told him she would have to dig through Storm's purse to find money; she wasn't sure she had enough cash of her own to pay for digs like that, and didn't want a hotel charge showing up on her credit card for Joe to see.

Okie had paid for the room himself, and came back to graciously carry an exhausted Storm from the Jaguar to the third floor while Rayne had her hands full with their bags.

• • •

The wait on the elevator had seemed to last to nearly infinity as Okie had set her on the floor and leaned her against him. Rayne had shot her daggers while Storm never even opened her eyes.

In all fairness, Storm was spent. Completely worn out. Her legs were so shaky, she'd barely made it to the car, even with Pork Chop and Okie on either side of her supporting most of her weight. She'd stunk of alcohol, smoke, leather—and sex. Rayne had looped one arm through a heavy bag just so she could hold her nose as she trudged into the hotel room behind Okie, completely cradling Storm in his strong arms again.

He'd helped Rayne undress Storm until they'd gotten down to her panties and then he'd waited in the only chair as she bathed Storm and helped her into clean pajamas. Rayne had stalked out of the bathroom, leaving a much more awake Storm wobbling against the wall. Okie had stepped in and took her hand, leading her to the bed and even tucked her in—like a child—as Rayne simmered.

She'd been furious with Storm. Cleaning her up was a necessity, and the right thing to do, so she'd done it—but she didn't do it nicely. *Storm had made her bed... let her lie in it,* Rayne had thought. But Okie obviously knew Storm better than she did, and whatever he knew gave him a soft spot for Storm and her depravities.

Or maybe he was just a really good man?

He'd given Rayne a grim smile and a nod and reminded her to lock the door behind him. And then he'd left.

Rayne's night had been mostly sleepless; tossing and turning as flashes of her experience with Seeder slammed through her head. How had it gotten so out of hand so fast? She berated herself for letting it happen. For not stopping him—for not stopping herself.

Even in the dark hotel room, with Storm fast asleep in the next bed, she'd hid her burning face under her pillow trying to smother the humility of her memory. She had wildly ridden the tattooed biker *like a horse* until she'd brought herself to a loud, wet orgasm, in front of the entire dance club!

FacePalm.

She was finally able to compartmentalize it into pieces... for her or Joe, she wasn't sure. But a) she kept her panties on, b) she never directly touched his package, nor did he ever put it inside of her, and c) they were both fully clothed.

Well, mostly.

Once she was able to stop the onslaught of sexy flashbacks and break it down like that, she'd thought she'd be able to finally fall asleep.

But then came the dreams. Haunting her. Seeder and herself. Storm and the bikers. The disapproval of Okie. The kindness of Pork Chop in the face of her humility.

Storm's exotic nude dance. Bikers sucking on her and putting their fingers in her most private places while she stood upon the pool table.

A gang-bang! Guns! Truckers! Bikers... it was just *too much.*

Storm was out of control. Or maybe this wasn't unusual for her, Rayne had only known her for five days. But this wasn't Rayne's lifestyle and it scared the shit out of her. She wasn't sure if she was scared of getting hurt, or of becoming like Storm. But either way it was too much. She was *out.*

Storm had awoken this morning to Rayne on the phone calling a cab to take her to a bus stop. She was going home—alone. And Storm wasn't happy about it.

"*You!* You're my problem," Storm screamed in answer. "After all I've done to get you here! And now you're just going to quit?" she said in a hateful voice. "We're finally here. Less than an hour from his company lot. You can see if he's alone or… or maybe catch that bitch with him. Don't be a *fucking quitter!*"

"I'm not a freakin' quitter. I'm a giver-upper," Rayne said quietly, mocking her, but not bothering to turn around. She dropped her brush into her bag and zipped it up and then looked through her purse, making sure she had everything.

"Giver-upper? What the fuck is that? *Teacher-talk?*" Storm laughed rudely. "And what's with the 'freakin' shit? Now all of a sudden you can't cuss either?" She shook her head at Rayne spitefully. "You're a *fake.*"

"No, Storm. *I'm* for real," Rayne answered in a low, quiet voice, but seriously starting to get mad now. "You know, I realized something this morning. I *never* cussed before. Maybe in my head, or when I'm mad at Joe… but *only* at Joe—and in *private!* But since we've hooked up, my mouth is so dirty I feel like I shouldn't even eat with it! Because of *you!*"

Rayne felt her grip on her temper slipping. She bit her tongue trying to stop the rest, but suddenly unable to, she continued, "I almost *cheated* on my husband because of you!" Her heart flipped as she realized she still may *have* cheated on her husband. Seeder's finger touched her once… there. Joe would probably consider that cheating, but Storm didn't know that. *Did she?* No. She was gone by then…No one ever had to know.

She continued her rampage, "I nearly made *road-kill* out of a biker because of you! I could've got *raped* because of you! *And* because of you, I called for help and Okie and Pork Chop had to come try to be heroes, just to find out I'm the little girl who cried wolf! How freakin' embarrassing do you think that was? Don't you realize how scared I was when I found you in that club with all those bikers? Okie and Pork Chop could've been hurt too. Don't you give a crap about anyone but yourself?" she screamed.

She threw her hands up in the air as she paused to take a deep breath and calm down. Storm was strangely quiet. Rayne almost turned around, but she waited.

After an awkward moment of silence between them, during which she expected Storm to apologize—but she didn't—Rayne continued, "All I wanted was a *friend*, Storm. Someone to help me though this *and* have some fun with. I didn't want to be a part of your dirty little freak show," Rayne finished, talking through her teeth, all patience gone out the window now.

She wished Storm would have just let her go before she'd ruined any chance at friendship they'd had—if she could even stand to be friends with someone like Storm. Poking at her had only made her say the things she couldn't take back.

Storm stomped to the other side of the bed, where she could face Rayne. Her face showed no remorse over what had happened last night. No regret. She could've gotten herself killed... or gotten them all killed.

Her almond-shaped eyes narrowed. "I get it, Rayne. You're fighting a battle between your *goody-goody-two-shoes* teacher life and your *I-want-to-be-naughty* hot little trucker's wife life..." she spat at Rayne. "And you can't stand it that your conscience is keeping you wet, horny and unsatisfied while I'm getting all the action."

Storm defiantly crossed her arms.

"Yeah, you're getting all the action. That's for sure. Fucking and sucking a dozen bikers," Rayne mumbled. "Wow. I should only hope to achieve so much in life," she almost whispered the last bit. But Storm heard her loud and clear.

"You couldn't *handle* it," Storm spat at her. "You couldn't handle *one* biker, you frigid prude. Your husband's out banging another woman because you're *frigid*. You probably got cobwebs growing between your legs. And now... *now* you're going to just run home with your tail tucked in behind you? He'll probably fuck *Blindside* five more times before he gets home to *you!*"

"Shut up, *slut!*" Rayne screamed.

"Fuck you, *bitch!*" Storm screamed back.

Rayne lunged across the bed and slapped her. Storm's head jerked from the force of it. Her eyes grew big and she gasped as she held her hand across the spot Rayne had hit her.

"No, fuck *you*, Storm!" Rayne grabbed her bags and stomped out the door, leaving Storm in shocked silence at her badassery.

Two

Rayne paced the sidewalk in front of the hotel, waiting for the cab. Her face burned in shame. She had never hit *anyone* before—ever. And Storm was just a little thing. She wouldn't have a chance if they were to fight. She felt like a bully. Or a criminal... *Oh shit, that's assault,* she thought. *I could lose my teacher's license if Storm presses charges.*

She tossed the bags on the ground, and rolled her shoulders, and then her neck. She was sore. From the tense driving at top speed in the dark chasing a biker last night, and the stressful situation at the club, and then carrying all their bags in, topped with very little sleep and the little showdown that had just happened, her muscles were screaming at her.

She stopped pacing and dug into her purse, looking for her cell phone. She turned it on to check the time—*where the hell was that cab?*—and listened as it chirped and whistled, letting her know she had several voicemails and texts.

She noted the time and then turned the phone off, and dropped it into her purse. The messages had to be from Joe, and she couldn't deal with him right now. She'd have to call him once she was on her way home—after she got her story straight in her head.

She sighed and then paced again, looking up toward the third floor, hoping Storm would at least come out on the balcony and they could say goodbye, and maybe still part as friends. She hated to leave her like this. *Maybe I should at least go back in and apologize,* she thought.

She looked both ways down the street. Still, no cab. She grabbed her bags and ran back into the hotel. She rode up the elevator in turmoil, not sure if she was doing the right thing. What if Storm opened the door and started swinging? She wasn't up to a beatdown, regardless of who would win.

Rayne hesitated, and then knocked loudly.

After a long moment, Storm slowly pulled the door open. She had a wet washcloth pressed against her cheek and she was sobbing. She lowered the washcloth and Rayne gasped when she saw a perfect imprint of her own hand on Storm's otherwise flawless face.

Omigod. I'm an asshole.

"Storm! I'm so sorry!" she said as she stepped in and let the door shut behind her. She dropped her bags onto the floor and reached for Storm.

Storm flinched and stepped back a few steps, the bed hitting her in the back of the knees. She awkwardly fell into a sitting position on the bed, and raised the washcloth to her face again, lowering her head. Rayne couldn't see her eyes or face in that position.

"Oh, Storm. I promise I'm not going to hit you again…" she whispered as she sat beside Storm and put her arm around her. "Let me see."

Storm slowly turned her head. Her eyes were red and teary—and wounded. She began to cry harder, her narrow shoulders heaving up and down.

"You were my only friend," she sputtered through her tears. "I can't believe you slapped me! And now you're leaving me."

Oh, geesh. Her *only* friend? Now she really felt like crap. Rayne pulled Storm's head against her shoulder and wrapped her arms around her, patting her back. "I'm sorry. I'm *so* sorry. I shouldn't have slapped you," she crooned to her. "Do you forgive me?"

Storm used the washcloth to wipe her runny nose and sniffed loudly.

"Will you stay with me?"

Rayne closed her eyes as she continued to rub Storm's back. *Dammit. I just want to go home,* she thought. *I want to be in my own bed…my own house…sort my shit out before Joe gets home.*

She took a deep breath before she answered.

"Storm, I'm still going home. But not because of you. I just *need* to be home, okay?"

Storm shook as she sucked in a huge triple breath… the crying sigh. It was pitiful. Rayne cringed. *I did that,* she thought to herself. *I did that to her. I'm not a badass, I'm a creep.*

"But we're so close. Don't go now! We've got to stick to my plan…" Storm whined through her tears.

Wait. What? Rayne's eyes shot up. "*Your* plan?"

"No! I mean *your* plan. *Our plan.* We watch him re-load and catch him with his hand in the honey pot on the flip-flop. That was the plan… right?" she whimpered. "And then we're headed home. Right behind Joe. If he stops to spend the night, you'll see if he's with… that other woman. Either way, you're still headed toward home, with me or without me. Why can't we just stay together?"

Rayne's shoulders went up and held for a second, and then dropped. It did make sense. If Joe was on schedule, he'd be dropping his load today at the company lot—although much later today—and it would only make sense to get behind him and see for herself what he was up to.

Three

"Alright. You win," Rayne muttered in a resigned voice.

"Shut up!"

Rayne raised her eyebrows and leaned back to look at Storm in surprise.

Storm laughed while she swiped at her face with the backside of the washcloth she'd been holding.

"That's an expression, silly. I just mean... seriously, we'll stay together?" she asked hopefully. Her face lit up, all signs of crying vanished in a split-second.

It was nearing check-out time and Rayne was dreading climbing back into the fancy little Jaguar. As close as they were to Joe's company lot, it would mean maybe an hour on the road, and probably three or four just sitting still somewhere, waiting.

Even if the leather was normally scrumptiously luxurious; right now it would be torture. Her muscles ached and was just sick to death of being folded up in that car. But she did want answers. And they were so close.

"Yeah. We'll keep to the plan," Rayne answered while reaching up to rub her own shoulders. "But he's not going to be dropping his trailer until much later and I'm seriously hurting. I don't think I can get into your car all knotted up like this and then sit for hours somewhere

182

waiting. You think we can talk the cleaning ladies into saving this room for last so I can stretch out and catch a nap?"

Storm got up and began slinging her stuff into her own bags.

"I can do better than that. I'm going to pay for you to have a *real* massage! There's a great authentic Chinese spa an hour from here that will get all those knots out. You'll feel like a new woman coming out of there. You'll be all stretchy-Gumby-like."

Rayne laughed and shook her head.

"No. You've spent enough money on me already. I'll be okay. Forget about it. I'll just do some stretches while you pack up. I can't let you buy me anything else."

Storm shook her head as she zipped her bag.

"Nope. I want one too. We're going," she said firmly. "You can leave the tip if it makes you feel better."

She stood up and grabbed her bag and purse.

"Load up, hooker," she said, and then smiled as she opened the door and bounced through it, without even a hint of stiffness from being laid out across a hard table with six different guys pawing over her the previous night.

Wow. And it didn't take long for her to forget all about our little tiff either, Rayne thought as she followed Storm out the door, trying to catch up with her spirited little bi-polar-ish friend.

Four

The sound of a waterfall and Chinese music filled Rayne's ears as she stepped into the spa. Her gaze took in a huge, classy, expensive-looking bronze Buddha statue, as her nose twitched at the smell of incense—it smelled like orchids. Sweet and flowery.

The shop was very clean. Lush thick carpet and nicely painted walls with thick crown molding framing them out. Beautiful Chinese landscape prints hung from the two side walls; one showed a curved bridge stretching out over a serene lake, with multi-colored koi fish swimming in the water, surrounded by water lily's.

Facing the door was a long marble counter, and behind that was a thick red curtain that hung from ceiling to floor.

As Storm dug through her wallet a small Chinese girl parted the curtains and stepped out. She was young. Early twenties. Her hair was so black it was almost blue, and hung in shiny, straight sheets down her shoulders and over her small mounds. It was held back from one ear with a small red flower. She wore a beautiful, black kimono, embroidered with red flowers that matched the one behind her ear.

This place was the real deal. Rayne worried about the price.

"Can I help you?" the young lady asked in very choppy English.

"Two massages please," Storm answered sweetly while she slid two one-hundred dollar bills across the smooth marble counter.

The young lady looked down at the money and smiled. She nodded her head as she looked back up at Storm. "Any special requests?" she asked, struggling over the word special and making it sound like 'swessool.' Rayne almost laughed, but caught herself and swallowed it down.

"Yes. Tā xūyào yīgè nánrén," Storm answered.

Wait. What? She knows Chinese? What the...?

The Chinese girl smiled wide and looked to Rayne, her eyes travelling from her face to her chest and down, and then up again. She looked away and nodded her understanding to Storm.

"What did you say to her, Storm?"

Storm gave a little laugh. "I just told her you need a deep tissue massage because you're very tense and sore."

Rayne shrugged. That was true. And she was actually starting to look forward to it. She stepped in behind Storm as the Chinese girl beckoned them around the counter and through the curtain.

• • •

Five

Once the curtain closed, the room they'd stepped into was dark, lit only with random candles placed throughout the room, sitting atop large rocks. Rayne stood still and grabbed Storm's shoulders, holding her in place until her eyes adjusted. She was typically somewhat night-blind, and today she was tired as well. She couldn't see much.

Finally, her eyes adjusted and she looked down to see they were standing on a very small section of wooden floor and then it dropped away to a shallow pond. Rayne had never seen anything like it... a room with a little bitty lake. She wondered how deep the water was; it couldn't be that deep... in a building? She saw real koi fish swimming a few feet away and stared in awe at them.

The Chinese girl waved a hand to them as though to say follow me, and then she stepped carefully onto a rock in the water. A large flat rock. Then she took another long step onto another rock. She continued until she was on the other side of the room, standing before a gorgeous carved door, rounded at the top. Next to the door, still in this water-filled room, was a small café-sized table with two chairs. It appeared from where they were standing that the table held a Chinese tea set.

Storm looked back at Rayne. "You got this?" she asked.

• • •
186

"Yeah. This is cool. I can see now. Isn't it pretty?" Rayne answered.

"Come on. She's waiting…" Storm nimbly hopped across the rocks to the other side and waited there for Rayne.

Once Rayne made her way across, the girl indicated for them to sit, and then she poured them tea into tiny little tea cups. Rayne thanked her and then sniffed the watery-looking tea. It didn't smell good, and she could clearly see tea leaves at the bottom of the white cup.

The Chinese girl said, "You drink tea. I be back." She stepped through the carved door, leaving Rayne and Storm alone at their table.

Rayne looked over her shoulder to be sure the door was closed.

"This smells terrible, Storm. I don't want it," she whispered.

Storm sniffed it too and wrinkled her nose. "To *not* drink it would be considered an insult. Let's just dump it in the water."

"No! Omigod. Don't do that! What if she sees? What if there's a camera in here or—" she said.

"Who gives a fuck?" *Too late…* Storm was already quietly pouring it over the edge of their little platform into the water.

Rayne took a tiny sip from her cup, attempting to drink it. She didn't want to hurt the girl's feelings. *Ugh.* It was awful. *No sugar?!*

She peeked over her shoulder again and then quickly mimicked Storm, dumping her tea into the water too. A school of orange and red Koi fish swam over, nipping at the top of the water, their mouths opening and shutting wide in their search for food.

"Shoo! You little beggars!" Rayne whispered loudly, trying to scatter them before the Chinese girl came back in and busted them. She leaned over, waving her hands at them to go away and felt herself leaning too far...she was going to fall into the water.

"Storm!" she squealed.

Storm snatched her by the back of her shirt and jerked her back, landing her ass back in the wrought-iron chair and then quickly took her own seat.

They burst out in giggles, and then quickly stopped, looking over their shoulders as they sat up straight and primly crossed their legs, folding their hands across their laps, with their purses dangling from their shoulders. When they realized they were mirroring each other, they both caught another fit of snickers.

The Chinese girl came back into the room and they quickly fell silent. She saw the disturbance in the once-serene water and eye-balled the fish begging for food. She looked at Storm and Rayne knowingly. Her face held a look of disapproval.

Storm rolled her eyes and then stood up, while Rayne tried to look busy adjusting her purse just right onto her shoulder—anything to avoid the accusing eyes of the Chinese girl. *I mean, tea is mostly water... fish do drink water. Geesh.*

The Chinese girl cleared her throat and then beckoned for them with her hand once again, and they followed her through the ornate carved door.

On the other side of the door was a dimly-lit, narrow hallway with five red doors. Each bore a brass Chinese symbol. Rayne assumed they were numbers.

The girl pointed to the first door and Storm winked at Rayne and then hurried in, quickly shutting the door behind her. The girl stood for a moment staring at the door, and then turned to Rayne. She impatiently waved her forward to the next door. She opened it and stood aside, and Rayne stepped in.

Six

The massage room was as beautiful as the rest of the spa. Long thick curtains completely covered the walls, blocking out all daylight. A narrow cabinet at the end of the room supported a small sink on one side, and a display of candles on the counter, all brightly lit. It sounded as though the waterfall was directly behind the curtain, muffled into a soft symphony with a partner of peacefully singing birds. The air smelled exotically spicy.

The massage table in the middle of the room was tastefully covered in crisp white sheets and a clean white blanket. It looked enticingly comfortable and spotless. The thought of a nap crossed Rayne's mind again.

At the end of the bed was a small red-wood carved box. It was closed.

The Chinese girl waited for Rayne's eyes to return to her and then said, "You take off all clothes and get under sheet?"

It sounded like a question.

"Yes…," Rayne answered hesitantly, while thinking, *What else would I do? Run around like a wild naked Indian and jump in your little lake?*

She barely suppressed a giggle while picturing herself doing something so crazy. It was still trying to sneak out as the Chinese girl nodded and quietly stepped backward, continuing to nod over and over as she left the room and quietly closed the door behind her.

Rayne finally let her chuckles out while pulling off her clothes and piling them on the bed until she was completely nude. Then she spun around, trying to decide what to do with her stuff. The room was so neat she didn't want to make it look messy. She finally settled on putting them on a short bench that was beside the door. She placed her shoes on bottom, and then covered them with her purse and panties, and then her jeans and blouse on top; neatly folded.

She stepped back to the bed and picked up the wooden box.

What's in here? She thought, as she opened the box to find a small fake red flower. It had a short stubby stem. She had no idea what she was supposed to do with it. She looked around the room and caught her reflection in a small mirror that was mounted just above the cabinets.

She walked to the mirror with the flower and pulled her hair back, and stuck the flower over her ear, like the Chinese girl wore hers. She shrugged her shoulders. *Damned if I know what else to do with it,* she thought, wishing Storm was closer so that she could ask her. She set the box on the counter.

Carefully, she crawled onto the massage table and squirmed down, trying not to mess up the sheets as she wiggled between them, and rested her head on a soft pillow. The bed was heated against her bare skin. She sighed…she'd pay to just lay here on this bed and take a nap if they'd let her. It felt awesome.

She laid very still and stared at the door, feeling weirder every second, lying there completely naked, except for the flower in her hair.

Just as she was about to reach up and pull it out, the door opened, and in walked a tall Chinese young man. He startled Rayne—she was expecting the same Chinese girl or another Chinese… *female*. She jerked the sheet up around her chin.

He smiled and held his hands up, as though in surrender and smiled.

"Hi. I'll be giving you deep-tissue massage today?" he asked and then nodded, as though answering his own question. His English was perfect, unlike the Chinese girl. Rayne recognized he was obviously American—of Chinese descent.

His smooth, clean-shaven cheeks sported dimples that gave him a soft, kind look. His almond-shaped eyes were smoky and sexy; caramel brown. His short hair was the same shiny bluish-black as the girls was, and his dark eyes shined brightly beneath thick black lashes. He looked fresh-faced and young enough to still be in college, and although tall and slim, the sleeves of his tight, white T-shirt bulged with muscles. His arms were free of ink but well-defined. His shirt was tucked neatly into freshly pressed, tight black slacks that clung to his thighs and his well-shaped ass. He looked young enough to still be in college.

Her cheeks burned as she realized she probably looked like a cougar checking him out. She wondered if it would be rude to ask his age. Every massage she'd ever had was given by a female… this was going to be awkward.

"It that correct? Deep tissue?" he asked again, rubbing hot oil between his hands. He looked like he knew exactly what he was doing. Very professional for a dude.

Of course they have male masseuses, you idiot. Stop being a dweeb.

Rayne realized she hadn't answered him.

She gave an embarrassed laugh and relaxed, pulling the sheet back down from her chin. She nodded her head in approval.

He pointed to himself. "My name's Tommy."

Am I supposed to tell him my name? Rayne wondered. She nodded at him and smiled.

"And yours?" he asked.

Duh, guess so. She gave a little laugh. "Oh. My name's Rayne," she answered.

He stepped over with a big smile on his face and plucked the little red flower from above her ear. "This looks cute, Rayne. But it'll get in my way," he said.

He reached over and picked up the red-wood box, placing the flower back inside of it, nestled to one side. He looked at Rayne with his eyebrows raised, and held the box open to her.

"You don't want to take your jewelry off?" he asked.

Rayne's face burned in humiliation. So that's what the box was for.

Omigod. I'm such an idiot. The flower was just decoration. FacePalm.

She quickly took off her bracelet and her wedding ring and dropped them into the box.

"I'm going to slide the box right under the bed. When you're lying on your stomach, you'll see it through the hole your face lays in," he explained as he squatted down and scooted the box underneath her.

"Thank you," Rayne mumbled through her embarrassment, hoping she would be lying on her stomach very soon to hide her burning face.

Seven

Rayne was soaking wet and throbbing. The muscles in her belly rippled in excitement each time Tommy, who stood at the head of the bed, reached over her and stretched his arms, slowly rubbing hot sensual oil from her shoulders down her back—circling and working out the knots and kinks—and then sliding down toward her ass, where he would squeeze her ass cheeks—explaining those muscles were in a knot—and then glide his hands down between her legs, keeping them on her inner thighs, but his thumbs coming closer and closer to the heat radiating from between her legs each time.

She wondered if he could feel it against his hands.

She was lying on her stomach and after having seen him thoroughly wash his hands at the small sink sunk into the counter before he'd started. She felt completely at ease—almost too much at ease, especially since she was face-down and he couldn't see her eyes. It made it less personal and embarrassing.

She involuntarily clenched deep inside of her, each time the heat of his hands came near, as though it were reaching for his warm hands. She'd had massages before—but not like this. She wondered if he was this sensual with all of his clients or if the money Storm had laid down on the counter had bought this experience. Either way, she was loving the attention and craving more.

* * *

"Flip," Tommy said.

It took a moment for it to register in Rayne's brain, and then she hesitated. She'd allowed him to remove the sheet from her entire body, as she was face-down, but flipping over meant he would be seeing all of her—or more of all of her.

"You don't want to flip?" he asked in a confused voice.

"No… I mean yes… I'll flip," she answered quickly. He'd worked all the kinks and knots out of her shoulders and back, and she already felt great—but hey… she wanted everything they'd paid for. And the feel of human skin against her own was intoxicating.

She slowly turned over, pulling her hair up and behind her, letting it fall over the edge of the bed.

She situated herself on her back, snuggling into the mattress, trying to forget her entire body was completely exposed, when she felt a cold, wet spot under her ass.

What the hell? Instantly she realized what it was; it was where her juices had dripped from her hot, throbbing core. She was mortified. She felt her body tense.

But Tommy immediately relaxed her again by running his hands through her hair, gently finger-combing as she kept her eyes closed; partly because it felt so good to feel a man's hands in her hair again, and partly because she didn't want to look up to see him looking down at her large bare breasts—and her mound with her lightly-colored strip of hair.

She sighed. His touch felt so good.

"You have a beautiful body," he said in a quiet voice.

"Thank you," she whispered.

His hands left her hair and rubbed straight down from her shoulders, over each breast and down to her abdomen, again and again and again.

Rayne's eyes popped open. Didn't they normally avoid the breasts? She'd never had anyone rub her breasts before. But when her eyes popped open, she was looking at the underside of his face and he was still calm and professional. No smile. No leer or grin. No come on. *Maybe this is normal at these fancy-schmancy places?*

She relaxed again, feeling like she was melting into a puddle, her body limber and warm, but her nipples taut and hard.

Then he changed positions, coming to her side. He picked up first her right leg, moving it apart from the left and then her left leg, moving it apart from her right, leaving her legs slightly spread on the bed.

Rayne's eyes popped open again and her head came up a little off the pillow.

He kept his eyes down and his face clear of expression as he began to rub one leg, massaging and kneading it. She dropped her head back down onto the pillow and forced herself to relax again, even though she knew he had a birds-eye view between her legs.

He rubbed from hip to toe and then moved to the other leg and repeated. But once he finished with that leg he moved closer to her midsection and reached down between her legs, slowly sliding his fingers along her panty-line—if she'd had on panties—again bringing his thumbs dangerously close to her clit.

Unconsciously, she arched her back as she felt the heat of his hands near her burning, throbbing core. She discreetly—she hoped—moved her legs a little further apart. She closed her eyes and couldn't help but let a little moan escape.

"You like?" he asked, as he kept sliding his hands *around* the part of her that was begging for his touch, massaging her inner legs, but never quite reaching her hot spot.

"*Mmmhmm,*" she whimpered.

His hands slipped and slid… and squeezed all around her mound. When he reached around her hips, in the same area, his hands wrapped under her ass cheeks and rubbed down, his slippery fingers barely sliding down through the crack of her ass, detouring to the sides just before he touched her—there.

She leaned her head to the side and opened her eyes. His black pants had grown much tighter. She could see a huge bulge in the front of them. She watched as he leaned in to the massage, pressing himself against the side of the table each time in rhythm with his hands.

"You're very aroused," he commented in a flat voice.

"So are you," she accusingly whispered back.

He ignored her statement and kept rubbing. Her body's reaction at seeing his hard-on was intense. She was fighting to keep her hips from moving and her arms from just reaching out and taking what she wanted.

"This isn't one of those massage places with the... er... happy ending, is it?" she whispered, trying to make it a joke. She wasn't sure if she hoped it was, or wasn't. But she seriously wanted to know.

He laughed as he continued her massage. "No. *Definitely not.* My mother owns this spa. She lets me work here for extra money while I finish college. I'm crossing her *boundaries* now... a 'happy ending' would get me fired for sure."

Rayne's lips squeezed together in a not-quite frown as she realized she would be leaving here intensely aroused and even hungrier for hot sex—once again. She couldn't help but let out a frustrated sigh.

She felt a stab of envy then, towards Storm. If she was Storm, she'd just take what she wanted and enjoy it. Hell, if she was Storm, she'd be too tired right now to even thing about the hot Asian guy currently rubbing her down. But she wasn't.

She was Rayne. The good little teacher. The loyal trucker's wife. *The fucking idiot.* She felt her envy turn into rage toward Joe, burning brighter and brighter every second, competing with the fire between her legs.

* * *

It was his fault. Her *husband's* fault that she felt so tormented. So sexually frustrated. And if that wasn't enough, the rage reminded her that he wasn't feeling that way. Nope. He was getting some on the side. *On the Blindside.*

She remembered her wedding band was off. It was locked away in a little box under the bed. She mentally threw the image she'd previously had of herself into that box with the little band of gold. That Rayne was gone. And Joe had chased her away. She could never be the same knowing what he'd done to her. And maybe she didn't want to be the same anyway.

Eight

"How old are you?" Tommy asked as he continued her massage, ignoring the dripping, wet drops that he had to see glistening down there.

There was no way he couldn't see her swollen lips and shiny juices puddling under her again from where he was standing. Rayne had to hand it to him, for a young guy, he was extremely professional... until now. *Who the hell asks that?* Especially since she's obviously older than him and lying there nearly spread-eagle and butt-assed naked.

"Over twenty, but under thirty," she answered in an almost-snarky tone, only so she could turn the question around to him. "How about you?"

"Twenty-two. I graduate college this year."

"Good for you. So why do you ask?" Rayne said.

Tommy shrugged, and then leaned against the table again, leaving his hard-on pressed against it for a long moment before backing up. Rayne noticed this time he closed his eyes during that long moment...

"I want to taste you," he admitted, with a shy smile... Rayne caught a glimpse of perfectly white, straight teeth before his mouth closed and his hands started moving again.

Nine

"Wait. What?" Rayne asked, shocked that he'd come right out and said that.

"I *want* to. Doesn't mean I *have* to," he said and shrugged again. "Take it as a compliment. You have a gorgeous body and I can smell you. You smell so good—and clean."

Rayne felt her cheeks warm. Both sets.

She was speechless, so he continued, "I swear to you, I've never said that to a client before. But I see you want it too. And I'm offering—not for money or anything," he was quick to add.

"Price is still whatever they charged you up front. I'm just talking about me and you... nothing to do with the spa. I don't want to lose my job—and my mom would kill me."

Rayne grinned at his mom comment. She felt like Mrs. Robinson, although she wasn't much older than him, she still felt older. She *was* a teacher. He *is* a student. If he was *her* student, it would be enough to get her fired; although she didn't teach college-aged kids.

And then there was Joe. She was still married for fucks sake. But she didn't feel married right now. Joe was having his fun, and probably had been for the last year. She wasn't sure why she kept holding back. It was over. He just didn't know it yet. That little part of her that hoped there was still a possibility she could get over his affair, or fix whatever was broken and get her marriage back... had almost disappeared. It was replaced with a fury for revenge.

Her mind warred with itself. *What if he wants to work it out? What if he begs my forgiveness?* She just wasn't sure Joe could forgive her if the tables were turned. And right now, the table was almost turned...

She couldn't deny her body wanted Tommy, and his pants looked near to bursting after his confession of wanting her. And he was twenty-two years old. *Hell, that's old enough to drink, vote and join the army.*

"I'm married," she blurted out. "Obviously. You saw my rings. But my husband is cheating on me and *I* haven't had good sex in a *long* time. I want to. I'm sure you can see that. But I've never cheated on him..." she admitted in a longing voice while looking at his bulging package, just inches from her reach.

Tommy nodded.

"I respect that. You're a good woman. I hope I can find a loyal woman like you for my own wife. But I'd treat her better," he quietly said.

"We don't have to have sex. I still want to taste you. Is that too close to cheating for you?" He rubbed his thumbs so close this time, that she thought he was diving in... her body defied her brain, as her ass lifted off the bed in anticipation, but his hands slid right by again, perilously close.

She closed her eyes and sighed in frustration.

To hell with Joe. She was drawing a line in her mind. Penetration equaled real sex and she wouldn't do that. *At least I think I won't.* Foreplay or oral sex didn't count. She may cross that line eventually, but for now... if Tommy was offering some relief without her having to cross her 'line,' she was in.

She just couldn't take it anymore. She couldn't stand it. Watching Storm in action had been torture up until now.

Her body needed attention too, or she was going to lose her flipping mind.

"Here?" she blurted out. Her mind made up, but still worried about getting him caught and losing his job.

Ten

In answer to her question, Tommy grabbed a towel, wiped his hands down, and then tossed the towel onto the counter. Then he slowly reached down and unbuttoned and unzipped his pants. His hips kept them from falling down as he stepped back toward the massage table.

Rayne's eyes got big and she quickly sat up.

"Whoa! I said... or I *meant* to say... I can't screw you," she blurted out, covering her breasts with her hands and pulling her legs together.

His eyes moved over her body, pausing at her lame attempt to cover her large breasts, and her legs closed in modesty now. His face was unreadable; it was changed. Gone was the cute, friendly college kid with the dimples, and in front of her now was a serious, but hot smokin' horny guy with fiery eyes and full lips. He looked like he was ready for battle.

A chill ran down Rayne's spine. Her brain said to jump and run...but...*no*. Her body was screaming for her to stay, and she was so damn tired of listening to her brain.

Without a response, he turned his back to her and pulled his white T-shirt over his head. His muscular back was cut and chiseled, and nearly completely covered with a dragon tattoo. It was amazing; the most beautiful and realistic tattoo Rayne had ever seen—if you can consider a dragon realistic.

The dragon's scales, iridescent greenish-purply-blue, shined and shimmered when his muscles moved under his skin. Its wings were drawn in, close to its body, but its tail wrapped up around the entire dragon, spiraling and coiling up Tommy's neck and ending at the base of his spine, pointing up. The dragon wasn't breathing fire, but there were tendrils of smoke curling up from its nostrils. It was breathtakingly fierce.

Rayne was speechless. In awe of him and the transformation that seemed to take place within seconds. Her body ached even more—she wanted some of that. But she was also afraid. She wasn't willing to screw him. She wanted to. But she just couldn't. And she wasn't sure if she could stop him. Or herself.

He walked to the foot of the bed and—finally—gave her a scorching closed-mouth smile, his dimples flashing to remind her he was still the same guy. Although he was still not answering her...

He leaned forward and gently grabbed her ankles with his muscular arms, slowly pulling her toward him. She didn't resist as he slid her down over the bed, the cheeks of her ass feeling the cool damp spot against her warm skin.

She wasn't sure what to do.

His sudden transformation into dangerously sexy had her heart beating like a trapped bird in her chest. Her body was screaming for her to just shut the hell up and take whatever he gave her, but her conscience was whining that he might take too much—more than she was willing to give.

Her clit throbbed, surrendering her brain to her body. *Just this once*, she thought. *No one will ever know...*

She let Tommy pull her to the end of the bed and drop her legs over the edge. His eyes looked stormy and dark as he looked into her blue-as-sky eyes. He didn't speak as his hands reached out to caress her breasts, much differently than the feeling of when he was massaging them.

He squeezed and rubbed her breasts as he stared at them in appreciation. Then he leaned down, with his hands still full and pushed one breast into his mouth where he gently bit down on the peak.

Rayne's eyes closed and her head fell back as he sucked first one, and then the other. She felt the fire start back up at her core. Picking up where it had left off when she'd almost bolted and ran.

She could feel a heartbeat in her clit now, it throbbed so hard.

She saw him reach under the bed with his foot, and heard him pull out something—she looked down to see a small bench—and then he gently pushed her back onto the bed until she was laying down again. She could still see his face as her head was propped up on a little pillow.

He lifted her legs one by one, placing the underside of one knee over each of his shoulders, and then he sat down.

He pulled her toward him until her ass was just barely hanging on the edge of the bed, and his face was directly in front of the apex of her legs. Before he even leaned in, she could feel his breath against her, and she moaned again.

It felt like his eyes were burning a hole through her as he stared between her legs. For a long, uneasy moment as he examined her most private area, Rayne wondered if he'd changed his mind.

Second thoughts maybe?

He finally met her eyes with a solemn look.

"You have *the* most perfect body. It rocks, girl. Your husband's an idiot, if you don't mind me saying. But I can respect your boundaries. No fucking. No sucking—from you. But you *are* gonna let me eat that pretty little thing for as long and as hard as I want? Agreed?" he asked politely.

Now it was Rayne's turn to be speechless, both shocked and delighted at the crudely-worded compliments with the extreme-polite tone.

What the? This guy was truly a mystery.

Her head wiggled up and down in its best impression of a nod.

Eleven

In a blur of movement, his hands roughly grabbed her inner thighs—almost painfully—and he thrust his smooth face into her wet muff.

Shocked at how quickly he'd gotten down to business, she gasped and jerked up on her elbows, staring open-mouthed as the top of his dark head bobbed up and down, moving in rhythm with his tongue that was taking long, sweeping licks. He was wild, almost feral... and oh yes, it felt so good.

His tongue felt abnormally... long. It felt like it was everywhere at the same time. Her head dropped back down to the bed and she threw her hands up behind her, grabbing the top of her pillow and squeezing. She abandoned any pretense of inhibition as she let her legs fall as wide open as they could. She couldn't hold them up anymore. They were already quivering with desire with just that little bit of attention. They landed on his elbows and he supported them without flinching.

As she gripped the sheet in her sweaty, trembling hands, he moaned.

She took that as a good sign and forced herself back up on her elbows to look again—she wanted to burn an image of this into her memory, something to use for her lonely fantasies later.

* * *

This time her eyes focused on the huge dragon tattoo covering his back. It was shifting with his muscles, rippling and surging, the scales changing colors in the warm reflection of the candlelight as he moved.

It was fucking hot. Everything was so surreal, her imagination got away from her. She sighed as she saw herself being ravaged by an undulating dragon in a circle of firelight. A strong, fierce dragon; one she had no control over. She told her conscience she couldn't stop a *dragon*—even if she wanted to—it was out of her hands.

She forgot all about baby-faced, college-boy Tommy. She forgot about Joe. She submitted and gave up thinking of anything—even herself—without regret or false shame, and without a whisper of a blush.

She imagined the dangerously fierce dragon hovering over her, taking her—devouring her—finally allowing her to surrender and let go.

At that moment, nothing else mattered. She wanted to give in to the moment, give in to *right now*... and she did...completely giving herself over to the dragon soaring over her wet, throbbing sex.

He slipped one finger inside her without pausing in his licking, drawing out a long sigh of ecstasy. She felt her inner muscles tighten around his finger, trying desperately to hold it there as he withdrew it and slid her juices up and down her sex, causing her to shake and quiver, only to slide his finger in again.

Rayne's head moved back and forth on the small pillow. She shuddered and slung one hand over her mouth, trying not to cry out—Storm was right next door!

He switched from licking to sucking, his mouth attacking her labia and clit, causing her to grip the sides of the bed. She could feel his animalistic moans rumbling through her and it turned her on even more to know he was enjoying her.

• • •

Another finger joined the first one and Rayne nearly went wild as he took turns jamming his tongue inside her and then licking up her juices, his tongue dancing wildly over her over-stimulated nub, lapping up her proof of desire, and his fingers driving back and forth, in and out of her.

Her hands were braced on the edge of the bed, knuckles white from her tight grip, and she wasn't able to stop herself from raising her hips up and down to meet each thrust of his fingers and tongue. She found herself moving into an almost sitting position, her naughty parts barely touching the bed, but her weight still supported by his shoulders.

She closed her eyes and lifted one hand, burying it in his hair and pushing him in as she pushed up… farther, closer, deeper… and she felt the edge of an orgasm build and build until soon she saw little bursts of flashing lights behind her closed eyelids. She was so close to ready. She bucked hard against his face and he picked up his speed.

Relentless; a frenzied barrage of tongue-teasing, licking, sucking, finger-probing and even a slip just around the edge of *that other place* had Rayne writhing and panting.

The sounds of sex overpowered the water and softly singing birds until all she could hear was sucking, slurping and her own moans and gasps.

She came long and hard, her mouth opening wide to let out something. Something loud; something between a startled scream, an erotic moan—and a prayer…

Twelve

Rayne smiled shyly as Tommy slipped his card into her hand. She hugged him and then shoved it into her purse. She prayed that Storm had finished her massage earlier and was waiting out front for her, in the lobby.

She took one last swipe at smoothing down her long blonde hair, and a deep breath, and then apprehensively opened the door.

No such luck.

Storm was leaned against the opposite wall, a big smile plastered on her face. Rayne stepped out and closed the door firmly behind her.

"Have a good massage?" Storm whispered with a brazen smile. She raised her eyebrows and tilted her head at Rayne.

Rayne shrugged, but held her head high. "It was a little rougher than I'm used to," she said, "but I liked it." And then she quickly turned on her heel and headed toward the carved door, hoping Storm was following.

It was time to find Joe.

Storm's heels clicked loudly as she ran to catch up with her. "Wait a minute! Slow down."

Rayne stopped abruptly and whipped her head around to look over her shoulder. "What?" she asked in an irritated voice.

Storm's eyebrows scrunched together in confusion at Rayne's new attitude. "Where you going in such a hurry?"

Rayne's face was serious. Relaxed, but humorless. She turned her head, not knowing or caring if Storm could still hear her answer.

"To slay some more dragons, Storm..." she whispered and then walked through the carved door, letting it shut behind her.

THE TRUCKER'S WIFE

Episode Six

WHO'LL STOP THE RAYNE?

One

"Just turn on the CB, Storm!" Rayne insisted. "Let's sort the mail, see if we hear him on there." She reached for the glove box door where Storm kept the CB Radio.

Storm irritably slapped her hand away and squirmed in her seat. "No! For the last time, I don't *want* to hear that chatter. And for the record, it's 'read the mail,' *not* sort it."

Geesh. Storm sounded like a spoiled child.

"Whatever. Look, we've been sitting here for almost three hours with no sign of Joe. I'm seriously getting pissed. If you turn the damn thing on, at least there's a chance of hearing him so we can figure out if he's been here yet."

Storm stared out the window at the lot. Several rigs were in line for loading or unloading. Without breaking her stare, she shook her head. "I just don't want to hear the CB chatter. It drives me crazy."

Rayne raised her eyebrows in suspicion. Every time Storm listened to the CB, it was when Rayne *wasn't* in the car. But when she suggested it, Storm didn't seem interested in chatting or listening. It was starting to whiff of dodginess.

And drives her crazy? A little late for that... Rayne was beginning to think Storm had always lived in Crazyville; no need to drive there, she brought it with her wherever she went.

She crossed her arms and sighed. *Three. Hours.* She felt like she was ready to jump out of her skin. When they'd left the motel that morning, she'd been all fired up, hoping to catch Joe with his slut, *Blindside*.

She'd felt ten feet tall and bulletproof, and was even a bit scared of what she might do when she did see them. But she *needed* to see them—together. She needed at least that for closure. She wanted to see with her own eyes, so she could at the very least give up all hope for her marriage—Wait. Did she even have any hope left?—and make some big decisions in her life.

She'd had enough of waiting. She loudly slapped the dashboard with both hands, startling Storm, and reached for her door handle. She was getting out.

"Wait!" Storm said. "Where you going?"

"I guess I'm going to walk in the office and ask if my husband has been here yet. I can't sit here and wait anymore, Storm. He could be miles and miles ahead of us by now. Or it could be hours more before he gets here. I need to be moving. I need to be doing something!"

Storm patted her arm. "Okay, okay… I'll go. That way you won't get recognized."

Rayne gave her a funny look. "Why would someone here recognize me? I've never been to this place before."

Storm hesitated. "Ummm… Maybe one of Joe's buddies might see you. It's possible he's shown other drivers your picture, right?"

Rayne thought about the picture of her that Joe kept in his rig, balanced behind the steering wheel on the dash. She remembered giving it to him and telling him to put it where she could see him; so she could watch over him. He loved that picture. He used to tell her all the time he was looking at it while talking to her before he went to sleep, laying in his cab trying to kill the hours until he could get to driving back home to her again.

She remembered, over a year ago, telling him he could just use his phone to see her in real-time while he talked to her. He had a smartphone. They could Skype or FaceTime. His answer was, "No. I'd rather look at your picture out here on the road. Seeing the real you gives me something to look forward to as I'm eating up the miles on the way home. I don't want to ever lose that."

Well, they'd lost that after all.

It had been a long time since he just kicked back and talked to her from the sleeper in his rig. Too long. She wondered if the picture was even still there. Probably not. The wife's picture in plain view might not go over well with a new girlfriend. She felt her heart give an uncomfortable little flip, and could feel her mood plunging from angry and jumpy, to just sad and tired.

She sighed and let go of the door handle, sitting back in her seat. "Go ahead then. You go."

Storm climbed out of the car, strutting with confidence toward the little office sign attached to the door at the front of the warehouse. But just before she reached it, she detoured and headed for a driver who was climbing down from his truck.

This guy definitely didn't look like a trucker. Wearing a pair of leather sandals—Jerusalem Cruisers, as Joe liked to call them—a colorful pair of long-swim trunks and a bright T-shirt, he looked like he was on vacation. A mop of longish-blond hair poked out the top of a sun-visor with the words, "Sun & Fun" printed across it. For a truck driver, he sported a nice, deep tan too.

Rayne watched with big eyes as Storm tilted her head and thrust out her hip, talking while waving her hands around. She had her back to Rayne, but Rayne could easily see the face of the driver. And he wasn't watching Storm's mouth. His eyes raked up and down her body, as he nodded here and there to her words.

A moment later, Storm was climbing up into the driver's side of his rig, with him following closely behind—too close.

The door shut. Rayne held her breath. *What the hell is she doing?* She couldn't trust that crazy girl to do anything—or to *not* do anything…

Not the time for a quickie, Storm. Get the hell outta that truck.

Ten minutes passed. Rayne was biting her nails. Just as she was ready to jump out of the car to check on Storm—and possibly pull Storm out by her hair if she was seriously getting it on with this guy right here and now—the door opened again and Storm climbed down. She ran back to the car, graceful even in three-inch heels, and slid into her seat.

Two

"He's gone," she said, panting. "On his way home. He's running deadhead."

"What does that mean?"

"Means he's going home with an empty trailer. He's not making another pickup on the way. I guess he changed his plans."

"How do you know?"

"That trucker, Beachbum. He told me. He knows Joe. He got on the CB and just asked him if he'd be seeing him here at the lot today. But Joe said no, he's already hours up the road—he didn't say exactly *where* he was, only that he dropped his load this morning. We can still catch up!"

Rayne's mouth dropped open. "Storm! That was *stupid* as shit. Now what if *Beachbum* tells Joe we were here looking for him?" She slammed her hands against the dashboard again. "Dammit!"

"No, he won't tell! I made sure of it. I gave him a quick hand-job and a promise for more. I swear, he won't say a word," she said, following it with a wink.

Rayne shook her head in disgust. Storm actually looked proud of herself. Rayne thought nothing could shock her after the biker's club… but yet… she shook her head again.

• • •

217

"I swear, Storm. Are we going to have to sew your shit up to get you home without having sex with another random stranger?"

Storm frowned. "I didn't know that was part of the plan. You got a problem with me having some fun now?"

Rayne shrugged her shoulders. Storm already knew she had a problem with her antics. No use going into it anymore. She didn't want to argue. "Look. I think I'm just starting to understand we're two very different women. Once we get home, maybe we can still hang out. But no more road trips. I'm just not into this, Storm."

Storm cocked her head. "Into *what*? You seemed pretty 'into it' when you left the spa yesterday, unless I'm mistaken," she said, holding her fingers up to make sarcastic air-quotes. "And you seemed pretty 'into' that biker at the dance club, too."

Rayne felt her face burn with shame. She took a deep breath and then answered, "Yeah. I guess you're right. And I could blame it on the alcohol—or a broken heart. But I'll own it. Those were *mistakes*, Storm. *My* mistakes. But that's not who I am. I'm *never* gonna be like you. That's just not my cuppa."

"Your cuppa?" Storm said, and laughed. "What the fuck is that? Like I told you the first day I met you... you *are* like me. We're trucker's wives. *Lonely* trucker's wives. We gotta do what we gotta to do," she snapped in a weird voice. A mean voice.

Hearing Storm repeat the word 'cuppa' made Rayne realize... that was Joe's CB handle! *Cuppa Joe*. Wonder why Storm had never mentioned that? If she'd heard him on the CB and heard other people talking about him, she'd have to know. She acted like she'd never heard the expression before, as in 'not my thing,' but then why wouldn't she just assume Rayne was talking about Joe?

Whatever. The many mysteries of Storm… She'd address that later. Right now, she needed to set Storm straight on a more important matter.

"No. Maybe *you* got to do what *you* got to do… But not me. I may not even *be* a trucker's wife anymore. But whether I am or not doesn't change me. I'm still *me*. I'm a teacher. With or without Joe, I still have that. That's who I am, and teachers don't go out on the road having random sex with every guy that turns them on."

She watched Storm's face transform. *Scary.* She looked pissed. Her jaw was set as she glared at Rayne through squinty eyes. "A little late for your high and mighty teacher speech, isn't it? When we find Joe, maybe we should tell him about 'your *mistakes*.' Or are you just going to let him think you've been a *goooood* little wifey out on a road-trip just trying to find her hubby?"

Storm smiled a hateful smile. Or was it a proud and smug smile? Either way, she looked as though she'd won an epic battle between them.

Shut the front door! What the hell was wrong with her? Hello, stranger…

Rayne cringed as though Storm had thrown the words at her, and her hand twitched. It was itching to slap the sneer off of Storm's face—again.

And what the hell did she mean by *we*? There was no way in hell she was letting Storm *near* her husband… whether her marriage was over or not, she would make sure there was at least one trucker Storm couldn't wrap her legs around. *Slut.*

She straightened in her seat, regaining her composure, and then answered in a very stern voice, "You don't need to worry about what I tell *my* husband, Storm. It's none of your freaking business. Let's roll."

She gave Storm the side of her face as she concentrated on buckling her seat belt. Then sat back, crossed her arms, and waited to hit the road.

Three

Storm shrugged and started the car. She slammed it in gear, screeching her tires on the way out of the lot. "Let's put the hammer down and boogie, girl!" Then she let out a loud *whoop*.

Rayne returned a *very* weak, "Whoo hoo." Under her breath, she mumbled the word, "Sybil." Great to have Evil-Storm gone, and Happy-Wild-Storm back... but seriously? How many faces did this girl have?

And she didn't share Storm's enthusiasm. They had no idea how far Joe had gone, or exactly how long he'd been on the road. They weren't even totally sure what highway or interstate he was on; they could only assume. Maybe he didn't pick up the scheduled load because he wanted to spend some extra alone-time with Blindside? *Maybe* they were going to stop at a hotel?

Her mind was spinning. They might never catch up to him. If he didn't pick up another load, that meant he should be home two days earlier. They could easily catch up if he was going straight home. But there was no way to know that for sure.

He was with her. *Blindside*. Rayne could feel it. Her jaws clenched and she felt nauseous. He probably planned to spend two extra days holed up with the whore somewhere while he assumed Rayne *thought* he was still working.

"Earth to Rayne!" Storm lightly slapped her on the leg. "Stop shutting down on me, hooker! We got this. Seriously, ease up. Even if he'd been there, and had his crackerhead with him, you aren't in any shape to confront him. You need to chill out. Get your head straight. What if you'd jumped on that girl and got arrested? That wouldn't go over well with your *teaching* job, right? Right?!"

She smiled at Rayne but got no response.

"Listen. He's got to stop and sleep—or whatever. We'll just drive faster, stop less, and sleep less. We'll still have some time to kill and be in his back pocket before he gets home. You wait and see."

She nodded as though agreeing with herself as she turned Southbound onto the interstate. They were headed toward home.

Four

Storm began to hum a little tune.

Rayne was bored. Three hours on the road and neither had said much to each other. Something had shifted in their friendship. Storm's good mood hadn't lasted long. She'd been quiet the last few hours. It felt weird.

Rayne fought with her imagination, trying to deny she was feeling a hostile vibe from Storm. Trying to tell herself it was her own paranoia. After all, she too had been quiet. Maybe they were both just tired. She was glad Storm was finally breaking the awkward silence, even if it wasn't exactly speaking to her.

She tilted her head listening to the melody of Storm's humming. It sounded vaguely familiar. Her face heated up as she finally recognized it. Her eyes dropped to look down at her dress—her purple dress—and matching shoes. She felt like a fool.

She crossed her arms and glared at Storm. "Are you humming *The Barney Song*?"

Storm's humming stumbled and she caught a chuckle before it erupted into a full laugh. She ignored Rayne's question as she reached down and flicked on the radio—for the third time since they'd been back on the road. It wouldn't be long before one of them would get antsy and turn it off again.

Like *now*.

Rayne reached down and poked the button—hard—to turn it off again. She resumed her glare at Storm. "Seriously? You *were* humming the Barney song! What the hell do you mean by that? Is it because he's fat?"

Storm sighed loudly. "Nooo... I didn't realize he was fat. Wait. Isn't he a she? Anyway, it's the purple you're wearing. It just made me think of that show. You know, Barney the *Purple* Dinosaur?!"

Rayne huffed. She was in no mood to play. Storm's snarkiness earlier in the car had her on edge. The more she thought about it, the more she thought it had sounded like a threat. A threat to tattle on her to Joe. *Not cool.*

Now she was taunting her about her dress? *Maybe I do look like an idiot...*

She looked down again at her clothes, a purple skin-tight dress and matching high-heeled shoes. She liked this dress. It felt powerful. And it made her feel pretty. Right now, she needed to feel pretty. Any minute they might be pulling up on Joe, and she wanted to look pretty and powerful when facing her—the other woman.

Or was she being facetious with the words to the song. "I love you. You love me... and some shit about being a happy family?" Either way, she was being insulted. She crossed her arms over her chest, seething.

Storm yawned—a fake yawn to try to change the subject—and then said, "This is crazy, Rayne. Maybe we're not going to find him after all. Want to stop for the night?" Storm whined.

Rayne's scrunched her eyebrow in confusion. *Here comes another Storm...* "Wait. You were the one that said we'd find him. All along, you've had no doubt. Why are you changing your mind all of a sudden?"

"I'm not changing my mind. I'm just tired. It's getting late, and he's probably pulled over sleeping somewhere too. We'll leave in the morning and keep heading the same way. If we find him… fine. But if we don't, I guess you can take care of this when you get home."

Rayne couldn't believe her ears. Every day, Storm had never faltered in her belief that they'd eventually catch up to Joe. Now she seemed uninterested. Bored with it. Maybe their friendship was over. But not before they found Joe, dammit. This was her last chance to catch him red-handed. She wouldn't get another opportunity once he got home, because she knew the moment she saw him, she'd lose her mind and tell him everything. She *had* to sneak up on him… before he knew that she knew.

"Look. I'm sorry about earlier. But you've been the cheerleader all along… always saying we'll find him. Don't give up now. We have to be right on his tail either tonight or by latest, tomorrow." She paused, waiting for an answer. Storm continued to drive and stare at the road. "I thought you wanted to help?" Rayne said in a pleading voice, hoping to keep the conversation drama-free and avoid letting Storm's crazy out.

"Yeah, okay. I do want to help. I feel bad—for you I mean. We'll keep going a little while longer," Storm answered, her voice sounding bored. "But let's stop and pee at the next rest area."

Rayne wasn't given any choice. It was Storm's car, and she sure wouldn't let Rayne take a turn driving. Other than the night chasing down the biker, Rayne hadn't been allowed behind the wheel at all. She needed to pee too— pretty bad actually—and maybe when they finished, she'd offer to drive and let Storm sleep. If Storm was tired enough, she might just let her.

Rayne sighed, and gave in. "I need to pee too. But I'm not really sleepy yet. I've still got hours left in me. Let's stretch our legs and then decide. Maybe you'll wake up a little if we stop and get out."

Good timing. The sign they were passing showed a rest area coming up in .25 miles. Storm flicked on her blinker and eased off the interstate without another word.

With her neck cocked at an angle and her lips pursed together, Storm looked like a completely different person—again.

Great. Another new face. Older. Serious. Indifferent?

Rayne would rather drive all night and *not* get a room. Things felt different between them now. She was dreading Storm paying for another night at a hotel for both of them. She wanted to ask her to stay at a Motel 6 or something cheaper. Rayne could afford to at least split the bill at one of those places. But she knew Storm would want to cruise into the fanciest hotel she could find. Way out of Rayne's budget.

This. Is. Getting. Awkward, thought Rayne. I wish we could just find Joe tonight.

Five

Rayne stepped out of the car and stretched. The rest area was deserted, other than a few rigs parked on the trucker's lane. The air smelled of diesel and gas. It was dark; only a few street lights to brighten up the area around the facilities and a few in the parking lot. The edges of the rest area faded into a deep black she couldn't see through. Spooky here.

She reached back in and grabbed her bag. Storm was still sitting behind the wheel, digging through her own bag.

"You coming?" Rayne asked. Now that they were there, that close to the bathroom, Rayne's bladder was ready to empty. She wiggled from foot to foot waiting for Storm.

Storm didn't even look up. "Yeah, I'm just trying to find my phone. Go ahead. I'll be right behind you." Her tone sounded dismissive.

"Okeydokey," Rayne answered in a sing-song voice, trying to not sound bitchy. She shut her door and headed toward the bathroom, worried about the tension building between them now. She really wished Storm shake it off long enough to at least walk in with her. These places gave her the heebie-jeebies, especially at night. Every time she walked into one, she imagined how easy it would be for a crazy serial killer to hide in a stall, and jump out and murder her.

• • •

She slowed down and quietly stepped into the ladies room, pausing to listen for any sounds. Other than the *drip, drip, drips* of a few faucets, she heard nothing but the night bugs chirping through the silence of the restroom.

Still, she bent down and looked for feet. *Of course, a smart serial killer would be squatted on top of the toilet seat, hiding his feet.* She felt the tiny hairs on the back of her neck stand up. She was scaring herself. She soundlessly blew out the breath she was holding.

Okay, stupid. Just open every door and check for crazy psychotic murderers first, so you can pee in peace, she silently told herself.

One by one, she swung the doors open, trying not to make a sound. Each one nearly took her breath away as she prepared herself for someone—or something—to jump out at her. Seven stalls. Seven doors.

Phew! No one here. She laughed at herself and began to pull toilet paper off the roll in long strips to cover the seat. The seat-protection dispenser was of course, empty. Just her luck.

Rayne looked at the ceiling as she relieved herself. It was taking *forever.* She didn't realize she had to go this bad... it felt like her bladder would never be empty.

Any minute, she anticipated hearing Storm come in. She wondered if her mood would flip again. She hoped so. No use in making the end of the trip a downer.

She finished and flushed and was pulling her dress back into place when she heard a car zoom by. It sounded like Storm's Jaguar.

Oh bloody hell. If it was a dude in a flashy car, they might not get back on the road for hours. She had no doubt that in Storm's frame of mind right now, she'd jump on anything swinging a dick.

She hurriedly washed and dried her hands, hoping to catch Storm before she hooked up with yet another random stranger. They didn't have time for any more of her bullshit.

Six

Rayne was confused. Wasn't this the parking lot they'd parked in? She looked all around, not seeing Storm's car. Not seeing *any* car...

She must've come out the wrong door. These rest area bathrooms sometimes had two entrances, and were confusing. She looked over her shoulder at the building, hoping to see a lighted sidewalk that would take her around to the other side. But there wasn't one.

She walked back into the bathroom and looked for another exit. Nope. Only one way in and one way out.

Walking faster now, feeling a little dazed, she hurried back out to the parking lot. Still, no red Jaguar. No Storm.

Shit!

Storm has probably pulled around to the trucker's lane and sparked up a little something with someone. *Dammit. I can't leave her for a second.*

Rayne was pissed. She stomped toward the trucker's lot, just knowing she was going to see Storm's car sandwiched between two big rigs, *and* knowing what Storm was probably up to. She nearly stumbled in her high heels as she turned a corner and tripped over a bag—her bag!

And not just one, but all of her bags. *What the hell?*

She couldn't wrap her brain around why her stuff would be laid out on the sidewalk. Where the hell was Storm?

• • •

What if someone had car-jacked her? Maybe more than one someone... maybe they'd needed the room for their own stuff.

Panic slid into place and she scooped up her bags and took off at a slow run for the trucker's lot, praying that Storm's car was there, hidden between the few rigs that were there. This was the one time she hoped Storm actually had pulled one of her tricks and was currently getting her rocks off in the cab of one of those trucks.

She ran past the first rig... no car. She gasped... but there were two more.

She ran past the second rig, her bags bumping uncomfortably against her, making it awkward to run, especially in heels. She was going to kill Storm for this.

But still, no car.

She dropped her bags where she stood. Panic really washing over her now like a cold sweat. She felt her heart beat quicken as several thoughts of what might have happened to Storm flashed in her head.

"Please....please.... let her car be behind this last rig," she mumbled to herself as she slowly walked to the edge of the next rig. She said a silent prayer and then took in a big breath and stepped out.

Not there.

Shit! Shit! Shit! Where the hell is she?

Rayne threw her purse over her head and looped one arm through it, but left her bags piled on the pavement, and raced back to the restroom facilities. She ran all the way around the building, nearly stumbling in the dark, her heels sinking in the grass. Still, no Storm.

She stopped in front of the restroom after her mad dash around it and sank down to the ground on her knees. She felt like she was going to pass out. Her heart was thumping hard. She frantically dug through her purse looking for her phone, barely able to see through the blurry veil that suddenly filled her eyes.

• • •

No!! Son of a Dick!

She realized she'd plugged her phone into Storm's car to charge, and left it dangling down into the passenger floor. She had no way to call her.

She felt a tear of frustration—and fear—slide down her cheek.

"Nuh uh. This is bullshit. Get yourself together, Rayne. She's coming right back. She'd been weird all day, and she's probably just messing with you. Don't let her see you cry," Rayne said out loud to herself, her voice hitching and breaking.

She swiped away the tears and cleared her throat and then pulled herself up off the ground. She squared her shoulders and walked determinedly back to where her stuff was. She'd be damned if she'd let Storm see her little joke shook her up.

Bitch.

Seven

Rayne had to face it. Storm wasn't coming back. It'd been thirty minutes. *Thirty minutes* of her sitting on a bench at the rest area with her bags piled around her! Not a single car had pulled in. She could hear the low rumble of the 18-wheelers in the distance behind her. Probably sleeping with the air on.

Once she'd slowed down enough to think, she'd realized Storm had to have put her stuff out herself, and taken her time doing it. It had all been stacked neatly, with the new designer purse Storm had bought her balanced on top, where it wouldn't get dirty from sitting on the sidewalk. Only a woman would think to do that.

Storm had left her. She'd just freaking *left* her here. She'd been acting weird all day, and now she'd gone and left her ass on the side of the interstate at a deserted rest area— well, almost deserted. There were still three rigs in the back. But that scared her more than comforted her. What if they were nucking futs? Human traffickers? Serial killers?

Freaking bitch!

She tried to stay calm as she thought through her options.

There *was* a payphone, but Rayne didn't know Storm's number. Such was one of the negatives of smart phones nowadays. No one remembered anyone's number. Just one push of a button and a request for Siri to "Call Storm" was all she needed to make a call, normally.

She gasped and began digging through her purse. She just remembered that little piece of paper with the lightning bolt that Storm had given her the first night they'd met. It had Storm's number written on it!

She dug everything out and piled it in her lap, and then turned the bag upside-down and shook it.

Damn. It wasn't there. She had no idea where it was.

She sighed heavily.

She could call Joe. She knew his number by heart. But she had no idea where the hell she was. And wouldn't that be something to explain to Joe in the middle of the night. 'Umm, yeah, honey. Sorry I haven't called you back, but I've been following you for five days out on the road, and I got stranded at some random rest area. Help?'

Yeah, right. Not gonna happen.

She didn't have anyone else she could trust to get her out of this mess. She dropped her face down into her hands. *What the hell am I going to do?*

An engine rumbled to life. She jumped, the loud noise in the otherwise nearly silent night startling her. She'd gotten used to the quiet—other than the *whoosh, whoosh, whoosh* of the passing traffic on the interstate far in front of the rest area, and the chirp of the crickets, it had been very still out here. The truck seemed unusually loud as it slowly pulled out of the rest area.

The truckers! Duh! They have CB's. Maybe she can use one to try to reach Storm.

Rayne stood up and gathered her bags, hurrying to the trucker's lot before the other two rigs up and left her.

Eight

"Not interested, honey!" The trucker yelled down through the window at Rayne.

This was the second door she had knocked on. The first trucker must've been sleeping hard. His engine was quietly running, masking her knock. She'd given up and tried this one.

"I'm not a lot lizard!" she yelled loudly back to him, hoping he could understand her through the door. "I need help. My ride left me here. Can I just use your CB, please?"

The door opened to an older man, probably in his early-sixties. Tufts of hair stuck out all over his head. His pale blue eyes were a sharp contrast to the white and gray halo of hair around his head. He was clean. His green-plaid shirt hung open over a crisp white T-shirt. Rayne caught a scent. Clean laundry smell. The smell of sheets hanging in the sun. Ivory bar soap, most likely. His smell was comforting and he looked like he could be someone's dad. Kind and concerned.

She heard a beep, and then the smell of pizza, or hot pockets... or some kind of microwavable junk food wafted out of the truck around him, smothering his clean scent and almost turning Rayne's stomach. She backed up a step.

The sleepy-eyed trucker looked her over carefully. Rayne prepared herself to shoot him down if his mouth started talking sex. But his face held nothing but worry. He cocked his head. "What'd you say, little lady?"

Rayne breathed a sigh of relief. *A good guy. Thank God.* Wait… Every trucker she'd met out on this trip has been a good guy. She realized truckers got a bad rap… for nothing. At least nothing she'd seen. She'd only seen kindness, helpfulness and respect coming from every trucker she'd encountered so far.

"My ride left me here. I don't know where she went. Can I use your CB to try to call her?" Rayne asked hopefully.

The trucker looked at the bags gathered around her and raised his eyebrow. "Don't you have a phone?" he asked.

"I do, but I don't know her number."

"You ladies have a little tiff?"

Rayne shook her head. "No. I mean… not recently. We were okay, I guess. We just stopped to use the restroom and she was supposed to follow me in. But she didn't. I heard her car take off and found my bags on the sidewalk. I have no idea what's going on."

He nodded to her words. "I see. Okay, climb on up here. I'll be glad to let you use my CB." He moved out of the way, leaving Rayne looking up at the empty seat beyond the door. Should she trust him? She didn't even have a weapon. *Maybe I should just go back and wait for Storm a little longer.*

She really didn't want to get in the cab… she could be trapped in there.

The trucker came back to the door and said, "Look at this here. I got a daughter your age. And grandchildren. Wouldn't dream of hurting you. Now climb on up here where it's safe, so I can get you back on the road and get me some shut-eye."

He held a large frame down where she could see it. The family in the picture appeared to be happy and normal. A trimmed-up version of the trucker was in the center of the photo, one arm around a sweet-looking woman about his age, and his other arm around a beautiful young woman about

Rayne's age. Eerily similar… long blonde hair and blue eyes too.

At their feet sat two boys and a girl. They had to be triplets. All the same size with white-blonde hair and big blue eyes. They were all looking up at their grandfather in adoration when the photographer snapped the picture. They appeared to be a big happy family.

She shrugged.

She left her bags on the ground, only keeping the purse still dangling around her, and climbed up. Shutting the door firmly behind her.

Nine

"Thank you again," Rayne whispered. "I'm so sorry for the trouble."

She huddled in the bouncing passenger seat, looking down as the road unfolded in front of them. She tried to pass the time by counting the yellow dashes before they rolled over them. It was making her dizzy. She looked away.

She was nervous. Hell, who wouldn't be? Riding down the interstate, locked into the cab of an 18-wheeler with an almost complete stranger. Anything could happen. But she didn't have much choice.

"No problem. Sorry it took me so long to get there. But you were safe with the Flying Dutchman. He'd never harm a soul. Got kids and grandkids. He's just out here trying to burn a few more miles before retiring with his lady. Good man."

Rayne smiled when she thought about the sermon she'd received from Flying Dutchman. He'd been very fatherly and super protective over her almost immediately. He offered to let her ride with him, but he was branching off to go a different route in just a few hundred miles… not the way she needed to go.

So after her trying to reach Storm and finally giving up, he'd put out a call for help himself. He said it would be better coming from him.

She'd had several offers to 'help her out,' that Flying Dutchman turned down or ignored. He wouldn't even respond to Rayne when she asked why not? Just solemnly shook his head and waited for more. When Smokin' Okie came on the CB and answered, Flying Dutchman seemed satisfied—and relieved.

She'd been far more relieved than him though. At least she kind of knew Okie—and he'd come to her rescue once before at the biker's club. There was that.

Two hours after her plea for help... and Storm not answering, Smokie had arrived. He had tried to raise Storm on the CB himself. But either her CB was off, or she was giving everyone radio silence.

He'd said he was heading her way—towards home—but Rayne was beginning to think he'd be heading whichever way was needed, just to be of help. It had seemed wherever they were, he was behind them. And now they were on the flip-flop... and so was he?

Pretty big co-ink-a-dink, she thought. Smokin' Okie was like a rig-riding cowboy in shining armor. Always there to save the damsel in distress.

Smokin Okie cleared his throat.

"So you want to explain to me what went wrong? I didn't expect your girls-trip to end this soon," he said. "Do you know why she dumped you?"

Rayne blinked rapidly. *So he doesn't know we've been chasing Joe?*

She didn't want to explain about her husband cheating, and their pursuit to try to catch him that ended up being a hook-up trip—at least for Storm. But she didn't want him to think she was like Storm either... just looking to get her rocks off. And, he was Storm's friend—not hers. It might even upset him for her to speak against her.

Shit.

"Storm was supposed to be helping me find someone out on the road—someone I know," she added quickly. "She and I have had a few disagreements, but nothing serious. At least *I* didn't think it was. But, I did tell her today I wasn't into her...um... lifestyle. Since then she's just been acting... I don't know... not like herself."

Okie gave her a quick look. His eyebrows scrunched together, as though examining Rayne for truth. "She's *not* herself right now. She's *Storm.*"

Rayne gave a little shake of her head. "Come again?"

"I'm not sure who she started out as when you left, but the night I met y'all at the truck stop, she was definitely Storm—one of her alters. And again at the biker bar... that was Storm too. I'm not sure why she left you at the rest area though. That's not like Storm. She's definitely the wild and crazy one, but she hates to be alone. She likes to have someone with her when she comes out to play. Maybe she transitioned."

"Wait. What?" Rayne had no idea what he was talking about. *Alters?* Someone with her to come out and play? She knew Storm enjoyed exhibition—or at least she didn't seem to mind having people watch her while she had sex. But what was an alter? As far as Rayne knew, that was something you'd find in a church. And transitioned? *What the hell is that supposed to mean?*

Okie looked at her again, tilting his head to study her face. "How long have you known her?"

"I met Storm the night before we left on this trip. So... six days ago?" Rayne answered. *And yeah, I know... I'm an idiot for jumping into a vehicle with someone I just met... and yet... here I am again,* she thought.

"Oh. You met *Storm.*" He nodded. "I had a feeling that was the case. You really don't know, do you?" he asked softly, his voice resigned.

"Know what? You're not making any sense to me."

Okie took in a deep breath and then let it out slowly, whistling through his teeth. Rayne watched as his grip on the

• • •
238

steering wheel tightened, his knuckles turning white, while his face seemed to turn hard; serious.

"Storm's not a real person. I mean, she is. But... it's complicated," he said.

Ten

Rayne felt like she was entering the Twilight Zone. Maybe hitching a ride with Okie wasn't such a good idea after all. He sounded bat-shit crazy.

"What are you talking about... not a *real person?*" Rayne whispered loudly. She didn't trust her full voice. This was getting creepy.

"No, no, no. She's a real person, but she's an *alter* personality. She has D.I.D., a fancy name that just means she has multiple personalities. Storm is one of them—the wild one. I think there are only two, other than her primary personality. But I'm not positive. Out on the road, it's usually Storm doing the driving."

"Are you kidding me? This sounds crazy." Rayne began to tremble. Could she really have been out on the road with someone so unbalanced as to have multiple personalities? That shit was real? She thought back to earlier when she'd mumbled 'Sybil.'

Omigod. She wondered if Storm had heard her. Maybe that was why she'd dumped her on the side of the road.

"It is crazy. But it's real. I've known Anastacia for years—"

"—Wait. Anastacia? Who's that?" Rayne asked, interrupting him.

"Anastacia is Storm. Or rather, Anastacia is the real person. Storm is one of the alters. Anastacia can't help it. I've done a lot of research on it, and she's one of the lucky ones. Or maybe she wouldn't think it was lucky... but she is subconsciously aware of her alters and what they do. She just can't control them. But she's slowly getting better, it seems. At least she doesn't lose time anymore. She's embarrassed about Storm's behavior, but has no way to stop her. At least not yet," Okie explained. "But if she transitioned back to her regular self, she may have been so embarrassed that she just left you there. And, *Anastacia* doesn't know you either. *Storm* knows you. Anastacia is very quiet. Kind of shy, actually."

Rayne couldn't wrap her head around it. She remembered seeing a Showtime series years ago, about a woman with multiple personalities... what was that called? Tara... something about Tara. This woman had multiple personalities too, and one of them was very wild and promiscuous. She'd forgotten all about that show. Heck, it was on TV, she'd never thought it was something that could actually happen.

Her mind was blown. She rubbed her hand down her face.

"Okay, so you're telling me she actually is crazy? Is that what you're saying? Because several times on this trip, I've thought she was a little mental."

Okie didn't looked pleased. He pressed his lips together, keeping his eyes on the road for a long moment before he answered, "Yeah. I guess you can put it that way. It ain't normal for someone to have three personalities. But... *Anastacia's* not crazy. She's a sweet girl. It's the other two that ain't right."

Oh shit. He was talking nonsense. How can someone be crazy, but not be crazy? He's acting like he's talking about three different people.

Rayne's eyes darted around the cab, not sure what she was looking for, but nervous. Her hands were trembling worse. She scooted over on her seat as far as she could go toward the door, without removing her seatbelt.

Okie noticed and sighed again. He reached over to pat Rayne's leg and she jumped. He pulled his hand back slowly and put it on the steering wheel.

"Look, Rayne. I know this is a lot to take in. It was for me too. When I met her, she was the other alter. She was in Trucking School with me and acted crazy as a pet coon. Me and the guys had a good laugh at her most of the time. But damn... she could drive a rig. She wanted that CDL license. Wanted to drive a rig professionally."

Okie shook his head as though the memories were not good ones.

"She did great on the classroom part. When it was time to put it all in practice, they partnered us up... me and her. I had to spend more time with her up close. She told me her plan of teaching *Anastacia* to drive a rig, becoming a truck-driver and wreaking havoc out on the road. She wants revenge for Anastacia. Talked all kinds of crazy shit. It was only when I *saw* her transition back to Anastacia that I believed it myself. Anastacia—or Storm—can't drive an 18-wheeler. Neither one of them. They haven't got a clue. Only *the alter* that came to class knows how. I saw her transition back to Anastacia several times. And Anastacia freaked. Nearly killed us in that rig."

He sucked in a big breath and blew it out.

"Anastacia told me the truth... it was my life at stake after all. She definitely made a believer out of me. The next day in class, the alter showed up as usual. I waited for Anastacia to come back and when she did, I dragged her to the instructor myself. Made her tell him not to pass her. Not to give her the license. I'm surprised he even passed me. He probably thought we were both lunatics."

Rayne crossed her arms tightly against her chest.

"So this... Anastacia... was willing to flunk herself out of Trucking School?"

Okie nodded. "Oh yeah. Anastacia's scared to death to drive a rig. She doesn't know *how* to drive one. The alter does. She couldn't control the alter coming out to drag her to classes, so she took care of it the only way she could. She told the instructor she was crazy. She was close to graduating when she begged him to fail her and red-flag her license in case the alter dragged her to a different trucking school. It worked. She hasn't been behind the wheel of a rig since."

Rayne chewed her bottom lip in concentration. Okie sure sounded as though he believed every word he was saying.

"So... If she knows she's crazy—or whatever—and her so-called alters get her into trouble, or into dangerous situations, why isn't she locked up somewhere? Why doesn't her husband or her family get her some help?" Rayne asked.

Okie jerked his head back in surprise. "Her husband? He's *dead*. That's what started this whole mess."

Rayne eyes widened. "Dead? But... Storm told me she was a trucker's wife... several times."

Okie gave a sharp laugh.

"Storm would say that. But *Anastacia* isn't a trucker's wife—anymore. She's a trucker's *widow*. Her husband died in a gruesome accident out on the road. Shiny side down," he said. "Anastacia may have had this disorder all along, but no one knew it until his funeral. It pushed her right off the deep end."

Rayne gasped.

"Yeah. It was awful. They were high school sweethearts. Married since she was eighteen and she was still in love with him. It devastated her. His dying was hard on her. *Real hard*. But even worse, they found a woman in the cab with him. He'd been cheating on her when he was out on the road. Apparently for a long time, too."

No wonder Storm refused to talk about her husband. How terrible...

Okie continued, "It breaks my heart for her…Anastacia, that is. It's been a few years, and she's still mourning him. The other two—the alters—they don't care. They only care about two things: fun and revenge. Obviously, Storm's the one always looking for fun."

Rayne shook her head back and forth. "Wow. This is all so… so *unfreakingbelievable*. I don't even know what to say. Damn, I could write a book about this trip. *My Trip With A Stranger…Taken by Storm*. But hell, no one would believe it. I'd have to market it as fiction," she said and laughed.

Eleven

Okie didn't laugh. His gaze stayed straight ahead, on the road. The cab filled with an awkward silence. Rayne felt bad. She began to fiddle with her wedding rings, twisting and turning them.

"I'm sorry. I guess it's not funny," she quietly said.

"No, it's not. Anastacia's sweet. She's a treasure. And she's absolutely horrified at what her alters do. And you've just seen the tip of the iceberg. That's why I try to stay close. Gave up my company job, and took a job contract-driving. Had to dump too many loads to save her ass. It's easier working for myself now. I only take the loads that aren't on a strict timeline. That way if I've got to turn around or dump a load, I've usually allowed myself enough time to do it. I try to help out whenever I can, although I can't always be there."

Rayne thought about the first night she'd met Okie. He'd been getting ready to go to sleep, yet he showed up and stayed there all night with Storm.

He sounds like her loves her. Rayne blushed as she thought about his and Storm's lovemaking—she'd watched that. *Weird.*

"So you and Storm... um... together. Does Anastacia know that's happening?"

"Yeah. She knows. But she knows Storm is going to do what and *who* she wants to do. She'd rather it be with me than a stranger. I just wish I could stop her from using Anastacia's body with every random dick she fancies. But I can't. No one can."

Okie paused. He sounded so sad.

"I know what I do with Storm isn't right. But I promised Anastacia I'd help. I'd look out for her. And when I'm with Storm, I just try to imagine it's Anastacia."

He shrugged. His smolderingly dark eyes shined. He turned his head and locked his gaze onto her for just a moment. She strained in the dark of the cab to try to see the deep gray and gold irises that she remembered from their first two encounters. It was too dark. She could only see his already-dark, thick lashes were more defined, wet and sticking together from unshed tears.

Rayne's heart lurched. She saw love in those eyes. And heartbreak. She saw a man who would do anything for the woman he loved. She wished Joe still loved her like that. He must have felt her checking him out... he self-consciously ran a big hand through his thick raven-black hair. Rumpling it further into a sexy rippled mess. He wore it well. He chanced another quick look at her and she smiled at him, a sad but understanding smile... from one limping heart to another.

He returned the smile—and a look of understanding passed between them.

Rayne had to look away then. He looked so much like her Joe. If it wasn't for Joe... and Anastacia... she'd be after Okie herself. Anastacia was a lucky woman.

"You really do love her, don't you?" Rayne asked. "I can see it all over your face and hear it in your voice."

Okie shrugged again, and one side of his mouth lifted into an attempted smile. Rayne watched as his square chin lifted just enough to give a peek of the dimple in his right cheek, still almost buried under the stubbly dark shadow of a few days.

He cleared his throat, and then coughed—a fake cough. And then swallowed loudly before answering, "I guess

I do. But I love *Anastacia… not* the alters," he admitted. "I consider myself lucky that Storm has taken a liking to me. That's gets me a little closer to Anastacia. But the other one… she doesn't like me at all. I don't put up with her crazy-assed bullshit."

Wow. This alter stuff was unreal. Almost too much to believe. Rayne wanted to know more. Still nervous about asking too many questions, she continued to twist her ring, letting his words hang out there for a long moment.

"Tell me more about them? I mean, the alters…" Rayne asked.

Okie tilted his head, gathering his thoughts. Rayne noticed cars and trucks were passing them in the fast lane. She wondered if he noticed he was only driving 50 mph. At this rate, she'd never get home. They were a good ten hours away from her home town as it was.

"Well, let's see. Storm, as you know, is *wild*. She likes to take risks. Loves to drive fast. And is definitely the nicer of the two alters. I think she's passively-aggressively trying to get revenge for Anastacia in her own way—or maybe just get even. For the cheating, that is. She'll talk to me about Anastacia almost as if she's her little sister. She's protective over her. She couldn't be more opposite a personality than her host."

"Host?" Rayne asked, her eyebrows drawing together.

"Anastacia is their host. It's *her* body they use." Okie stole a glance at Rayne. "Damn girl, this must sound like a science fiction movie to you. I swear to you, it's true. I'm not making this shit up."

Rayne still had her doubts. "Yeah, does kind of sound like *Revenge of the Body Snatchers*," she said and laughed. "But I'm still listening. What about the other alter? What's she like?"

Okie blew out a breath. "*Phew!* She's a handful. Like I said before, she fancies herself a trucker. She's tough. And she's all about revenge too… but not passive aggressively.

She's out for blood—well… not blood. She hasn't hurt anyone physically yet, other than a few fistfights."

"Fistfights?!" Rayne exclaimed. "With who?"

Okie laughed. "Women, mostly. But there's been a few men. I avoid her. She doesn't come out for long. But when she's out, there's trouble. She's a mean one. Storm and Anastacia seem to work together to try to keep her in. Normally, it's Storm that steps out to put her back. Anastacia's not strong enough. Only problem with that is Storm sees herself as the neutral party. Kind of like a middle sister. Sometimes, she goes along with whatever the other alter is up to. Kind of helps her accomplish her plans. Or at least plays along… until someone gets hurt. And then Storm disappears. She's not violent and if she finds herself in the middle of a situation, usually you'll see her transition back to Anastacia. Kind of giving her back the reins."

A snapshot of Storm crying flashed through Rayne's mind. "Does Storm ever cry?" she asked.

Okie laughed. A loud, deep rumbling laugh. "No. Storm's not a crier. If the shit gets too deep she'll just disappear—transition—and leave Anastacia in the lurch. And when that happens, Anastacia is usually crying, either embarrassed or unable to deal with the chaos Storm has her in."

Rayne thought back to the morning at the hotel, when she'd slapped Storm. *Omigod. Was that Anastacia?* She *had* cried and acted totally *not* like Storm, and then like a light switch, once Rayne had comforted her and said she was sorry, she'd flipped her mood up and began acting wild and happy again—in the blink of an eye.

And again at the truck stop when they were eating, the night they'd met Okie. She'd seen a very different side of Storm before he'd arrived. A quiet and sensitive side. That must've been Anastacia too. And this morning, when Storm had threatened to tell Joe about the things Rayne had done on the trip, and her humming the taunting little Barney song… That was a whole new side she'd never seen before. Spiteful and bitchy. Maybe that was the other alter?

Rayne was becoming a believer too.

Twelve

Rayne wasn't sure if it was because she now knew Okie was in love with Anastacia, or just his gentleman ways, but she began to feel safe once again—and tired. But she had a few more questions before she'd ask him if she could use his sleeper.

"What about her car? Does Anastacia have a job? A 2015 Jaguar is nothing to sneeze at. How does she pay for it?"

Okie sadly shook his head again.

"She *did* have a job. She was a pre-school teacher. She loves kids. She was hoping to start a family soon when her husband died. Then she lost it. The alters showed up, and at first she'd lose time. She had no idea where or who she'd been. She ended up getting fired."

Rayne gasped. "A teacher? *I'm* a teacher! Storm never said a word to me about her being a teacher too!"

Okie shook his head. "That's because *Storm* isn't a teacher. She couldn't care less about kids, and she doesn't know shit about teaching. Storm's just a party girl. She dances, she drinks, she shops... and she screws. That's *all* she's about."

He sounded angry. Rayne felt sorry for him. Of course he'd be angry... he was in love with a woman that was MIA half the time and worse, when she went missing, Okie

• • •

had to hear about and/or see her screwing other guys. That had to sting.

He continued, "Storm's the one that bought that stupid, snazzy car with the life insurance money Anastacia's husband left her. Not that she doesn't have more money... she's rich. She got a huge settlement from the company of the other driver—over a million dollars."

He nodded his head as he looked at Rayne with his eyes wide. Then he continued, "The brakes failed on his rig after the driver had reported several times that he thought there was a problem. But *the man* just kept pushing him to finish one more route, and then another and another... saying they'd take care of them the next trip in. But they didn't. Those worn-out brakes took three lives that night... Anastacia's husband, his girlfriend and the driver."

Okie sounded tired of talking. He mumbled a last few words, "And out of the ashes of their deaths arose two new lives—the alters."

Thirteen

Rayne didn't want to ask him anymore questions right now. He seemed down… depressed about the whole thing. Or maybe he was just tired, like her. She had plenty of questions to ask later and after all he'd shared about his feelings and about Anastacia, she wanted to share her story with him too. She wanted him to know why she was out on the road… because of her cheating husband.

But she'd wait until after she'd gotten some sleep before telling him. She didn't want him to think she needed someone to snuggle up and console her. If he offered, she wasn't sure she could say no; she could use a strong shoulder and some sympathy.

She stole a glance at the sleeper cab behind them. It looked clean and comfortable… and tantalizing. She thought about stretching her body out, getting all the kinks and knots out from being folded up and strapped in to a seat for so long.

Yes! That sounded good. She took a big sniff. It smelled fresh in the front of the cab. She assumed he'd switched out his bedding since she and Storm had been in the cab five days ago.

"Okie, what's your plan? You going to drive straight through or stop somewhere to sleep for a while?" Rayne asked, hoping for the former. She couldn't—wouldn't—sleep

• • •
252

beside Okie. First of all, he was too damn sexy. Secondly, she was married, and he was in love with Storm... er... Anastacia.

"Naw, girl. I'm good on my coloring book. Had my shutters down a full eight hours before I heard your call for help. I'll keep driving. If you're tired, help yourself to the sleeper. I'll wake you up when we're close, in case you want to fix yourself up a little or something."

Maybe or something... but fix myself up? Yeah, right. Rayne gave a little laugh.

All she wanted was to see her own home, her own bed, and her own pillow. Hopefully at least a full day before Joe got there. She wanted a long, hot soak in her tub and then wanted to sleep in. She wanted a fresh head and plenty of time to think about how she was going to confront Joe about his cheating—and also explain to him where she'd been and why she hadn't returned his calls... which would tie in to the whole confronting-Joe-cheating-thing—

—Stop!

She couldn't start thinking about that. She needed sleep. Right now. If she let her mind go down that rabbit hole, she'd be awake all the way home.

She unsnapped her seat belt and climbed past Okie, muttering a sleepy, "Thanks, Okie. For everything," on her way.

"No problem, Rayne. You just get some shut-eye. I gotta stop to fuel up in about six hours or so... don't worry, you can stay in the cab and sleep. I'll lock it up and keep you safe."

Rayne barely heard him. She was drifting off to sleep as soon as her head hit his pillow. *Something about fuel... okay... G'night,* she thought.

Fourteen

Rayne felt a scream clawing up from deep inside of her. She opened her mouth and it flew out, just as her body lunged toward the party row of the trucker's lot.

Okie barely caught her, his strong arm around her middle. He nearly lifted her off the ground as her feet fought to move.

"Shit, Rayne. What the hell's the matter? Where you going?" he yelled.

Rayne swung her arms wildly. "Let me go! That fucking bitch! I'm going to kill her! Let me go!"

Okie wrapped the other arm around her too, holding her from behind. He was dodging and ducking, avoiding her fierce swings and the jerk of her head.

"Settle *down* a minute! Rayne! Settle down, and I'll let you go. Just talk to me a minute, girl!" Okie swung his gaze around, hoping no one was watching him restraining Rayne. This would be hard to explain. Hell, he had no idea himself what was happening. "You can't run off half-cocked like that. Who the hell are you after?"

Rayne went limp in his arms and began to sob. Okie slowly lowered her to the pavement, settling her between his long legs and loosening—but not letting go—his grip around her.

• • •

"*Shhh...* that's it. Calm down. Tell me what's *wrong*, girl," he whispered, his mouth pressed against her ear as he held his head against hers and his legs pressed against her, holding her in place to prevent her bolting again.

She stilled a moment, and then turned and threw her arms around his neck, falling into him. Her face was blurred with hot tears and her hair was a mess.

"Okie! Omigod, I'm such an idiot!" She howled, beating her fists lightly on Okie's back in anguish. "I've lost him. I've lost him now..." she cried.

He let her wail. And he didn't stop her from hitting him... but he flinched with every blow of her small fists on his back.

When her cries turned to whimpers and blubbers, and her fists uncurled, her words became clearer between the weeping, "Fucking bitch..." *Sniff...* "My husband..." *Snivel...* "...she tricked me..." *Sob...* "...all her fault... and all along it was her—she's his *lover!*" And the crying escalated to a howling bawling once again.

"Whoa. I need you to calm down, Rayne. Let's get you into the cab and move away from the fuel pump before someone comes out here to see what in tarnation's going on. Heck, I need to figure out what's going on myself," he said loudly over her cries. "Come on, get up."

She didn't answer—or move a muscle. She was a puddle... limp with exhaustion, mentally and physically. Broken. Unfixable. She just wanted to give up. It was all a bigger mess than she had thought. Fooled. Not just by Joe either. *Yeah, they're probably laughing. The stupid fool... that's me.* She cried harder.

Okie struggled to stand, not getting any help from her... but he managed to pull them both up off of the pavement. He scooped Rayne up in his arms and quickly moved to the side of the rig, looking all around as he walked. He climbed the steps to the passenger side and amazingly, almost effortlessly, set Rayne in the passenger seat, pushed her feet safely away from the door and slammed it shut.

Then he hurried back down and around to the driver's side. He put the truck in gear, slowly rolling it to the trucker's lot and putting it in park, and then he turned to Rayne. He reached into the sleeper and came back with a box of tissue. Pulling several out, he handed them to her.

"Now, tell me what's got you so torn up, little lady."

Fifteen

Rayne sat up in the seat and looked out the window. She could still see a bit of the red sports car from where they were parked. She looked for Joe's rig, but if it was here, she couldn't see it from the rig blocking the full view of the car.

She pointed her finger. "Is that Storm's car, Okie?" she managed to say, around her broken and hitching voice.

Okie looked to where she was pointing. His head moved back and forth a little, scrutinizing what he could see.

"I'm not sure. The little bit I can see looks like the same color and possibly a Jaguar, but I don't know. You think she followed us here?" he asked, confused.

Rayne gave a quick three-breath sigh… the crying sigh. Always happened after a big, ugly cry. Usually meant the end of it, where she could think and talk again. She wiped her face and blew her nose—not caring if Okie heard.

Gross. She was a mess. But she couldn't find it in her to care even a little bit.

What the hell does it matter? It's not like I can be any more embarrassed than I already am, she thought.

"Okie, my husband's been cheating on me. That's why I came on this trip, to try to catch him red-handed. Storm was trying to help me—or so she said. She told me she'd heard on the CB that Joe's girlfriend was some crackerhead who went by the handle: Blindside. When I woke up, I remembered her saying Blindside's name was really *Stacy*. So I figured it out. 'Stacy' is a nickname for Ana*staci*a! So, Storm, or Anastacia, or *Blindside*... one of them is the woman my husband's been screwing."

Okie's mouth was hanging open. Rayne waited for him to catch up. Finally he blinked rapidly, and shook his head. "Wait a minute. If Storm... or Blindside... whoever... is sleeping with your husband, than how is it you and her were together on a road-trip? How'd that work exactly?"

Rayne nodded her head quickly. "I *know*! It sounds crazy, doesn't it? Why do you think I freaked out? My head is about to blow off."

She ran her hands over her face and kept going, smoothing her hair down as she tried to think how to best summarize the whole story. She needed to get out of the truck and see if that car was Storm's. Because if it was... she was going to give a beatdown. But she needed Okie with her. She was surprised to realize that she was actually afraid of Storm now—or Blindside... if she truly existed.

She cleared her throat.

"The last night my husband was home, he sent me to the truck stop after some deodorant. He had to leave again right away and wanted to go to bed. We'd been fussing, and he'd been acting weird for a long time, so I was already suspicious. He'd turned me down again for sex and my feelings were hurt. I drove *his* truck. At the truck stop, Storm ran toward the truck—*now* I know, she must've recognized the truck and thought I was Joe. But *then*, I didn't know. She saw it was me—a stranger to her—but struck up a conversation. We went to the party row... things got hot and heavy, but I stopped her. She left me her phone number. Then, that night when I got home, I saw Joe had a hickey on his neck. I called Storm the next morning and she suggested we hunt him down and catch him with his girl."

If anything, Okie's eyes were even wider. "Wow. That's...um... quite a story."

Rayne's stuck her head out toward him in disbelief. "Seriously? *That's* quite a story? What, you don't believe me? But you expect me to believe *your* story? The woman you love has split personalities, and you sleep with one—or two—of them and pretend they all go by different names? Yeah? That one is more believable?"

Okie shrugged, lifting his hands up with his palms in the air.

Geesh. Rayne looked down at her lap. She didn't have the heart to go full-throttle bitch on him. He was just too nice.

"Look. I'm calm now. Let's just walk over and see if that's Storm's car. If it is, we'll see what's what. Cool?"

Okie reached up and rubbed his finger over each of his eyebrows, avoiding Rayne's gaze. Finally, he answered, "*If* that's Storm's car, you got to promise me you'll let me do the talking. I've got more experience dealing with all of them. Okay?"

"Yeah. Okay," Rayne agreed. If he could get the truth out of her, fine. That's all she wanted—for now.

Sixteen

Rayne peeked into the window. There was her phone, still hooked up and dangling in the passenger floor. She tried the door, but it was locked.

"It's her car, Okie. Now where the hell is she?"

"She's got to be in one of these rigs," Okie said, pointing his finger at the long row. "Might be best to wait until she's... um... done... doing whatever she's doing."

Rayne bobbed her head from side to side. "Oh hell no. I'm finding her right *now*. I want my phone. And I want answers." She stomped off to the first of the rigs and stopped just under the cab, listening. All was quiet.

She stomped around the rig to the next and was surprised to see the logo on the door. It was Joe's company. She stood open-mouthed, staring up at the door as her body started to shake. Okie came around the corner of the last rig, and saw her staring up at the truck.

His forehead wrinkled as he squinted up at the words painted on the door.

"What?" he asked.

Rayne pointed a shaky finger at the logo. "That's who my husband drives for."

"That's a huge company, Rayne. I see those trucks all over the road," he answered reassuringly. He put a hand on her shoulder and squeezed. "Probably just a coincidence."

• • •

Rayne stood ramrod still; until she didn't. Her legs began to almost bounce back and forth. Her pulse quickened and her heart raced.

"After the past five days, I don't believe in coincidences any—"

"Shhh! I hear someone." Okie moved closer to the rig, Rayne stepped closely behind him. They huddled under the passenger door with their heads tilted.

"I don't give a shit what pictures you have! You did this! Rayne would never do some shit like that on her own. She loves me!"

"No. She *did* love you... now she thinks you're a cheating asshat. You broke her heart! Why do you think she hasn't called you? She's *done* with you, Joe. Finished!" a voice screamed at him—a voice that was definitely Storm's. "And even if she wasn't, do *you* still want your sweet little teacher-wife after what she's done. Or should I say *who* she's done? Look. Just *look* at these pictures!"

The air became quiet then. A pause in their arguing. Was he looking?

Rayne's insides twisted. Memories of their trip raced through her mind. The screaming saddle—the strobe lights... were there flashes too? Pictures being taken?

And at the dance club... she saw Storm taking pictures of her with Seeder, the biker. She'd drunkenly—stupidly—posed as she danced too close to him. But did Storm see her on Seeder's lap? Did she take more pictures of Rayne with her dress hiked up, riding the denim of the fierce biker?

And the massage. She'd thought no one would ever know. She was weak, and hurt. She gave in to the temptation... and the stolen orgasm was so intense, she'd thought she seen lights.

FacePalm.

She remembered a long red curtain covering the wall that separated her room from Storm's. Maybe there was a door behind that curtain. Maybe Storm stepped through and took a picture? She did have a knowing-smirk on her face when Rayne had come out.

She felt sick.

What was Joe looking at? What was he thinking? It didn't even matter that he had cheated first. She never meant to do any of that. Regardless of the pain he had caused her, she'd never want to return that pain to him. That wasn't her. She wasn't that person. She wished she could rewind the entire week back to the night Joe came home. She'd have never stopped at the Quick Dip—never met Storm.

Her marriage was definitely over now... even if she could forgive Joe, he'd never forgive her. Joe was always a bit jealous and protective over her. She was his. Or she had been. Until now.

Rayne and Okie jumped as a loud crash sounded against the window. They both crouched down.

"Take your fucking phone and get out of my rig! Just like I told you before... *I. Don't. Want. You.* Even if I didn't have a beautiful wife, I wouldn't touch you with someone else's dick. Get the hell out, and don't ever come back up in here again."

Rayne's heart thumped. Okie took her hand, trying to pull her away. She resisted. She wasn't going anywhere.

"She *saw* your neck, Joe. She saw the love-bite on I put on you. *And* the condoms in your bag!" Storm laughed evilly. "Oh wait! You didn't know about those, huh? Yeah, your wife found some sparkly, multi-color condoms. She wasn't delighted, to say the least."

"You fucking psycho! You know *nothing* happened. You set me up. If you hadn't of sneaked into my cab again and surprised me, you wouldn't have gotten a chance to smuggle condoms into my bag, *or* lock your sick mouth onto my neck. I swear, you're lucky you're a woman," he growled loudly. "If you were a man, I'd have beat your ass then, and

I'd beat it now," he said in a slow, threatening voice... loud but calm.

"Now get OUT!" he roared, all calmness gone. His scream scared Rayne. She'd never, in all the years of their marriage, heard him scream so loud. She cringed and Okie tried once again to pull her away.

She slapped his hands away. "No," she whispered loudly. "*Shhh!*"

Rayne was shocked. This was a twist. She felt her world tilt again. Joe *hadn't* cheated on her! The hickey was a fake—or forced anyway. The condoms weren't his. She felt like a fool. She'd been tricked. Lured into ruining her own marriage by a psycho bitch that wanted her husband. She wanted to kill Storm.

The door lurched open then, sweeping over the top of Rayne and Okie's head fast enough to blow their hair. They ducked even lower until they heard Storm take the first step.

Okie jerked upright and backed away. Rayne stood too, stepping just far enough away to allow Storm down the ladder. Her back was to them. She had no idea she had an audience as she huffed and jerked herself down the few steps and then jumped down to the pavement.

She gasped when she came face to face with Rayne, but recovered quickly. An arrogant smile covered her face, and her eyes narrowed. She flicked her head, making her long chocolaty waves bounce over her shoulder. She laughed at Rayne.

Rayne's arms were stiff at her side, her hands knotted into fists. She could feel her nails biting into her palms. Her muscles quivered and her nostrils flared as she stared at the crazy bitch who'd single-handedly ruined her marriage. She closed the gap between them with one step. They were eye to eye—

"Rayne, that's *not* Storm!" Okie warned.

"Yeah, I know," she growled over her shoulder.

• • •

To the woman in front of her, she screamed, "Nice blindside, bitch!" just before rearing back and throwing a punch. It hit dead center and hard, bone hitting bone to make a loud *pop!*

Rayne watched in satisfaction as Blindside flew backward, landing on her ass, with blood running in rivers down her face.

Broke nose in exchange for a broken marriage? It's a start, thought Rayne.

Epilogue

Joe's legs bounced as he nervously awaited the results. Rayne reached over and took his hand, squeezing it. She sat straight up in the hard chair, proud to be sitting beside her husband, but stiff from worry.

The metal door opened and a nurse stepped out. She looked at Joe and smiled. "Come on back, Joe and Rayne." She held the door open as they stood up and Joe gave Rayne's hand a return squeeze.

He took a deep breath, and then led Rayne to the back of the clinic—the specialty clinic he'd been visiting every time he was in town for the past year. The clinic that he'd spent nearly every penny of their savings on.

Tests. Treatments. Long waits. More tests. More treatments... it was over now. They just needed the final results, so they could plan the rest of their lives together.

Rayne had been shocked when he'd told her his secret. It explained everything... his bad moods, his avoidance of intimacy, his willingness to take any and every run that was offered to him. He needed the money... to pay for the treatments. She felt bad for assuming he was just penny-pinching and nagging all the time. He'd had his reasons.

And they weren't because he was mad at Rayne. Or that he didn't love her anymore. And he definitely still desired her.

Everything had been revealed that night at the truck stop after Blindside and Rayne had come face to face.

Rayne was almost glad it had all happened. At least the 'storm' that had rained down on them had washed away the lies and the unintended deception. It had cleansed their marriage, bringing forth the truth, and bringing them together. It had uncovered a year of falsehood and negative assumptions. A year of hurt feelings and needless spats.

She just wished Joe had told her from the beginning. She would've supported him… she'd have been *with* him at the treatments. But he'd explained he felt like this was something he needed to do alone… at least to start with. But they'd learned their lesson. Never again would they ever keep anything from each other, or go it alone. Good or bad, they were in it together.

He and Rayne stiffly sat down on the loveseat placed directly in front of the mahogany desk. Joe's eyes darted all around the room and then landed on Rayne. He smiled nervously.

"The doctor should be in any moment," the nurse said. She closed the door behind her, leaving them alone in the chilly room.

Rayne shivered. She wasn't sure if it was the cold air or that she suddenly recognized that voice and it brought back a bad memory. She'd heard that voice on Joe's voicemail. It had interrupted him while he was leaving Rayne a voicemail and said something about putting his clothes back on; Rayne remembered the hurt she'd felt when she'd thought it was her husband's girlfriend.

He saw Rayne shiver and wrapped an arm around her, rubbing her arm with his hand to chase away the goose bumps. His other hand tightly held hers.

Her heart swelled. Even if it wasn't good news, she was happy right now…right here. Just sitting beside him, his arm around her, and her hand in his. *Together.* That was the most important thing. She had her husband back, after she'd

● ● ●

266

thought she'd lost him at the end of that road trip. He still wanted her, amazingly. He'd always wanted her. She'd forgiven him of what she'd thought he'd done, and he'd forgiven her of what she had done, because of the lies that pushed her to it. He'd seen the pictures, and refused to ever speak of them again. She loved him so much more for that.

The door opened, creaking loudly, and the doctor entered. He smiled politely as he leaned over to shake Joe's hand, and then Rayne's.

He took his time getting settled as Joe watched his every move.

He slowly placed a file on his desk and leaned back in his chair, as though he had all the time in the world.

"I've got the results," he finally said, looking at the nervous couple.

Joe blew out a breath he must've been holding. "Just tell us, Doc."

He squeezed Rayne's hand tightly and looked into her eyes. Squeezing his lips together in a firm line, he gave a firm nod to his head, and then said, "Regardless of the result this time, Doc, I'm done with these crazy treatments. This is our last shot... no pun intended," he said and then laughed, embarrassed at his pun.

"Well, I know it's been uncomfortable... and a bit embarrassing for you, Joe. But it worked. The treatments were very successful. Your little guys are no longer low and slow," he paused and winked. "Your numbers are way up. In fact, one of those little guys won the race!"

Rayne jumped to her feet and gasped, her hands coming to rest on her stomach. She turned to Joe, whose eyes mirrored hers... shiny and wet.

He stood and placed his hands over hers, staring down in awe. They held their hands there, together, protecting the treasure they'd waited so long for... and worked so hard for.

Joe's eyes found Rayne's. They both beamed from ear to ear. "Congratulations, little Momma," he whispered through a thick voice, and then he grabbed his wife—his now *pregnant* wife—pulling her to his chest as they both wept with joy.

THE END

From the Author

While this series *is* fiction, D.I.D. is a <u>real</u> disorder. It stands for "Dissociative Identity Disorder." If you're interested in reading more about it, try *"Sybil"* or *"The Three Faces of Eve."* Both are true stories, and both books were subsequently made into movies. Also, on NetFlix, you'll find an interesting fictional series called "United States of Tara," which was part of the inspiration for this series.

Please note, this story was in no way criticizing or making fun of the serious disorder, D.I.D. In fact, I hope it brings more awareness and compassion to those suffering from this illness, as well as understanding from the friends and family of D.I.D. victims.

While my fictional character, Rayne, didn't find much compassion for Storm in this series, you'll see her find a bit more in the next trilogy, which stars Storm, a.k.a. Blindside, a.k.a. Anastacia. I hope you'll continue to read, to see if Okie can weather the *Storm*, break past the *Blindside*, and find his happily ever after with *Anastacia*.

About the Author

Ember Penn is a writer of a several genres, each under a different pseudonym. She grew up with a book in her hand, surrounded by square cornfields, wheat farms and dirt roads.

Readers of her other genre asked her to pen a *steamier* romantic tale filled with adventure and suspense. This book is for them.

If you'd like to know when the next book is coming out, you can be notified via email by Ember Penn's *Head's Up List*—No name required.

Type: **http://eepurl.com/XQNH5** into your browser to sign up. Ember will give you a *head's up* each time there is a new release, and she **won't** share your email addy, or write it on the truck stop wall.

Please return to the online store in which you purchased this book and leave a review. She'll be waiting with her ears on to hear your response to *The Trucker's Wife*.

Made in the USA
Middletown, DE
05 August 2015